BURIED IN BALTIMORE

LOUISE TITCHENER

Louise Titchener

Hard Shell Word Factory

© 2001, Louise Titchener
ISBN-ebook: 0-7599-0039-6
ISBN-paperback: 0-7599-0042-6

Published April 2001

Hard Shell Word Factory
PO Box 161
Amherst Jct. WI 54407
books@hardshell.com
http://www.hardshell.com

Chapter 1

"TONI!" Alice's voice whined through the open window.

"Who's that?" My sister Sandy stalked across my guest bedroom and peered down at the street below. Wild-eyed, Alice stood on the stoop. She wore a grimy pink sweatsuit, tight in all the wrong places. Clumps of matted gray hair festooned her shoulders.

"Toni, please! I ain't got no place to crash. I feel sick. Think I'm gonna puke."

Sandy shot me a horrified look. "Don't tell me she's a friend of yours."

"She's a street person around here. She lives on handouts."

"Toni, have a heart. Let me in."

Sandy's eyes widened. "Don't tell me you've ever let her into your house!"

"Once or twice on super cold nights."

"Are you out of your mind?"

I pushed the sash up and leaned out. "Not tonight, Alice."

"Toni, please, please. There's people trying to kill me."

"Sorry Alice, I've got company."

"Okay, Toni. You'll be sorry for treating me so bad." Head sagging into her shoulders as if she were a weary old turtle, Alice slouched into the darkness

Sandy asked, "What did she mean about people trying to kill her?"

"It's a delusion." I stared after Alice. "Ever since I've known her, she's talked about an assassin trying to get her."

"Jesus! How long have you been chummy with this nutcase?"

"About three months. I met her just after I moved in. She panhandles for drinks around here. Poor old gal. Except the homeless shelters, she really doesn't have any place to go. Maybe I should have let her in."

"Is there something wrong with my ears? Toni, for God's sake, get away from that window before another piece of human trash floats up to your door."

My scowling sister had her arms crossed over her chest. Normally, Sandy wouldn't set foot in my house. But she'd just had a row with Al, her husband. Since, according to her, she couldn't stand being under the same roof with him now, her choices were few.

"So, where are the kids?" I asked.

"I left them in Little Italy, with the folks."

"Won't that interfere with Mom's life of drudgery? How can she stir the Credella Cauldrons with your three underfoot?"

Sandy snorted. "When will you get it through your thick head, Toni? Maybe we didn't like growing up as kitchen slaves in the family restaurant, but Mom likes to cook. Though how she'll manage this weekend with Billy, Matt and Alex, I'm not sure."

I agreed with that. Sandy's three boys are just like their thick-necked dad—noisy, bad-tempered and pig-headed.

Maybe I'd better tell you about myself. My name is Toni Credella and I'm twenty-nine and dyslexic. Four years ago I shot and killed my husband Nick with his service revolver. He and Sandy's husband were boyhood pals and got their police training together. The night Nick died he was beating me up. Though a jury acquitted me on grounds of self-defense, my family didn't. We're reconciled now, sort of, but it's been a rough four years.

"I'm beat. Mind if I crash?" The springs squawked as Sandy dropped onto the bed. She and I are both short, busty brunettes, but marriage and kids have padded her with a few too many pounds. She grimaced. "I'm afraid to ask where you dug up this bed."

"Same place where I picked up all the rest of the furniture in my castle—Good Will and local auctions. Relax, nothing's going to crawl out of the mattress." I gave her shoulder a pat. We argue all the time, and I despise her husband. But Sandy's still my big sister. "Sweet dreams. I'll see you in the morning."

I left her and headed downstairs. When the city of Baltimore sold me my early nineteenth century row house for a song, it was an abandoned property with Contemporary-Urban-Horror decor. Bums and druggies had spilled food, dirty needles and obscene graffiti.

But underneath the dirt and broken plaster the place had high ceilings, a fine old marble fireplace and possibilities. Sort of like Alice, I thought. If you cleaned her up she might not be a bad looking lady.

When I walked into my kitchen, I felt proud. It was really beginning to shape up. Sure, the cabinets were antique and I'd scrounged the appliances at Good Will. Yet, now that I'd scrubbed everything down and painted it white, it didn't look half bad.

Whistling, I got to work laying black and white tile on the ruined floor. An hour later it was about time for the evening news. That's when the phone rang.

"Toni?"

"Yes." Recognizing my favorite local detective, Gus O'Dell, I worked to keep a cautious note out of my voice. O'Dell and I had become friends when he helped me out of a tough situation a few months back. But the friendship was uneasy because we both knew there was an unresolved man/woman thing between us. I was still coping with the damage from my marriage with Nick and wasn't ready for a man/woman thing yet.

"You still up?"

"Sure. I'm working on my kitchen."

He clucked. "Harriet Homeowner strikes again."

"So? I never thought I'd be able to own my own house."

"If you can call that dump a house."

"Don't start, O'Dell. All day I've had my sister Sandy making cracks like that. It wouldn't be any trouble to hang up on you."

He gave with a heavy sigh and I realized how tired his voice sounded. Bone weary. Exhausted and discouraged. "Sorry. Toni, I know it's late, but can I come over?"

I raised an eyebrow. This was a first for Gus O'Dell. Oh sure, when we'd first met he'd asked for a date. When I'd refused, he'd backed off and had seemed to accept a "just friends" status.

"Not tonight. Like I said, my sister is here."

"Would you be willing to go out for a beer? I need to talk." Long pause. "I'll pick you up."

"Something wrong?"

"Nothing blasting off for the moon wouldn't fix."

"That bad?" O'Dell had done me favors. Despite the sexual vibes between us, he'd never pushed and he sounded bummed. "Sure. I'll meet you outside. Just tell me when."

Not wanting to bother my sister, I didn't spend a lot of time prettying myself up. When Gus O'Dell came by in his unmarked BPD Cavalier, I sported my customary dress up outfit—jeans, sneakers, a baggy pullover and a corduroy blazer left over from my days as a young abused matron. Except a pair of gold hoop earrings, I wore no jewelry. My hair blew around my face. As I moved it out of my eyes, I shivered in the September wind and watched leaves and bits of litter swirl off the curb on my street.

"Are you supposed to drive this thing when you're off duty?" I asked as I climbed in.

"No, but tonight I'm in the mood to shit on rules. This crummy job is eating my soul. Or don't you think my soul is worth a free ride in a cheap Chevy?"

"Don't ask me what souls are worth. If it's more than I can count on my fingers, I'm lost."

Twenty minutes later O'Dell and I sat with our backs pressed against the wall at a seedy bar close to North Avenue. Grime filmed the vintage overhead lights, and the guys on the barstools looked as if they'd taken root.

"Why'd you pick this place?"

O'Dell took a long swig of his Rolling Rock. "Suits my mood. Pleases me to know that at any given moment some punk is vandalizing a car around the corner."

"Then your mood must be rotten. You didn't say word one all the way down here."

O'Dell is tall and skinny, with the kind of bony, half-loony face that Tony Perkins sported in *Psycho*. Only O'Dell never looks crazy. Most days his demeanor runs the gamut between bored and cynical. He made me think of an iron kettle on a gas flame turned up high, its lid locked tight over scalding steam getting hotter by the second.

"Prescient," O'Dell muttered. He cast me a sideways glance. "I bet you're surprised I know a word like that. Pretty good for a homicide cop with no education, wouldn't you say?"

"You're asking me? I can't read, remember?"

"You can read. I've seen you."

"Just barely."

"Stop putting yourself down, Toni. You know you could have any guy you wanted."

"Sure. What's this all about, Gus? What's got you so down?"

"Just a typical hellish workday. Starts out with a Korean grocery store that's been robbed half a dozen times. Only this time the owner's there with his shotgun. Blood everywhere and the two thieves, a couple of teenage kids, leave the premises in body bags. Only now the owner is scared their pals might come after him. He's right to be scared, but I have no way to protect the man.

"After that my day goes from rotten to untreated sewage. A shootout between a couple of kids at Flag House. After that, a domestic with no survivors. Finally, I end this duty from the pits of hell with a dump job." He spat out the words.

"Whatever it is, it doesn't sound good."

"Unidentified body found buried under a pile of bricks near Fells Point. Been there for years. According to forensics it used to be a young girl, white, early twenties."

"Where in Fells Point?"

"Close to rotted docks between a parking lot and that burned out warehouse they say is the oldest building standing in Baltimore. Know the spot?"

I nodded. "When did you find her?"

"I didn't. It's a construction site. They were cleaning out the area to begin building a sixteen story condominium. She's my case now, though. I haven't been able to track down her identity."

I pushed my beer away. What had happened to this girl? It could be so many things—an angry boyfriend, a chance meeting with a crazy. Maybe she'd been a runaway who'd accepted a ride with Mr. Wrong. Now, she'd never tell her story.

"You know," O'Dell muttered, "most cases really don't get to me. I've grown a pretty thick shell. But after a day like this I want to quit and open an antique store."

"You in antiques?" I laughed.

"Yeah, you're right. Baltimore has too many antique shops. Crime now, that's a growing field. Speaking of which, how's your decorating business going? Putting up lots of wallpaper?"

"Tell you the truth, wallpaper's kind of out. I'm getting calls for faux painting, though. Tomorrow I do a ceiling in a lawyer's office." I picked up my beer again. "Actually, now that you raise the subject of my shaky employment picture, I got an idea the other day."

"What idea?"

"Maybe you could give me some advice," I hesitated, then plunged in. "How hard is it to get a private investigator's license?"

O'Dell stared at me. As I gazed back, I noticed a nerve start to tick in his jaw. "Why would you want a private investigator's license?"

"I didn't say I wanted it."

"You wouldn't ask otherwise."

"It's a way of making a living, isn't it?"

"A lousy way. And I thought you might cheer me up. Toni, with your record, you haven't got a chance of getting a detective's license."

"If you're referring to my husband, I was tried for that and acquitted on grounds of self defense."

"Doesn't matter. Every police officer in Maryland except me would like to see you behind bars, so forget it."

No longer was I interested in trying to ease the sting out of Gus O'Dell's bad day. I stood. "It's late and I'm ready to turn in."

"I suppose now you're pissed because I'm not encouraging you to make a fool of yourself applying to be a private investigator."

"I'm not mad, I'm just tired. Take me home, please."

"Sure." Wooden-faced, O'Dell plunked some bills down on the pock-marked table. "Women," he muttered.

We walked out of the bar like we were both wearing starched underwear. The night had turned colder. The shops on the strip of city block outside the bar looked so sleazy and abandoned, I almost expected a tumbleweed to roll past. Across the street the pink neon outline of a nude woman winked in the window of an adult book store. Next to it a movie theater with broken panes in its marquee advertised an art film. No customers stood at the ticket window.

"Toni." O'Dell's voice was gruff.

"What?"

"Listen, I didn't mean ..."

As he spoke, we rounded the corner to the shadowy side street where he'd left his car. The tinkle of breaking glass rang out. My head jerked to the left and I spotted a dark figure on the curb side of the Cavalier.

In a blink, O'Dell was in front of me, shoving me back with a thrust so hard I sprawled to the pavement. A gun had sprung into his other hand and he was sprinting toward his car shouting "Stop, police!"

The dark figure galloped the other way, clutching some sort of club or baseball bat. He was quick, but O'Dell moved like a greyhound. As I pushed myself off the ground, Gus shoved his gun into his holster and tackled the man with the bat. After the briefest of flurries, he had him pinned against the side of a rusty Suburban parked fifty yards down from the Cavalier. The bat lay on the pavement, rolled a little distance from O'Dell's, arched, wide-spread feet.

I heard them yelling at each other and trotted forward to get a better look.

"Motherfuck! Get your hands off me!"

"Don't give me that shit, asshole!" O'Dell was rigid, aggression rolling off him in waves. He slammed his captive flat against the Suburban's side panel. They were both panting, their ribs heaving and the muscles of their bodies strained. I heard little grinding noises as they struggled against each other.

O'Dell was winning. "Having a little fun with your baseball bat? Tonight you smashed the wrong piece of glass!"

I recognized the glass breaker right away. It was a skinny black kid in jeans and a torn jacket. He'd been panhandling near the bar. When we'd walked past he'd asked for money, but we'd ignored him. It's what happens when you live in a city where panhandlers flock like starving pigeons. You pretend you don't see them.

He went limp, and then gathered himself up and spit full in O'Dell's face.

"Jesus!" O'Dell yanked out his gun and jammed the barrel of his revolver into the kid's ribcage so hard he squealed. In one fast hard motion, O'Dell flipped him around and dragged his arm behind his back until I heard the bone in his arm socket crunch.

The sound sent a sliver of ice through me, as if I were feeling the pain myself. "Gus, he's only a kid!"

"Did you see what this little fuck just did?" O'Dell snapped on a pair of handcuffs.

Behind my breastbone I felt a sick trembling. My stomach clenched. "Yes, but ..."

O'Dell's face was a mask so rigid and scary it shut me up. In my mind's eye I saw another face twisted with fury. I saw my husband Nick coming at me with his fists balled.

"That's called assaulting a police officer," O'Dell snarled and frog marched the kid down to his Cavalier. Yanking it open, he shoved him inside. An instant later I heard him call for help on his radio.

Rooted to the street, I stood shivering. I felt as if I'd stumbled into a horror show where a friend pulls off his kind mask and reveals a monster. A minute or two later O'Dell emerged from the car dragging his captive with him. All the fight had gone out of the kid. He hung his head. His hands dangled in the cuffs like a broken puppet's. He was weeping and moaning.

"Are you going to just stand there in the middle of the street?" O'Dell yelled at me.

"What else should I do?" I wished I'd never agreed to go out for a beer.

"Get in the Cavalier."

"It's full of broken glass."

"Suit yourself."

About five minutes later a cop car rolled around the corner. The door opened and a white-haired officer in uniform unrolled his six-foot length. Even in the dark, his low-slung belly and meaty Irish mug made him look as if Central Casting had sent him. I recognized him. His name was, appropriately enough, Duffy.

"Got yourself into a bit of a ruckus," he remarked as he ambled over to O'Dell."

"Nothing I couldn't handle," Gus muttered.

Duffy ran an experienced eye over Gus's captive and then eased around the Cavalier to look at the window broken on the passenger side. "Tsk, tsk. I should think a young man of your wide experience would know better than to park an official vehicle in a favorite trashing spot like this."

"Maybe I was in the mood to get trashed."

"Maybe you were, but that's not what they're going to want to hear back at the station when they have to file a request to get this vehicle repaired. And you out on a date with a pretty young lady, too. Guess I can see why you wouldn't want to transport her in your own heap of rust."

For the first time, Duffy seemed to see me. As he looked over the top of the Cavalier, his eyes slitted into cushions of lined flesh. "Do I know you, young lady? You look familiar."

"My name is Toni Credella."

A charged silence ensued. Duffy knew me all right. He'd worked with my husband. Deliberately, he turned back to O'Dell, focusing this time on his prisoner. "All right, my boy," he said with mock cheer, you won't be breakin' anymore windows for a day or two. You're coming down to the station with me."

TWO HOURS later I sat alone in my kitchen, only the light over the stove burning. A noise distracted me from my brooding and I looked up as Sandy came through the archway in a rumpled tee shirt and neon pink socks.

"It's three o'clock in the morning."

"I know the time. What about you? What are you doing up at this hour?"

"Who can sleep with all the noise out on that street?" Sandy made a face and crossed to the stove where she looked critically at the kettle. She took it to the sink and began scrubbing it. "Police sirens, fire engines, people tramping back and forth," she muttered. "Do you realize there's a jerk who wanders around playing a harmonica?"

"That's Harmony. He's a street person."

"Are you on a first name basis with all the street creeps around here? By the way, your pal Alice came by again. Between her and the motorcycles and the harmonica guy, I don't know how you stand it."

"I'm used to the noise. Hey, it's not so quiet in suburbia. You have fire engines and motorcycles."

"Not like this. Where did you go, by the way?"

"Out for a beer with Gus O'Dell."

"Ah ha!" She shot me a knowing grin. "So, how's Mr. Dangerous-Dark-and-Sexy? You two jumping on each other's bones yet?"

My laugh was short. "Not yet, and after tonight, not ever." I described the evening and what had happened when O'Dell apprehended the kid.

"So?"

I rolled the ceramic mug I'd been drinking water out of between my palms. "I've never seen Gus O'Dell like that before. I'd never seen him arrest somebody when he was really angry. He was scary."

Sandy padded over to the table. "You mean, he reminded you of Nick."

"Yes, he did." I thought of how my husband would come home sometimes after a rough night on the beat. He would be surly, foul-mouthed, vibrating with some inner rage he could only unleash on me. He'd been terrifying those nights, and eventually they'd cost him his life—at my hands. "Sandy, I don't ever want to get involved with someone like that. Not ever again."

Sandy heaved a big sigh. "Toni, are you ever going to get over what happened with Nick?"

"I don't know. Maybe not. Right now it doesn't look good."

"Hey, you can't want to be alone for the rest of your life."

"Maybe I do. Maybe I was meant to be alone. Besides, look at you. The folks hold you up to me as Mrs. Happy Housewife. Yet here you are with your kids parked on mom and dad."

"That's nothing. Al and I will probably get back together in a few days. The big asshole," she added darkly. "It's you we're talking about. Toni ..."

Pounding on the front door and a high-pitched wail interrupted whatever she was going to say.

"Toniiiii!"

"Oh my God, it's that crazy woman again!" Muttering curses, Sandy slapped out of the kitchen and down the hall.

It took me a couple of seconds to pull myself together and follow. When I arrived at the front door, Sandy was yelling at it.

"Get the hell out of here! If you don't stop bugging us, I'll call my husband. He's a police officer. He'll fix you good!"

"Sandy, for crying out loud!"

She shot me a look. "You are not letting that crazy woman in here, Toni."

"She's harmless."

"She's a nut, and I'm not staying another night in this loony dump of yours. It's worse than living with mom and dad. It's even worse than living with Al."

"Jeez Sandy, you really know how to hurt a person."

"Very funny, but it's the truth. First thing tomorrow, I'm out of here." Sandy stomped back upstairs.

Ignoring her, I opened the front door. I'd expected to find Alice slumped on the marble stoop. My thought was I'd call a cab, give the driver five bucks and send her to one of the shelters that would take her in.

The street was empty. "Alice?" Leaving the door ajar, I stepped outside. The wind raked cool fingers through my hair and set a sign to creaking on the pet shop opposite. Street lamps spilled puddles of yellow light on the cracked pavement, and a scrawny cat slunk into a narrow passage between two brick buildings. Alice was nowhere in sight.

Chapter 2

"TO WHAT do I owe this unexpected delight, Honeycakes?"

I don't visit the offices of Breed, Wardall and Haworth very often. When I do, it's a kick to see Randall sitting behind an acre of polished mahogany in one of his GQ-type suits.

After I shot Nick, Randall Haworth defended me. Lucky for me, he's an ace lawyer and an even better friend. When my parents disowned me, Randall took my messed-up self under his wing. He found me a place to live and steered me toward the decorating business that still feeds my face—occasionally. If it weren't for him, I wouldn't have survived those years. In more ways than one, I owe the man my life.

"I'm here on business."

"On business?" Randall lifted an eyebrow.

"I need your professional advice."

"Does that mean you'll pay up when I bill you $150 dollars an hour for my valuable time?"

"Are you kidding?"

Randall glanced at the Rolex decorating his handsome black wrist and then pushed back his oxblood leather wing chair. Its castors rolled smoothly over the Turkish rug which added color to the otherwise cool neutral tones of his office.

"It's almost lunch time. What do you say we discuss this professional matter over food?"

"I'm broke."

"So what else is new?"

FORTY-FIVE minutes later, Randall and I ordered lunch at The Brass Elephant, a gorgeous old town house just north of the Mount Vernon area where Randall lives.

Lest you get any false ideas about the two of us, I'll explain that Randall, aside from being a beautiful ebony prince, is gay. He lives with a blond artist named Johnathan.

"This place is so beautiful." I squinted at the fancy plasterwork on the high ceiling. "How can people eat in sterile little shopping centers when there are places like this?"

"Sweetheart, they prefer the sterile shopping centers because of Baltimore's crime rate. Already more than 250 murders. You know that, Sweets. But aren't we a wee bit off the topic?"

"Not at all. We're right on the topic. I need your advice. How does a person go about becoming a private eye?"

Randall's jaw dropped. At that moment the waiter brought our order. After the guy set my Caesar salad and Randall's grilled salmon on the crisp pink tablecloth, Randall found his voice. "You're joking."

"I'm not. I'm serious. I want to know how to get a private detective's license."

"Make a phone call."

"I did that, Randall, honest. I didn't want to bother you about this, so I spent the whole morning dialing and holding. You know how hard it is for me to get anything out of the phone book. I started with the Bureau of Licenses," I continued. "They told me to call the police department. I did and they referred me to the State Police. Finally, I talked to a sergeant something-or-other who said I had to have been a cop or worked five years for another licensed detective before I could apply."

"That's right." Randall stabbed at a bright green bean.

"Are you glaring at me like that because you think I'm crazy?"

"You got it, Babe. How did you get this killer bee in your bikini panties?"

"Now you sound like Gus O'Dell."

Randall stiffened. He and Gus didn't get along. "You still seeing Mr. Dead-Eye-Dick?"

"No. He's not my type. Too violent."

"That's the first intelligent thing you've said all day. I shouldn't have to explain why this detective idea is crazy, but I will. Four years ago you killed a Baltimore City cop."

"Randall," I hissed, glancing from side to side. This was not a fact about my life I cared to advertise.

"WHAT MAKES you think the powers-that-be would ever grant you a detective's license? Even if you were qualified to be one, for God's sake."

"Randall, is there any legal reason why I couldn't?"

"The Superintendent of the State Police may deny a license to any applicant he deems of poor moral character. Given your history, you're not going to get his thumbs up."

"Does that make it impossible?

He sighed. "It would depend on who made the final decision. But like I said, you'd need five years experience working for a licensed PI first."

I dropped my fork. "Randall, help me."

"Toni, I love you. You know I'll do anything I can for you. Encouraging a hare-brained idea like this is not my idea of friendship."

"Randall, you don't understand. I'm looking at thirty. I need to do something with my life."

"You are doing something. You've got your own place now, a business. You're beautiful and smart. You'd have no trouble finding a decent man if you wanted one. Just open your eyes."

"Randall, I can't be like my sister, happy with a ranch house in the suburbs, a bunch of kids and a thick-headed husband with a beer belly."

"Count your blessings."

"Sure, but I have to have something, Randall. I need some direction in my life that feels good."

"And you think working as a private investigator is going to be it? Oh Baby, most of what those guys do is boring as shit. They spend their lives sitting around in cars twiddling their thumbs, waiting to snap a Polaroid of a cheating husband. Take my word for it."

"At least let me find out for myself. Let me try it. Randall, I know I'm always asking favors. But this will be the last. Please."

He rolled his eyes. "Against my better judgment."

"What?" I felt myself brighten.

"There's a guy who owes me a favor."

"Yes?"

"His name is Angus Maloney."

"Is he Irish or Scotch?"

"Judging from the way he used to drink and pick fights, he's ninety percent of each. He's a private investigator in town, has an office not far from here." Randall pulled out one of his own embossed business cards, scribbled an address on the back and slid it across the table. "You can tell him I sent you. Beyond that, you'll have to rely on your own powers of persuasion."

"Such as they are."

"They're good enough to get you into trouble. Are we through here?"

"Sure. Oh Randall, thank you!"

As he counted out the tip, he shot me a speculative look. "There's something else."

"What?"

"There's more than one reason why I'm glad to hear you aren't so thick with Augustus O'Dell. You might as well be the first to know. Detective O'Dell and I are about to enter the ring in opposite corners."

I blinked at him. "What's that supposed to mean?"

"He's pressing willful destruction, attempted robbery and resisting arrest against a young man named Jerome Robinson. Claims he caught the boy breaking a window on an unmarked police car."

The scene from a couple nights back was still vivid in my mind. "I was there at the time, as a matter of fact."

"So I hear. Jerome's mother has asked me to represent her son. O'Dell dislocated the boy's shoulder, and she's filing counter charges of police brutality. I've agreed to take the case and I may have to call you as a witness."

"Oh Randall, no." I flattened my spine against the chair slat.

"Why not? Hey Toni, Jerome is black and so am I. It's no secret that police hassle young black males. If half of what Jerome's mother claims is true, O'Dell was way out of line."

"You're right, he went kind of crazy, but I think what happened with Jerome was unusual."

"Do tell. Well now, that changes everything, doesn't it!"

"Really, Randall, Gus wasn't himself." On the way out of The Brass Elephant, I explained about O'Dell's dump job.

Randall narrowed his eyes. "I know the area. Just west of the old warehouse, isn't it?"

"Yes. When Sandy and I were kids we used to play there. We climbed on piles of old bricks. To think that girl's body might have been lying beneath our feet." I shuddered. "You know as well as I do what a tough job O'Dell has. Sometimes cops see too much for their own good."

"Jerome Robinson has a rough life, too. He grew up in the

projects with no father and no hope."

"He was breaking windows."

"Windows are one thing, body parts are another. Jerome deserves better than to be slammed around by some hyperactive cop who's acting out because he's had a bad day. You, of all people, should agree. Brace yourself, Toni. You might be my star witness."

I DECIDED to stay in the neighborhood and look up Angus Maloney, but when I knocked on his door nobody answered. I spent the rest of that afternoon working at home. Several times I dialed Maloney's number. Nobody answered.

After I ate a tuna sandwich for dinner, I felt restless. I knew I'd been neglecting Mom, so I climbed on my bike and peddled over to Little Italy. Three generations of Credellas have run a restaurant there and it hasn't changed much since the day it was first opened. Mom, as usual, hovered in front of a cauldron of tomato sauce in the basement kitchen. Above us, in the restaurant, my father, as usual, strutted around playing benevolent host.

"Toni, my baby!" Mom wiped her hands on her apron and gave me a hug. "You look pale." She stepped back to eye me. "So skinny. You're not sick, are you?"

"Of course not. I'm fine."

My mother is a little woman with an anxious expression and graying hair. She waggled her head. "I don't know. So many bad diseases going around these days. I worry about that AIDS."

"Don't worry." Since I wasn't a drug user and didn't even have a boyfriend—O'Dell was definitely out of the picture now—AIDS was not even a remote threat. However, I chose not to mention my lack of a love interest so she wouldn't start moaning about how terrible it was for a nice Italian girl my age not to be married.

"If you're not sick," she declared, "then you're not eating right. You sit down and I'll feed you something good."

"Mom ..."

"You sit down, Toni, and I'll bring you a nice dish of stuffed shells."

My mother's cooking is heavenly, so I didn't put up too much of a fight. While I ate, she bustled around the kitchen and passed along the family news. She talked about Sandy and her troubles with Al.

"His bad moods are all because he don't like his job. He hates the city, he hates the crime. Every night he comes home a grouch."

"Then maybe he shouldn't be a police officer."

"Maybe he shouldn't, but Al's no brain surgeon. How's he gonna' support those kids? Oh those boys, they are lively ones."

"Yeah, lively like a box full of tarantulas," I muttered under my breath.

"Spiders? Yes, you're right." She chuckled. "They like the Spider Man and the Iron Man. Oh yes, and the remote control cars. So noisy." She changed the subject to Pop and the new cook he'd hired to help her out in the kitchen and how she really didn't need him.

"You do need him, Mom. It's about time Pop stopped letting you do all the work."

Tentatively she asked, "You want to go up and say hello to him?"

I didn't. For three years after my trial my father wouldn't speak to me. Now we're reconciled, but just barely. Tonight I wasn't in the mood to do the remorseful-daughter dance.

"Toni," she said, "you remember Mario Caprini?"

"Sure." When we were kids, Mario and I used to hang around together. But he'd gone off to college, married and moved out of state. And I'd met Nick.

"Well, Mario, he's back in town."

"Oh?"

"His marriage, it didn't work out so good. He's divorced, living with his mother 'til he finds his own place, and working an engineer job near here." Mom looked at me expectantly. "I ran into him buying bread at Appicella's the other day. He still remembers you."

"Well, I remember him, too. Why wouldn't I? I'm not brain-damaged." Knowing where that conversation was about to go, I changed the subject. When I left it was close to seven o'clock and sunset. I should have headed back to Federal Hill. Instead, I pedaled across Eastern Avenue to the stretch of harbor that for decades has lain abandoned between the Inner Harbor and the historic watering holes of Fells Point.

Dodging traffic across Fleet Street, I saw that the landscape was a'changing. Instead of a rat-infested parking lot flanked by piles of abandoned junk, the area had been cleared and paved with curving new roads. Skirting a concrete barrier, I cruised past cranes and earthmovers to the water.

"Wow!" I exclaimed when I spotted the network of expensive docks that had just been laid in next to a spiffy stone seawall. Straddling my bike, I stared to the left where dozing gulls blanketed the cleared but still toxic chrome plant property. I hardly recognized the seedy haunts of my childhood.

When Sandy and I were kids these junk-strewn fields with their rotting old piers and floating debris had been a place for secret, forbidden adventures. Hot summer days we'd poke around among the piles of old boards, rusty bedsprings and broken glass. Sometimes we disturbed alcoholic bums who sent us sprinting for home with their curses ringing in our ears. Often, we scavenged bits of treasure from the past like broken cups and unmatched old earrings. Since the city morgue had once been down here, rumors flew among the kids that a person might stumble over a skull or a detached hand.

Now, dry cleaned by bulldozers and ironed by blacktop rollers, the property lay like a featureless game board waiting to be dotted with hotels and yuppie restaurants. Breathing the gamy harbor fragrance, I looked to the left and spotted a bulldozer.

The sight of it reminded me of O'Dell's story. I shivered. That must be the place where a construction crew had unearthed what was left of a young girl's body. I stood listening to the cries of the gulls. A tug pushing a barge chugged past. Behind it, a sleek white sailboat ghosted on the wind.

I got back on my bike and pedaled east. A couple of minutes later I leaned my handlebars against the chain link fence surrounding the construction site. The work crew had all gone home. Behind me the setting sun lay on the black water in a ball of red-orange flame. Almost, I expected to hear it sizzle.

I turned my head and stared at the spires of the city bathed in pinky-orange glory. A car appeared on the horizon and cruised slowly down the new road. My eyes watered from the sun, so I focused on the car. As it closed with me, I recognized its profile—an unmarked Cavalier.

"What are you doing here?" O'Dell said after he pulled up and climbed out.

"Just taking a bike ride."

"It's not safe down here after dark. No streetlights, no people, no protection. You don't know what kind of creep you might run into."

"Obviously."

"How could I forget the famous Credella wit?"

"So, what are you doing down here?"

"Investigating a case."

"Your dump job?"

"No, this time the meat is a lot fresher. They found her this morning face down on top of a pile of dirt." He took a notebook out of his jacket pocket and flipped it open. "You might know the lady. She's a street person who hangs out in your new neighborhood. Name's Alice, Alice Ritco."

Chapter 3

"ALICE, DEAD?" The news punched me in the gut.

"You knew her?"

I nodded. "When was she killed?"

"According to the ME, she'd been dead about 48 hours."

"Oh, God." I told O'Dell about my last encounter with Alice, how she's begged me to let her in and I'd refused. "If I hadn't sent her away, she might still be alive."

"Yeah, and where's your hair shirt? You can't take people in off the street. Your sister was right."

"You're a cold-hearted bastard."

"Mary Poppins wouldn't make a good homicide cop, now would she? I'm going in to have a look around. If you like, you can come in with me and tell me what you know about Ritco."

I hesitated, not wanting to get cozy with O'Dell again. On the other hand, I wanted to know how Alice had died and where. And I needed to talk to him about Jerome Robinson. "Okay."

O'Dell had a key to the padlock closing the chain-link gate on the construction site. While he undid the lock, I eyed his narrow backside. He'd left his suit jacket in the car and rolled up his sleeves. I noticed several glints of gray in his short brown hair. He wasn't getting any younger. Nor was I.

Either the lock was sticky or the key didn't fit. As he wrestled with it, I saw anger and frustration building in the set of his shoulders and the bunched muscle on his lean forearms. I remembered his violence with Jerome. It had exploded out of him like a caged tiger.

The lock fell open and O'Dell swung the gate outward. "Coming?"

We walked in on a rutted dirt road peppered with egg-sized gravel chunks. Eerily silent, earthmoving vehicles squatted on the barren landscape. To our right, bulldozers had hollowed out a pit resembling a giant open shoebox. Cement pilings poked up from the scraped dirt floor.

I asked, "What are those for?"

"This used to be water. We're standing on fill. Planting a building of any size on it is tricky. Those pilings will stabilize the foundation."

"Is this where they found Alice?"

"No. It's where they dug out the bones of the girl I told you about."

"The dump job. Anything new on that?"

He shook his head and turned to a pile of dirt flanked by stacks of what looked like gray plastic kitty litter pans. "That's where they found her."

O'Dell told me that Forensics had already checked out the site. Nevertheless, he wanted to refresh his memory. He walked around, eyeballing the placement of equipment and gravel piles and taking an occasional measurement. While he worked, jotting observations and figures in a notebook, I told him what I knew about Alice. There wasn't much.

"Ask me, Alice Ritco is probably better off dead," O'Dell remarked when I finished my brief, pitiful account. "What kind of a life could she have had? No home, no family, wandering the streets in an alcoholic haze, sleeping in shelters and begging for handouts. If someone hadn't put her out of her misery by bashing her on the noggin, she'd have died of exposure or liver failure or AIDS."

"She was hit in the head?"

"First, she was strangled. ME says there was no sexual assault."

"God!" I pictured Alice, her lank gray hair a dispirited frame around her ruined face. Who would bother to kill her so brutally? "If you really believe Alice is better off dead, why are you here after sunset trying to figure who murdered her?"

O'Dell dropped to one knee, turned on a pocket flash and sifted through a handful of dirt. When the glittery object he'd caught sight of turned out to be a sliver of mica, he flicked it off his fingernail. "I'm just doing my job." He rose and dusted off his gritty palms. "I'm a born hunter. If I weren't tracking down slimeballs and collaring crooks, I wouldn't know how to get through the day."

"A couple of nights ago you were talking about quitting police work and opening an antique shop."

"That's all it was, Toni, talk. I couldn't make a living at that. Even if I could, I probably wouldn't like it. Too tame."

When I cocked my head, he added, "Granted, my job is shitty.

All the same, I'm addicted—the feeling you get when you're on the trail, and later when you actually nail a creep. Anyhow, it's the only thing I can do, the only thing I'm good at. It suits me." He rolled his tight shoulders. "I wouldn't fit in at a bank or an office, and construction is too tough. Besides, I wouldn't look good in a hard hat."

"Police work isn't making you happy, Gus. Maybe it's not even healthy for you—you know, mentally. The other night what you did to that kid ..."

O'Dell looked at me coldly. "That kid was busting up other people's property. Maybe I was a little too rough with him. On the other hand, maybe giving him a wake up call is the nicest thing I could do." He took a step toward me. "I know what you saw worried you, Toni. I'm sorrier about that than you know. I can't change history, so let's forget it and talk about Alice Ritco. I'd better warn you. Since you may be the last person who saw her alive, it's possible you could be called as a witness."

He'd warned me, so I couldn't put off warning him. "There's a chance I could be called as a witness in another case." I told him about Randall's plans to take Jerome Robinson as a client.

For a dangerous minute O'Dell was silent. He spent another thirty seconds cursing under his breath. When he ran out of swear words, he said, "I knew that over-priced shyster had it in for me."

"Randall Haworth is not a shyster."

"No, of course not. He's your pal. The guy doesn't like me hanging around you, does he?" O'Dell's slitted eyes glittered.

"Considering my past, Randall doesn't think you're the type of man I should get involved with, no."

"You're talking about that husband of yours knocking you around. Do you think if you ever let me close to you, I'd hurt you, Toni?"

I couldn't come up with an answer. The truth was I had no idea. I've learned not to trust my instincts about men. Even after all these years, they and what they're capable of baffles me."

"Jesus! I suppose if Haworth goes through with this, you're going to testify for him."

"I wouldn't have much choice, would I? I was the only witness to what happened."

Gus looked down at his feet, then off to the side, anywhere but at me. I was trembling, but I tried to sound firm and not show how upset I felt.

"We're done here," Gus said. "I'll see you home."

"I've got my bike. I'll ride home."

"Not in the dark, you won't."

"I'll ride home." I shook off the hand he'd laid on my arm. In the end, we both got our way. I rode my bike back to South Baltimore and Gus trailed me. His Cavalier hovered in the street until I was inside my door. When I looked out the upstairs window, it was gone.

I DIDN'T SLEEP well that night. First thing the next morning I headed for Angus Maloney's office on Read Street. Leather shops, antique stores, health food establishments, coffee houses and new age book shops are conspicuous in the area. I passed Dreamland, a vintage clothing store which caters to the exacting tastes of drag queens. An evil looking pair of screaming pink platforms, size twelve caught my eye.

Since Maloney did business close to Dreamland and Randall knew him, I figured he might be gay. However, his grimy brick building was seriously short of Randall's trademark elegant décor.

As I buzzed the office on the third floor, I noted the corroded mail slots. Above them, dirty beige paint had loosened from the wall in flaky strips—probably historic enough to be laced with lead.

"Hello?" After an invisible hand buzzed me up, I trudged three flights and peered around Maloney's half-open door. Bedraggled chairs furnished his reception area. A battered desk took up one corner, but no receptionist sat behind it. Overhead, a bulb behind a fly-specked shield shed weak light over the grime-green walls.

Had Randall been playing a joke on me? "Hello?"

I heard a faint rustling in the room beyond. Somebody with a whiskey base cleared his throat and ruffled papers. Chair legs scraped against a protesting wood floor.

"Just a minute, just a minute." A figure filled the doorway, big, bear-like. "Young lady, I have to tell you, if you're here about the job, that's a helluva' way to dress for an interview."

I glanced down at my jeans and sneakers. "There's a dress code for detectives?"

The hulk in the doorway, his face still half hidden in shadow, snorted. "Who said anything about detective? I advertised for a receptionist."

Behind me, a tall, bottle blond swinging a costly leather briefcase yanked the door open and shouldered past. She wore a sexy short-skirted business suit and a no-nonsense expression. Pointing a long red fingernail at the man I assumed was Maloney, she said, "No more of this crap, Angus. I'm not having it!"

"Not having what?"

"Calling up Andy and making a date with him for Camden Yards. You know you're supposed to clear that with me."

"Hells bells, Karla! It's only a baseball game."

"Andy has a Scout meeting Thursday night. You know the terms of our settlement. Andy's weeknights are my turf. Keep your ugly, flat feet off it."

Maloney's big face went almost as scarlet as his rooster comb of hair. "Seems to me you're the one who's invading turf. Who invited you?"

The two had squared off as if I weren't there. I glanced from Karla, who had the varnished appearance of a pricey stockbroker or lawyer, to Maloney who looked like a furry red bear dressed in L.L. Bean castoffs.

I was considering backing out, but Karla, after spearing Maloney with another pointed warning, turned on her Ferragamos and whipped out.

As we listened to her heels tick down the steps, Maloney and I gazed bleakly at each other. He wished I weren't there, and so did I. "Ain't love grand?" he growled.

"Don't ask me. I wouldn't know."

"That makes two of us."

"I gather the lady is your ex?"

"You gather right. Now, who are you?"

"Name's Toni Credella." I handed over Randall's card. "Randall Haworth recommended I come see you."

Maloney frowned. "You not answering my ad for a receptionist?"

"No sir. I'm here because I'd like to learn how to become a detective."

Maloney had a broken nose and a jaw so square it could have been the front end of a shoebox. He made me think of a cartoon character—Joe Palooka or Superman with Lucille Ball's coloring.

His face looked as if it had been chipped out of stone too hard for anything but angles and rough edges. Maybe the artist with the untutored mallet had been after Greek perfection. What he'd achieved was craggy individualism.

Maloney's body was big and rough looking, too. He had to be well over six feet, with a barrel chest that strained at his blue button-down collar shirt. His khaki pants hung low on hips too small for the rest of him. His pant legs dripped over dirty sneakers.

The man could have played a wild Scot whirling a claymore or a mountain man too overgrown and uncouth to be at home with any society but that of his mules. I might have been tempted to imagine he was as dense as his shoulders if it weren't for his eyes. Pale green and half hidden by his bushy brows, they examined me shrewdly.

"Would you repeat that, please?"

"Sure, I want to learn how to be a detective. Randall said you might be willing to take me on."

Obviously, Maloney was going to tell me to get out of his face. I knew I must look idiotic. Why didn't I think to get dressed up in a business suit before I came? My cheeks began to burn.

"Were you ever on the police force?"

"No."

"But if I'm not mistaken, your husband was. Before I quit the BPD, I knew your husband."

"I suppose that means you won't hire me."

"The reason I won't hire you has nothing to do with the fact that you iced your husband. This is a one-man operation. I can't afford to hire help and I can't take the time to train an amateur with no experience. Leave me your card. If things change, I'll call."

"Sure," I said. I scribbled my number on a scrap of paper, threw it on the desk and walked out. Sure he'll call, I thought as I pounded down the steps. When hell freezes over, he'll call. What a dumb idea this was!

A COUPLE of days later Angus Maloney called. It was seven in the morning, and I had just staggered out of bed. I was trying to retrieve a singed English muffin from my arthritic toaster when the phone brrrrred.

"You still interested in a job with my agency, Miss Credella?"

"Sure." I knew my astonishment could be heard in my voice.

He went on gruffly. "To be honest, I didn't expect I'd get back to you, but I'm in a spot. A couple of jobs came up I couldn't turn down, but there's another case I agreed to. The client may pull out if she doesn't see quick results. The guys who usually fill in for me in situations like this aren't available."

He was certainly going to a lot of trouble letting me know I wasn't his pick of the month. "It's okay. I don't mind being the last name on your dance card."

Rumbly male chuckle. "You insulted?"

"Mr. Maloney, I'm thrilled you remembered my name."

"In that case, maybe we can do some business. This is the deal. Client's name is Marnie Brockloff. Her lawyer husband, Brooks, is a partner at Goldner, Morton and Brockloff."

I knew the firm. They had refused to take me on a *pro bono* basis when I'd been broke and on trial for my life after I shot Nick. Maloney went on to explain that Marnie Brockloff suspected her husband of cheating on her. She wanted him watched and followed. This would entail a full report on all his meetings with women.

At this point, of course, I should have excused myself. Not only do I not have a car, I am severely dyslexic. Though I have been working hard on my reading and writing skills, the thought of penning a report scared me.

On the other hand, I had mortgage payments and my decorating business wasn't making it. The hourly wage Maloney mentioned, though a pittance by anyone else's standards, sounded like riches to me. Beyond that, I really wanted a shot at the detective game.

"Sounds fine," I said and listened carefully to the rest of Maloney's instructions. After he hung up, I fidgeted around the kitchen. Lawyer-Brockloff left his house at eight-thirty. He took the Jones Falls, an expressway that's a high-speed version of bumper cars at morning rush. How was I going to follow him on my bike and stay inconspicuous?

I spent the rest of the morning stripping layers of paper off the west living room wall while I mulled over this question and other matters. Like, how would I bring myself to testify against O'Dell? I speculated about the jobs Maloney had taken which put him out of action both day and night. Didn't the man have to sleep? In the end, though, it was Alice Ritco I couldn't get out of my head.

I met Alice the day I moved into my house. Sandy thinks my

place is a dump now. Then it was unspeakable—holes in the kitchen where appliances and even copper plumbing had been ripped out, filth coating the floors and walls, the smell of urine and mold fouling the air.

Facing the job ahead of me that first day, I wondered if Sandy and my whole family were right. Maybe I really was crazy.

I wandered outside into the July heat to get out of the smelly old wreck that was supposed to be my new home. I was sitting on the marble stoop with my head in my hands when Alice tapped me on the shoulder.

My first glimpse of her wasn't exactly entrancing—the stringy gray hair, the gap-toothed grin and bleary eyes. She wore a tired black tee shirt and flesh-colored tights that from a distance made her look as if she might be naked from the waist down. On Alice, not a pretty sight.

"I need to tell your fortune, hon. Cross my palm with silver."

"I don't have any silver."

"A five dollar bill will do."

Don't ask why. I reached into my pocket and handed her the bill I'd planned on using for groceries.

"Everything's going to be okay, hon." She tucked my money into her waistband, revealing a roll of yellow flesh above the elastic.

"It is, huh?"

"You betcha. You're going to be jim dandy. You did good coming here. You going to find everything you need in this place, so don't worry your pretty head none. Now, I got to be on my way. See you."

Alice's prediction cheered me up. After that I saw her everywhere. She was a neighborhood fixture, hanging out at the Cross Street Market, walking the streets at all hours, cadging quarters from tourists as she checked out the waste bins at the harbor. Almost always, she was cheerful, calling out nonsensical greetings, cracking jokes.

Now I couldn't stop thinking about Alice. Mid-afternoon I threw on my trusty corduroy blazer and jogged down to the First Presbyterian Church on Light Street. Their soup kitchen sign warns, "Nobody admitted until 2:30." Regardless, lines start forming around noon.

At one time the church may have been red brick. Now a purplish black stains its masonry shell. It sits so close to the street that the sidewalk flows right into it. It's as much a part of the block as the storefront businesses that come and go on either side. When I arrived, the food line stretched all the way down to Nail Magic, a new manicure place specializing in fancy designs dusted with glitter.

As I jogged past, several of those waiting their turn for a meal made smart remarks. One called my name. I waved and hurried on down the concrete steps. Alice was a rarity among the people who patronize the kitchen. Almost all are men. Some are white-haired with Santa Claus beards. A few look young. Some are crazy, or alcoholics or drug users or all three. Some aren't very smart and have been plain unlucky. Though the soup kitchen guys are different physical types and races, they all have that hangdog look that goes with open admission of failure.

The church basement was crowded and noisy. A damp cloud of steam table food-smell hung in the air. A row of tables along the back wall held metal cafeteria containers and a giant-sized coffee-maker. Platters of wrapped sandwiches sat next to plastic utensils rolled in paper napkins. As men shuffled along with trays, ladies in aprons and an occasional male retiree dished out lunch. Today's menu featured cheese on white bread and vegetable soup.

Looking for Reverend Mitchum, I threaded my way through the tables. I spotted him in a corner talking to one of his new volunteers. She was a young woman who, judging from the business clothes beneath her apron, had to work at one of the office buildings ringing the harbor. It's nice to know some of those people still have a heart.

As I came up, she resumed ladling soup. Mike gave me a big smile. "Come for a square meal to put some meat on those skinny bones?"

"Not me. I had a delicious lunch of tomato juice and peanut butter on onion-flavored matzoh crackers."

"There are times when you worry me, Toni."

"Now you sound like my mother."

"Not such a bad way to sound, if you ask me. What brings you here?"

He's a funny guy, Reverend Mike Mitchum. Somewhere in his mid-thirties, he's a big, fair-haired fellow who, no matter what the weather, wears khaki pants, plaid shirts, and golf jackets. He and his wife, Carol, both look as if they grew up on a midwestern farm. He could have played football and she could have been a cheerleader. Yet here they are in the heart of the evil city, dealing with the dregs of society. Doing a good job of it, too.

Everyone I know likes Mike, including even the most hostile and hopeless of the down-and-outers he serves. The church ladies of South Baltimore adore him, and he's had good luck drawing in the yuppies who've gentrified the area close to the harbor. Maybe it's his mild blue eyes and cherubic smile. That smile beamed at me. Unfortunately, I had to wipe it away by asking about Alice.

"We got the news yesterday. Terrible thing. Poor lost soul was harmless. I hate to think of her dying like that."

"Reverend ..."

"Mike, call me Mike. Reverend makes me feel like the old man of the altar." His smile crept back.

"Mike, how will she be buried?"

"It's thoughtful of you to ask, Toni."

I was not thoughtful. If I'd taken her in she might still be alive. I would never forget Alice slinking off into the night like a whipped dog. But I held my tongue. No point in laying my guilt feelings on Mike Mitchum. He had enough problems to deal with right in this room.

"A lot of people considered Alice a nuisance, but folks felt sorry for her, too. We plan to take up a collection in church and around the neighborhood," he said.

"I'd like to contribute. I don't have much, but I'll give whatever I can. Alice was so alone. She deserves a decent burial at least."

"That's good of you. Though the collection I spoke of will just be for flowers. Alice wasn't actually as alone as she seemed. She had a daughter who'll pay for her funeral."

"She did?" I was amazed.

"Oh yes. Dr. Doris Ritco."

"Doctor?" I was even more amazed.

"Doris has made several generous contributions to the church on her mother's behalf. She and I are planning a memorial service for Alice next Monday. I intend to drive out to see Doris this afternoon to discuss the arrangements." He cocked his head. "Since you had a special relationship with Alice, maybe you'd like to come with me?"

"I'd like that. Hey, isn't that Jimmy and Harmony I see over there?" I'd caught sight of a skinny young man wearing a blue knit watch cap centered on a wild fringe of black curls. He got the nickname Harmony because he always carries a harmonica around and stands on street corners playing it for change. Now he was helping a man in a motorized wheelchair down the wooden ramp set up to allow the handicapped into the church basement.

Mike lifted his head. "Indeed it is. Haven't seen them around for several days. They were friends of Alice's. I'm sure they know what happened to her. Word gets around fast on the street. But they might not know about the memorial service."

I followed Mike through the crowd to an empty table at the edge of the room. By the time we arrived at it, Harmony had already left to join the soup line. Jimmy, the guy in the wheelchair, watched our approach quizzically. His broad face was made more so by a rapidly receding line of light brown hair which hung in a thin fringe around the collar of his fatigue jacket. Jimmy always wore old olive drab army clothes which emphasized the blocky mass of his upper body. Aside from a droopy brown moustache, he was clean-shaven. Below his level brows his pale blue eyes were sharp and observant.

I first met Jimmy and Harmony when I saw them cheering Alice on down at the harbor. Maybe, I'd better explain about Baltimore's Inner Harbor. There's an open theater area between the food and shopping pavilions which serve tourists, conventioneers and suburbanites out for their annual city spree. Every year singers, acrobats, dancers and musical groups audition for a license to do their thing there. They get tips from the audiences they attract. Some performers are pretty good and have gone on to greater fame.

The musical groups, particularly the funky ones, sometimes receive help from the more uninhibited members of their audience who spontaneously join the show. I've seen some really amazing dirty dancing down at the harbor, much of it from senior citizens. Alice was one of these.

Whenever the music inspired her, she'd wander out to the middle of the amphitheater and strut her stuff, much to the mixed amusement and consternation of onlookers. You had to hand it to the old girl. She never let the nervous titters and whispers bother her. Lost in her own private euphoria, she'd close her eyes, wiggle her butt and, prance, storklike, to the beat.

"Good to see you," Reverend Mike said, reaching out and shaking Jimmy's hand. "It's been a while."

"I've been busy, one thing and another. Took your advice and went to see that doctor down on Read street."

"How'd that work out?"

"Don't know yet. She prescribed something, but she says it'll take a while for it to kick in." Over Mike's shoulder, Jimmy shot me a faint grin. "Hi Toni."

"Hi, Jimmy. How's it going?"

"Not good, not bad. Heard about Alice. 'Spose you have, too."

We talked about Alice for a couple of minutes, sharing memories. Like a lot of homeless men in Baltimore, Jimmy is a Vet. Only, he's not homeless. Since he lost the use of his legs in a Vietnamese jungle, he collects a disability check and rents a place near the Cross Street Market. Nevertheless, I see him out on the street with a homeless sign propped on his lap accepting dimes and quarters to supplement his income.

Harmony ambled up to the table and set down the tray he'd loaded with his and Jimmy's lunches. "Smells good," he commented to all of us in general. He put half the food in front of Jimmy's place. "Vegetable soup's my favorite."

"Then you're in luck today," Mike said kindly, and pulled out a chair for Harmony who dropped into it and reached eagerly for his bowl. Not that he needed Mike's help. Harmony is somewhere in his early twenties and as nimble with his hands and feet as he is prolific with his harmonica. He can juggle and turn cartwheels at the drop of a hat and often does if there's any chance somebody might throw a quarter into his trademark watch cap.

Unfortunately, Harmony's mental state is even more unpredictable. He's schizophrenic, tossed out long ago by his parents and abandoned by a cost-cutting government willing to do no more than dole out pills. He's okay when he takes his medicine. That didn't used to be often. Since Jimmy started watching over him, Harmony has been seeing better days. The two help each other. Harmony adores Jimmy and follows him around like a devoted puppy.

When Jimmy told Harmony about the memorial service for Alice, the kid's face fell. His overflowing soupspoon paused between his plate and his mouth. Harmony's pointed chin, wide, mobile mouth and slanted dark eyes and brows make him look like a skinny, badly dressed elf. Whenever I see him, I think of stories my first grade teacher used to read to us kids about Robin Goodfellow. "Poor

Alice," he said. He caught my eye. "She liked you, Toni."

"I liked her, too." Guilt thickened my throat. "I'll miss her."

"We'll all miss the poor old girl," Mike commented. He patted Jimmy's shoulder. "Good to see you two. Take care now."

After Reverend Mike left us, I asked Jimmy if he'd mind if I sat down. Harmony and Jimmy were neighborhood characters, as Alice had been, so of course I knew who they were. But I wouldn't exactly call us friends. A couple of times I'd dropped change into Jimmy's cup, and once I'd given Harmony a dollar after a particularly soulful harmonica rendition of *Home on the Range*. But except a wave or an offhand greeting, I'd never really talked to either of them. Still, we'd had Alice in common, and we'd all seen each other around.

"Why should I mind?" Jimmy answered in his flat way. "Take a load off your feet. Glad for the company."

"She's a looker, isn't she?" Harmony remarked to his friend between loud soup slurps. He was shoveling food into his mouth as if he had the Grand Canyon yawning inside that skinny belly of his.

Under his brows, Jimmy shot me an amused look. "That's the thing about Harmony, he speaks his mind."

"I don't mind if it's compliments. Thanks, Harmony."

"Welcome." Avoiding my gaze, he jammed a cheese sandwich between his teeth.

I turned back to Jimmy who was consuming his soup in small sips that seemed oddly delicate in a man with his size and brooding demeanor.

"I saw Alice down at the harbor with you guys quite a lot."

Jimmy tore a small hunk off his sandwich and dipped it into his soup. "She used to hang around with us. Sometimes when Harmony was doing his juggling act, she'd pass the hat and we'd give her a percentage."

"She ever tell you anything about herself, her background?"

"Why do you want to know?"

"I can't stop thinking about her."

Jimmy nodded. "Yeah, I know. I still think about some of the guys I knew back in 'Nam, even dream about them." He shot a somber gaze around the church basement. The ragged crowd hadn't thinned any. The clink of spoons and rattle of plastic wrap being stripped from sandwiches echoed off the pale green cement block walls.

"She used to talk about how she grew up a farm girl on the Eastern Shore. According to her, she was doing fine until her husband ran off with another woman and she started drinking."

"How'd she wind up in Baltimore?"

Jimmy shrugged massive shoulders. "Who knows? Maybe she came here trying to get work."

"She came because nobody wanted her back home." Harmony had finished off his food and was looking around the table in a disappointed way. Jimmy tore of a small hunk of his sandwich. Harmony accepted it with delight.

"Since I don't move around much, stuck in this chair like I am, my stomach doesn't work so good," Jimmy commented.

"Mine works fine," said Harmony and downed the food in one gulp. His dark eyes looked at me with the brightness of a bird's. "Alice came to Baltimore because she was scared of something. The night before she got killed, she told me someone was trying to get her. I guess he did." Harmony pointed a bony finger around the room. "Maybe that someone is here right now. Maybe he's looking at us and planning on who he's going to get next."

Chapter 4

"OH, I'VE known about Alice's daughter for a long time."

Reverend Mike piloted his shiny new blue church van out Falls road. The two-lane strip of cracked asphalt runs through one of the more scenic sections of Baltimore County. I looked out the passenger window at pet emporiums, bicycle shops, and arty furniture stores. All were perched back from the winding road against hilly greenery. Dotting the land between the newer business developments were turreted old wood mansions and farmhouses dating back to the area's rural days.

"How did you find out about Alice having a daughter?" I asked.

"The old girl told me. I have to admit, at first I didn't believe her story. Thought she was just delusional about having a kid with a medical degree. Then Doris came to see me. She wanted to make a donation to the church just to make sure her mother always had a place to go. She's been giving us money ever since."

I mulled this over. "So Alice wasn't as alone in the world as we all thought. If she had a kid with money, why was she out on the street? Wouldn't the daughter help her?"

"It wasn't anything like that, Toni. Alice led the life she picked for herself."

"You mean she wanted to be out on the street panhandling quarters and checking out garbage cans?"

"Hard as it is to believe, yes—that's what I mean. And it's not just her, either. I'd have to say the same of a good many of my other clients."

By clients, of course, he meant the people he fed in his soup kitchen, the homeless alcoholics and schizophrenics he and his saintly wife cajoled out of doorways and off grates on bitter winter nights and ferried to his church basement so they wouldn't freeze. Reverend Mike sounded quietly resigned.

From my angle, his forehead and cheeks were round and smooth as a baby's. Above the open collar of his golf jacket I detected just a hint of a double chin. Below his sandy eyebrows, his eyes were as clear and guileless as a young child's. I figured he'd seen more misery than I could imagine—maybe just as much as O'Dell had seen. Yet the world's afflictions hadn't made Mike bitter or cruel. He just went on trying to do something about them.

"What's your secret, Mike? How do you see so much woe and still go on being such a nice person?"

He grinned at me. "Thanks for the compliment, but what makes you think I'm nice? Is it my big blue eyes?" He batted his wispy lashes at me.

"It's just seeing you in action and being around you. You're not dumb. You know how lousy things get out there. Yet you don't seem unhappy."

He nodded. "Happiness is a big word. But you're right. Despite all the trouble, I'm content with my life. The world's troubles touch and move me, but so far they haven't stained me. I owe a lot to Carol for that. We have a good and loving life together. And, of course, I have my convictions and my relationship with God."

I didn't know what to say about his relationship with God, but I did know what he meant about his marriage. Whenever I saw Mike and Carol together, it was obvious they loved and supported each other. They had built a personal life that apparently cushioned them from the rocky road they'd chosen.

"Why do you ask me about happiness, Toni? Is it yourself you're worried about?"

I shook my head. "Actually, I was thinking about a friend. He's a man who sees a lot of bad stuff in his line of work. I'm afraid it's making him sour and mean."

"Then maybe he should find a different job."

"He's not going to do that."

"Do you want to send him to me for counseling?"

"No offense, Mike, but he wouldn't go."

"Then maybe, if you care about this man, you're the one who's going to have to do the counseling. Tell him he needs to find something good in his life, something he can hold onto when things get dark."

"We all need something to hold on to, don't we?"

Mike nodded. "Now you've got it, Toni. That's the secret."

Things were getting heavy in the van, so I changed the subject. "What kind of doctor is Alice's girl?"

"She's a chiropractor."

"Is that like a real doctor?"

Mike chuckled. "Depends on who you ask. She certainly appears to make money like one. But Doris is a little different from other chiropractors I've met."

"How?"

"You'll see. We're almost there."

A couple of minutes later a large, arty sign beckoned us off the road. Though I didn't have time to sound out its words, I recognized the black and white figure behind them. It was the Chinese symbol for life's spiritual opposites, yin and yang. Mike turned into a gravel parking lot.

As he switched off his ignition, I spotted the same sign on a low slung redwood building. "New Wor ..." I said aloud as I tried to make sense of the spidery letters.

Mike knew about my reading problem. "New World Health Clinic," he said, helping me out.

"What's new world about it?"

"See if you can read the smaller words listed underneath."

I squinted, then shook my head. "No way."

Mike gave with his rich chuckle. "Chiropractic, Ohashiatsu, Colonics, Reflexology, Aromatherapy and Kripalu Yoga."

"I know what aromatherapy and chiropractic are, and I've heard of Ohashiatsu. What's colonics?"

"You've heard of spiritual cleansing? Well colonics tackles the cleansing issue on a much more physical level. Let's go in."

I still wasn't quite sure what he meant, but I was afraid to ask. Once past the double doors with their red lacquered oriental-style half-moon pulls, we were in another world. Beyond the terra cotta tile in the entry, an oatmeal colored carpet ran up against natural wood walls. Lush greenery dangled from the ceiling beams in peat pots and sprang from corners in bushy, flowering profusion. Rainforest and jungle spices freighted the damp air. Birds twittered amidst the soothing rush of falling water. I looked around, half expecting to see a waterfall.

"It's a CD," Mike informed me. "The sound is piped in through speakers."

"Can I help you?" The receptionist sat at a desk so thickly camouflaged with plants and flowers that I hadn't noticed her. As

Mike and I drew nearer, I saw that she was somewhere in her twenties. She'd drawn her long, straight blond hair smoothly back from a makeup-free face and wore a loose yellow shift with a gauzy weave. Her bare arms sported a dragon tattoo and several exotic bangles. A half dozen earrings pierced each ear, and a fine gold circlet decorated her right nostril.

We gave her our names then sat down to wait for Dr. Ritco. Soothed by birdcalls and the smell of sandalwood, I fell into a kind of trance. I have no idea how much time went by before the receptionist beckoned us behind a shoji screen and into Doris Ritco's office. A moment later she came in to greet us, and I heard myself make a strangled sound. It was like seeing Alice alive again.

"You look just like her," I said after we'd shaken hands and introduced ourselves.

She gazed at me from intelligent hazel eyes and nodded sadly. Doris Ritco was a younger, slim, well-dressed and well-groomed version of her mother. "You're not the first person to make that remark." She pointed to a framed picture on her desk. It was of a little girl holding a puppy. A young woman, obviously her mother, gazed down at her lovingly. At first I thought the woman must be Doris. Then I realized from the clothes and hairstyles that the photo had been taken sometime in the sixties. The woman had been Alice. Alice in another world, another life.

"What happened?" I stared at the woman in that picture. She held a hand up to her forehead to keep the sun out of her eyes. Its light gilded her hair. The summer breeze stirred curls around her shoulders. I thought of Alice the way I'd seen her last, her filthy hair matted, her alcoholic voice thick with despair.

Doris Ritco shrugged. "My father ran off with another woman. She started drinking, having affairs. My grandmother took me. Then I was lucky enough to win some scholarships so I could go away to school. I didn't see or hear from my mother for years and thought she might be dead. When I opened my practice here in Baltimore I hired a detective to find out. You can imagine how I felt when I finally found her."

How had Alice felt, I wondered. Had she wept for her ruined life?

Doris Ritco sighed and put a manicured finger on the linen collar of her shirt. "I tried to help her, tried to persuade her to change."

"I can certainly testify to that," Mike said.

Doris shook her head. "But she wouldn't. She said she was too old to change."

"Did your mother have any enemies that you knew of?" Harmony had said that someone was stalking Alice.

Doris shook her head again. "She thought everybody was her pal. That's one of the reasons she gave for not wanting to live with me. She said all her friends were on the street, and she was happy."

I picked up the photo and studied it more closely. "You know, it was probably true. Whenever I saw Alice, she was almost always cheerful."

"But look how she died!" Doris exclaimed. "If she had friends, they weren't there for her when she needed them."

I set the photo down and stuck my hands behind my back. I hadn't been there for Alice when she needed me. And I had been one of those she'd considered a friend.

I didn't sleep so well that night. Nevertheless, dawn's early light found me staked out behind a clump of overgrown evergreens in Guilford. I was determined to prove to Angus Maloney and Gus O'Dell and Randall Haworth and anybody else who doubted me—including myself—that I could be a detective. Through pin-point holly leaves, I eyeballed the fancy pile of gray stone Brooks Brockloff called home.

Guilford is the classiest neighborhood in the city. It features big old brick and stone mansions set back from shady curving streets on roomy azalea-dotted lawns. Though its outer edges rub shoulders with some of Baltimore's rougher neighborhoods, the oxygen in Guilford feels different. It breathes like old silk-smoothed by professional success and inherited money.

Baltimore's poor black population and rising crime rate makes the Guilford types nervous. Occasionally there's a burglary or a stickup on their hallowed streets and they go ballistic.

Last year an older couple was found murdered in their seven-bedroom mansion. The neighbors threatened to uncircle their Mercedes Benz's and head west. Then it came out that the wealthy couple had not been murdered by a crack-crazed black teenager but by their grandson.

I thought of this as I eyed Brooks Brockloff's front entrance.

Bad things can happen behind nailhead studded doors designed to look as if they belong on the other side of a drawbridge. You don't necessarily get rich by being a lovely person.

A short, thickset man came out toting a leather briefcase. Though he had a receding hairline and glasses, he carried himself like a man in his prime. I knew he had to be Brockloff. In his unbuttoned navy cashmere overcoat and tasseled loafers, he looked the look and walked the walk. The vanity plate on his pearl gray Lexus read Lawman, but it might as well have read "Lotsabucks."

As his car started down the street, I spotted a pallid face peering out the front windows of the Brockloff manse. Mrs. Lotsabucks checking to see if I was on the job. I squinted, trying to get a better look at her, but she quickly withdrew. My only impression was a stiff set of bony shoulders.

I peddled after the Lexus. So I'd pass for a bike courier, I wore a helmet and backpack. The Lexus proceeded at a discreet pace along St. Paul, then made a right onto University Parkway. Furiously, I peddled through traffic, weaving my way through delivery trucks and breathing in noxious fumes from gleaming Beemers and rusted station wagons. By the time I caught up, Brockloff had parked at a meter. I sighted him disappearing into one of the tall apartment buildings which look out over the north end of the Johns Hopkins campus.

After skidding up alongside the Lexus, I checked the time on the meter. Even if you're a lawyer with important connections, you don't play Russian roulette with Baltimore's parking meters. City finances being what they are, iron bandits sprout from every available curb. A horde of uniformed vultures salivating at the thought of slapping a twenty-dollar ticket on your windshield hovers nearby. Brockloff had paid for forty minutes.

I got out the notebook and pen I'd stuck in my back pocket. While my heart slowed from my rush through traffic, I did my best to jot the time and location. Despite my dyslexia, I've developed a sort of code I, at least, can usually read.

Since Brockloff didn't intend to be in the building long, I considered simply waiting for him to reappear outside. But I was born curious, and the pale princess in the window had paid to find out how her husband spent his hours away from the house.

I took an empty brown envelope out of my backpack, scribbled something illegible on the front and pushed my way through the apartment building's swinging glass door. A gray-haired clerk in a green and gold uniform stood behind a marble-topped console.

"I'm here to deliver some papers to..." I peered at the scrawl on my envelope. "Hmmm, it's kinda hard to read. I think It's a Mrs. George Braa..."

The clerk leaned over and peered at the envelope. "It's a disgrace how they don't teach people to write proper letters in school these days." He shook his head.

An old lady about four feet tall and wearing an out-of-date fur coat came pattering through the front door. A tiny pop-eyed dog with a breathing disorder was pulling her. Huffing and snorting like an asthmatic in a field of goldenrod, he dragged her across the marble floor. She slid at his rear as if she were a sack of flour on two-inch heels. As she coasted along, rearing back to keep her balance, she fluttered a hand at the desk clerk. "Fluffy is feeling his oats today!"

"The elevator is just coming down from the eleventh floor now, Mrs. Meyer." The clerk turned to me. "Could the name on your envelope be Meyer?"

"I don't think that's it." As the elevator doors pinged open and Fluffy dashed between them, I backed off. "Listen, I'll check with my dispatcher and get the correct name. No sense bothering people here 'til I've got my information straight."

Five minutes later I was at the bottom of the building's parking garage, lurking to one side of the pair of keyed elevators which allowed residents to bypass the lobby to get to their cars. I tried to remember the time when I'd checked Brockloff's parking meter. I don't wear a watch, but my instincts warned that about fifteen minutes had elapsed. For all I knew, Brockloff was back outside in his car and I was losing him.

At that moment the elevator wheezed open. Two elderly women with blue hair walked out. On instinct, I slipped in behind them and pressed eleven.

When the elevator gates parted again, I stepped into a dimly lit hall which smelled of mold and last night's TV dinners. Trying to make like a detective, I cocked my ears and swiveled my head for clues. A damp spot on the carpet in front of 1109 rewarded my efforts. Stepping around the spot, I pressed my ear to the door. "Wheeze, wheeze, puff puff, yap yap." I'd tracked down Fluffy.

I knocked and thirty seconds later the door cracked in front of a latched chain and Mrs. Meyer peered out. Between her feet, Fluffy snarled at me.

"Sorry to disturb you, ma'am, but I'm trying to make a delivery on this floor." I glanced at the envelope in my hand. "I'm looking for a Mr. Brockloff. Would you happen to know which apartment is his?"

"Stop that, Fluffy! Did you say Mr. Brockloff?"

"Well..." Giving the envelope another puzzled glance. "The writing isn't too clear."

"You must mean Mrs. Brockloff. I'm afraid you won't be able to visit her. She died months ago. Dropped dead at our Valentine's Day party, poor thing."

"Oh." Between Mrs. Meyer's feet, Fluffy still growled. His crazed eyes bulged.

"Of course," his mistress went on, "her son still comes around. Oh, not to visit her, of course. There's someone else living in her apartment now. He comes to visit her friend across the way in 1106, Mrs. Sekorski." She shot a pointed look up the hall. "He visits her at odd hours. For all I know, he might be there this very minute."

"Thanks." I knew for a fact that he was. After Mrs. Meyer closed her door, I mooched up to 1106 and pressed my ear to the paneled wood. The metal sliding against metal grind of someone turning the knob on the other side made me jump back. I hightailed around a corner just in time. Brockloff came out wearing a jaunty smirk and headed for the lobby elevator in the opposite direction.

When he was gone I tapped on 1106. I had no idea what to expect. Maybe Mrs. Sekorski was another little old lady. Maybe Brockloff, still in deep mourning for his mom, was visiting her in the role of surrogate-son. On the other hand, possibly everyone who lived here wasn't a retiree. Could be Mrs. Sekorski was a bleached blond chick fresh off the Block.

The woman who opened to me was neither, and a little of both. Though she had to be closer to sixty than the big 5-0, and therefore at least a decade or two older than Brockloff, she'd worked hard to lessen the impact. Dyed auburn hair hung loose around her shoulders. A crimson and peacock blue Chinese silk robe swathed a full, but well-preserved body and her face glowed from stubble burn and a recent tumble in the sack. She smelled of sex.

"Yes?"

"I'm trying to deliver an envelope to a Mrs. Brockloff."

The aging redhead licked her lips like a cat clearing away the last traces of clotted cream. "You're too late, dear. She's dead." *And I'm not,* her smile said. Score one for Brooks Brockloff.

Chapter 5

BY THE time I hit the street again, Casanova Brockloff was gone. I spent the rest of the morning parked outside the twenty-story tower which housed his firm.

As I lounged on my bike at the curb, trying to keep warm in the thin September sunshine, I mused about important life issues—namely sex. Actually, I'd been thinking a lot about sex lately. Mainly, I suppose, because I wasn't getting any. But also because it had been such a disaster for me.

After I shot Nick and Randall convinced the jury to acquit me on self-defense, I couldn't acquit myself. Nightmares terrorized me. I'd been badly burned by the man-woman thing. For a long time sex didn't interest me.

Then I met O'Dell. He was the first man in years who'd attracted me. Now, even though I couldn't stop thinking and worrying about him, I'd ruled him out. Did that leave me with any other hot romance prospects? I shook my head. Even when men showed an interest in me, my first instinct was to brush them off.

Yet, my conversation with Reverend Mike the day before lingered in my mind. Maybe the idyllic relationship he had with his wife wasn't in my stars. Still, the gleam in Mrs. Sekorski's eye and the flush on her withered cheek hadn't escaped me this morning. Brockloff was a jerk. But even sex with a guy like him was better for that woman than a whole bottleful of vitamins. I'd despaired of ever finding the perfect lover, but was I ready to call it quits entirely?

At noon the flow of people out of office buildings thickened. Gaggles of secretaries streamed through glass doors.

A few minutes later Brockloff appeared. He'd shed his overcoat. After striding down the stone steps, he headed briskly west on Lombard. I climbed onto my bike and followed.

Brockloff's destination turned out to be the Mariott. Either he was meeting a client, or the rest stop at the office had primed him for another love shove. A few minutes later I was filled with admiration to discover that it was the latter.

After parking my bike, I ambled into the hotel's lobby in time to see Brockloff disappearing up the elevator with a frizzy-headed blond who was as much too young for him as Mrs. Sekorski had been too old. This man was making a heroic effort at bridging the generation gap.

While I waited for the lovebirds to reappear, I downed a diet coke and a couple packages of peanut butter cheese crackers from the lobby gift shop.

I used the ladies room and was surprised and interested to find it swarming with a family of gypsies. After the mother and at least eight children of varying genders sampled every toilet and washbowl and decimated the paper towel supply, they streamed back outside. Their destination was a rusty Volvo station wagon with sagging springs.

As it swallowed the last little gypsy, a blue and white cop car roared up and my brother-in-law Al poked his big stupid head out the window. I pushed my way through the revolving door.

I was too late to hear what he'd had to say to the Volvo's driver. The man roared off with a squeal of brakes and a puff of blue exhaust.

"Running out of jaywalkers to hassle, so now you're giving kids a hard time?" I accused.

Al's head jerked in my direction. "As if my day hasn't been lousy enough, now I run into you!"

"Seeing you doesn't brighten my life, either. Why were you wasting taxpayers' money bothering those people?"

"Listen, bleeding heart, half the merchants downtown have complained about gypsies ripping them off, so I'm only doing my job. What's a bad girl like you doing in a nice place like this?"

Al's never going to believe I shot Nick in self-defense.

"Lending the lobby a little class."

"Then maybe you should brush the orange cracker crumbs off your shirt, Cupcake. I hear you bought yourself the worst dump in Baltimore."

"Yeah, it's so bad Sandy was willing to go back to you to get out of it."

Al glared. "Sweetheart, someday your mouth is going to get you into the kind of trouble your face can't get you out of." With that, he roared away.

Forty-five minutes later Brockloff reappeared with an extra

bounce in his jaunty stride. Five minutes after that the blond, looking considerably less jaunty, emerged from the elevator. I followed her. Sure enough, she took a different route, but wound up going inside Brockloff's office building. I went up and peered through the glass panel on the office where Brockloff was a partner. She was just settling into the receptionist's console.

"I wrote down the name on her plaque," I told Maloney when I stopped by his place that night to make my report. "It's Miss Lovelace, believe it or not. I bet anything Brockloff pressured her into sleeping with him. She was probably afraid she'd lose her job if she turned him down."

"I don't know," Maloney retorted. "Sounds as if the guy has a way with women."

Instead of meeting my new boss at his fleabag office, I'd gone to his fleabag apartment, as he'd requested. Maloney lived in a building off Park. His place was in one of those cut-up old mansions that rents cheap because it's close to a homeless shelter. Yet its high ceilings and ornate plasterwork still recalled the days of its turn-of-the-century splendor.

I admired a marble fireplace where Maloney had propped several snapshots of a fair-haired little boy I guessed was his son. One of them showed Maloney and his wife and son posing with big happy smiles.

Aside from the snapshots, there wasn't much of a personal nature in the living room. As I noted its elegant proportions I reflected that Randall would have had an apartment such as this looking like a palace. Maloney, on the other hand, hadn't exactly maximized its potential. His furniture consisted of a stained couch and a ratty canvas chair.

"I guess you're not exactly into home improvement," I commented.

He stopped pacing back and forth in front of the couch where I'd perched. "What are you, a critic? The decorating police? When my wife threw me on the street, she didn't shove any of our fancy couches and chairs out the door after me."

"Hey, I'm sorry. Sometimes I speak without thinking. I don't want to offend you, honest. I want to work for you."

He slapped his hands on his hips, which were still noticeably too narrow for the rest of him. He wore the same loose khaki pants and shirt he'd sported the day I went to his office to apply for a job. If he hadn't looked clean, I would have wondered if he ever changed his clothes.

"I'm working a construction site tonight, so I need to grab some chow. Tell me the rest on Brockloff in the kitchen, okay?"

A thoughtless landlord had painted Maloney's kitchen a dingy blue. The pipes showed in several places and the sink and refrigerator were historic, to put it kindly. While I sat at a small table and continued my account, Maloney peered into a painted wood cabinet. He extracted a can of Spaghetti O's, a can of baked beans, a can of hash and a can of minestrone soup. His five fruits and vegetables of the day?

"After his lunch break, if you want to call it that, Brockloff stayed in his office until three."

"Hard working guy. Probably in that time he raked in more dough than I see in a year. Then what?"

"He came out and headed for the Block."

Maloney dumped the Spaghetti O's into a battered enamelware saucepan. "The guy is into variety."

"Guess so." The Block is Baltimore's infamous downtown sin strip.

"Brockloff went into a club called The Volcano. He came out ten minutes later with a redhead on his arm. They disappeared into an alley entrance next to a storefront with an adult book display.

The hash in Maloney's skillet had started to sizzle. "Was this redhead a 38D with raspberry colored hair teased up about a foot off her head?"

"I couldn't begin to guess her bra size. You're probably close, though. She a friend of yours?"

"Let's just say, I know the city well and Merlene is unforgettable. Want some minestrone and hash? There's plenty for two."

"Sure."

"Beer with it?"

"Just a glass of water, thanks." I noticed Maloney didn't offer to share his Spaghetti O's. The man knew when to be openhanded.

"Okay, what next?" Maloney dished the food. He pulled out the chair opposite me, straddled it and dug in. Washing dishes wasn't going to be a problem. His china and silver were paper plates, styrofoam soup bowls and plastic utensils.

"Nothing. Brockloff and Merlene came out a half hour later. She went back to the Volcano and he headed for his office. He left shortly before five and drove straight home." Actually, I couldn't be completely sure of this since I hadn't always been able to keep him in sight on my bike. But when I arrived at his house, his Lexus was parked in the drive.

"Well, three in a day, that's pretty good," Maloney said. "Lucky bastard," he muttered under his breath. Meditatively, he wolfed down his hash.

I did the same. It was good—a nice mix of salt, grease and nitrates, and I was hungry.

"You did very well," he said.

His praise made me glow. Actually, the secretary and Merlene had been easy, just a matter of trailing behind Brockloff. But if I hadn't shown some initiative, I wouldn't have found out about Mrs. Sekorski. "Does that mean you're going to let me work for you on other cases?"

"We'll see." Maloney took a swig of beer. "For now, I want you to follow Brockloff until Friday. Keep a record and at the end of the week make a full report."

"What kind of report?" My heart fell.

"Just a written account of times and places and names when you have them." He glanced at his watch. "I have to be at the construction site by seven-thirty."

"What are you doing there?"

"Keeping an eye on the place. Old lady was murdered there a couple of nights back. It's on the waterfront where city bigwigs hope to lure the yuppies. Murder is bad publicity."

I knew he must be talking about the site where Alice had been killed. "So, you're a night watchman?"

Maloney grimaced. "I don't wear a uniform or make the rounds. Somebody else does that. I'm just staked out in my car. If I see anything that looks like trouble, I dial a number on my car phone."

"Must be rough sitting in a car all night."

"It pays the bills. In my line of work money tends to flow unevenly, in case you hadn't already guessed."

"Would you like me to spell you? I could sit in a car just as well as you." Actually, I couldn't since I didn't have an automobile and couldn't drive. But I didn't think of that until the words were out of my mouth.

"You?" Maloney shook his head and started gathering up our empty plates. Since tidying up meant tossing everything into a plastic garbage bag, I helped. "What would you do if somebody came along and gave you trouble?"

"I'd be locked inside the car."

"There are people in this town who aren't shy about breaking windshields."

"I can take care of myself."

"You mean, like this?"

Maloney's big hand shot out, grabbed my wrist and whirled me around. Before I even knew what was happening, I was lying on my stomach at his feet. He'd broken my fall with one hand. The other hand held my arm twisted around behind my back, so I couldn't move.

"Hey! What's the idea! Stop that!" Fear such as I hadn't known in a long time knifed through me. My heart pounded. Blood churned in my ears as if my head were an out-of-balance washing machine. Black spots appeared before my eyes.

Next thing I knew, I was lying on Maloney's couch and he was staring down at me with a worried look on his big Irish face. "You okay?"

"Yeah, I mean..." I tried sitting up, but my head still felt woozy and I fell back.

"Hey, I'm sorry about roughing you up. I didn't mean to hurt you. I just wanted to show you what could happen."

"You showed me." I felt my cheeks go hot. Actually, I was the one who'd shown Maloney what a chicken-hearted wuss I was, fainting just because he'd put a hold on me.

"I'm really sorry," he insisted. "When you blacked out like that I wanted to kick myself."

"Hey, forget it. I guess you just scared me."

"You were more than scared. It was stupid of me to forget about..." He hesitated, then cleared his throat. "The reason you fainted like that was because..." I knew what was coming and braced myself.

"Did it have anything to do with what happened between you and your husband before..."

"Before I shot him?"

"Yeah."

"I don't know just what it was you did, but Nick used to do something like that to me now and then. He liked to show me how helpless I was."

"I see why you shot him."

"I didn't mean to kill my husband. He was drunk, hitting me. I just grabbed his service revolver off the kitchen table. Somehow, it went off. When I realized he was dead, I called 911 and then went into shock."

"The way you behaved just now, I imagine. But in my line of work it's not a good idea to faint whenever a bad guy lays a hand on you. You can see where I'm coming from."

I could see, all right. Maloney had decided I wasn't fit to work for him. I struggled into a sitting position. "I wasn't prepared for what you did. If I were in a dark alley or staked out watching for bad guys, I'd be expecting trouble. I'd react differently."

"Trouble doesn't always give you a chance to prepare. Often as not, it's sudden and unexpected."

"I know, but...look, I really need this job. Please give me a chance."

"If something happened to you on my time, it would be my fault. I'd know I'd sent someone on a job who couldn't protect herself. I don't need that on my shoulders."

"Then teach me how to protect myself."

He sighed. "I'll say this for you. You're persistent."

"Also punctual and hardworking. I need this job badly. I really want to work for you."

"To work for me you should know how to handle yourself physically." Maloney's green eyes ran over me, assessing. "You don't have much meat on your bones, but you look strong."

"I am strong. I'm extremely healthy." Riding my bike around Baltimore, I certainly got plenty of exercise.

"Okay, if you're willing to learn, I'm willing to teach you."

"Teach me what?"

"Aikido." He glanced at his watch again, then grabbed a yellow folder off a stack on top of the mantel and handed it to me. My reading skills are not the greatest. I knew the first word in thick black letters was BALTIMORE. I recognized the last word, ARTS. The

MARTIAL in the middle took some silent sounding out. The address at the bottom I didn't even try to decipher.

"Meet me there Saturday morning around ten," Maloney said. "You can deliver the material on Brockloff the same time. It'll be a fun morning of sex and violence.

Chapter 6

DARKNESS HAD crowded out the light when I left Maloney's place. I climbed on my bike and headed south at a brisk pace.

As my wheels turned, I mused about Brockloff and Maloney, and even about Nick. Yes, I think of him too often. Eventually, my thoughts returned to Alice. On impulse, when I hit the harbor, I headed east instead of continuing south and wound up at Beans and Bread in Fells Point.

It's one of the many soup kitchens scattered around the city. Located in a run-down row house on a side street close to the market, Beans and Bread is staffed by volunteers. I know a guy who volunteers there. He says you can tell the time of the month by the length of the lines waiting to get fed. At the beginning of the cycle, when the SSI checks come out, the place is deserted. "They're all off ordering filet mignon at the Ritz."

This was the wrong end of the month. The line of down-and-outers snaked around the corner and well back into the alley.

Inside, the same cast of characters I'd seen at Reverend Mike's crowded the place's tiny rooms.

"Alice didn't make it down here too often," Marge Creech told me when she was able to get a couple minutes break from dishing out hot dogs and creamed corn.

Marge is a grandmotherly type from East Baltimore. After she feeds her half dozen cats and bakes brownies for her tribe of grandchildren, she schlepps down to help out at Beans and Bread. She says she does it because "it's my Christian duty." I think she does it because her heart is as generous as the bosom which slopes down to the bulging waistband on her pale green Banlon slacks.

I know Marge from when she waited tables in my parents' restaurant. She always went home with the biggest tips just because of the sheer homey warmth of her personality. Marge is retired now, but she's still feeding the hungry.

"You know the place where they found her body is only a couple of blocks from here?" I asked.

Marge's multiple chins bobbled sadly. "Yeah, I heard. What a way to go, face down on a pile of dirt where they used to stick the loonies."

"Loonies?"

"You're too young to remember, hon, but I know all the buildings used to be around here. That construction site where they went and found Alice used to be a mental hospital. It got tore down in the sixties."

"Really." I flashed back to the excavation where O'Dell had told me they'd found the twenty-year-old remains of a young girl. Those bricks had probably come from that mental hospital. Did O'Dell know about it?

"You know what I been thinkin'?" Marge asked. "All the time I've been slinging hash for these men here, I've been wonderin' if one of them could of done it. I mean, they all knew Alice."

"All?" I glanced around at the men gobbling down their hot dogs.

"Well, most of them. Alice wasn't shy with the fellas. She got around."

"She ever tell you anything about herself?"

Marge puffed out her lips. "Said she used to be a farm girl until her man left her and she started in on the booze."

That jibed with what Doris Ritco had told me. I wondered about Alice's husband. It must have been a long time since he'd walked out on her. Could he have anything to do with her murder?

"If they're not already crazy, it's the booze that gets them all," Marge was continuing philosophically, "either that or the drugs."

"Did you know Alice had a daughter who's a chiropractor, Marge?"

"If she did, she never said. It's possible, though. Anything's possible in this city. Which makes me think about you, Toni. You got yourself a boyfriend yet?" Marge gazed at me in kindly inquiry. The bare light bulb on the wall fixture behind her head glowed through her teased waves and turned them into a pale taffy halo.

"I'm still flying solo, Marge."

"It's a damn shame, pretty girl like you." She clacked her tongue. "Hon, you should have a pack of kids by now, just like my Ernestine. She's not much oldern' what you are and she's got half a dozen and another in the oven. Time's flying, Toni. You won't always keep that pretty young face on you. A woman's a poor piece without no grankids to comfort her in her old age. Take my word on it."

"I don't have to, Marge. Everybody else I know is saying the same thing."

I LEFT BEANS and Bread and rolled my bike down the cobblestones of Thames Street. As I admired the fat red Moran tugs at rest in the harbor, I pondered my life. I looked back on a collection of blunders. There was no pattern, no meaning. Somehow I had to make my life mean something. I felt in need of company and considered stopping in at The Cat's Eye for a beer.

Knots of young girls in tight jeans and leather jackets streamed past me followed by similarly dressed males wearing backward baseball caps. Couples came out of bars, their hands stuck in each others rear pockets. A pair kissed and cooed under a streetlamp. Like eager pianists, their fingers ran up and down each other's backs. Once Nick and I had been like that. I turned my bike around and headed home.

Inside my house, I dialed O'Dell's number. To my surprise, he answered.

"Oh, it's you," I blurted when I heard his voice.

"Who did you expect would pick up the phone in my apartment, Toni? Claire Boothe Luce?"

"She's dead?"

"Then it would be mighty strange if she answered my phone."

"I thought you'd be at work."

"You called to speak to my answering machine? Don't swamp me with flattery."

I cleared my throat. "I found out something, and I wanted to make sure you were aware of it, too." I told him what Marge had said about the mental institution.

"Yeah, I knew that. It was an old psychiatric Institute and mental hospital called The Harzine Institute. It was built in the 1890's."

"That girl's body you found, maybe she was an inmate or worked there."

"Not likely. When they took the Institute down in the sixties it had been more or less abandoned for a couple of decades. What makes you so interested in a case that's ancient history? If you want to play detective, think about Alice Ritco. She's somebody you knew and her corpse is a lot fresher."

"I can't stop thinking about that young girl. Maybe her murder and Alice's are connected somehow." As I threw this out, I wondered where it had come from.

"That's a crazy notion. No crazier than you doing legwork for Angus Maloney, though."

"How'd you know about that?"

"Baltimore's a small town. He told me himself. I go to his dojo three times a week to work out."

"His dojo?"

"Maloney's a black belt in karate and aikido. He teaches self-defense for the BPD and down in Washington, too. He runs his own dojo in Hampden. That's not where I first met him, though. When Angus and I first ran into each other, he was QRT, just like me."

"Quick Response Team? Was he a sharpshooter, too?" O'Dell's main claim to fame is his marksmanship. Everyone who knows anything about guns tells me he's the best.

"Maloney knows how to pull a trigger, but his talent is hand-to-hand combat. He's not bad at scaling walls and kicking in doors, either."

"How come he's not still on the force, like you."

"Ask him. Why all the questions, Toni? You interested in Maloney?" O'Dell's voice had taken on an edge.

"Of course I'm interested. I'm hoping to work for him, maybe even get to be a private investigator myself."

"Yeah, well you know what I think about that."

"You told me."

"Okay, work for Maloney, but don't get any romantic ideas. If you do, you'll only get hurt. He's still hung up on his ex-wife."

"My romantic ideas are none of your business, O'Dell."

"You mean you do get them? Comes as news to me. Speaking of news, another piece crossed my desk today. Your other boyfriend, Randall the Black Avenger, is going after my balls. It's official. He's charging me with police brutality in the Jerome Robinson case."

I had been blotting that from my mind. "I warned you."

"Thanks a lot. By the way, you're going to be his chief witness. Listen, duty calls. I gotta' go out and practice my brutality. You know, bash in some heads and break some arms. See you in court."

The line went dead. What a lousy day this had been. I asked myself why I should care about the bitterness in O'Dell's voice. I shouldn't. But I did.

As I replaced the receiver my gaze fell on Maloney's brochure lying on the counter next to the sink. I smoothed and opened it. Inside, nestled in a sea of thick black print was a picture of Maloney. Dressed in a white karate suit, he was flipping another guy on a mat.

I sat down at the kitchen table and sounded out the words. A half an hour later, this is what I had learned: Angus Maloney was recognized by the Japan Aikido Association as a 4th degree black belt. He also held a 2nd degree black belt in Judo and a first degree black belt in Karate.

He was nationally certified as a "Police Self-Defense Instructor" with the United States Karate Association. He was also certified as a "Psycho-Motor Skill Design Instructor" with the Justice System Training Association. He was an instructor of self-defense for the United States Customs Service in Washington, D.C. Three years ago he had opened Baltimore Martial Arts where he offered a wide range of supplies and instruction. That was where he'd told me to meet him Saturday morning. I glanced back at the picture of the guy going splat on the mat. He didn't look too happy. Was that what Maloney had in mind for me?

NEXT MORNING Casanova Brockloff went straight to his office. No stop offs for a quickie at the old folks building. Well, yesterday had seen a lot of activity on the stud front. Even a champ needs an occasional breather.

It was a gray morning with a damp chill that boded rain. I was glad I'd worn a sweater under a waterproof anorak. As I straddled my bike on the curb across from Brockloff's building, I pictured Maloney spending the night parked near that construction site and wondered how he endured the spooky boredom of it.

It's funny I happened to be thinking about Maloney, because just then I looked up and spotted his ex-wife. Dressed in a classy black raincoat, she was just emerging from Brockloff's building.

There was nothing surprising in this. The glass and poured concrete tower was stuffed with lawyers. Why shouldn't the ex Mrs. Maloney work in there too?

It was only ten-thirty, a little early for her to be going out to lunch. But she could be going to court, or heading to some other law office to haggle over a divorce settlement.

I watched her march down the street in her sexy high heels, long blond hair bouncing against her shoulders. She wasn't headed toward the Clarence Mitchell Courthouse and she wasn't carrying a briefcase. I pushed off and followed.

She didn't go far. Ten minutes later she disappeared into the revolving glass door outside the Mariott. Hey, wasn't this where Brockloff met his receptionist?

Pretending to study a poster on an easel, I watched Karla Maloney check in and take her key to the elevator. Then I watched her elevator stop at the 9th floor.

Who was she meeting? Could it be Maloney? No, somehow I didn't think so. Of course, her reason for being here could be professional. Either way, what business was it of mine?

I was turned toward the exit, intending to hurry back to Brockloff's office building, when what to my wondering eye should appear but Brockloff himself.

I scooted behind a collection of potted ficus. He hurried past me to the desk, took a key and then caught the elevator. Mesmerized, I watched it climb to the ninth floor. That's where it stopped, and he'd been the only passenger.

By five I'd finished my workday by trailing Lover-boy-Brockloff back to his Guilford mansion. Instead of going directly home, I detoured toward the Pratt Library. As I peddled through the darkening streets, avoiding manholes blowing steam, I passed Maloney's building. What was I going to tell my new boss about his wife and Brockloff?

At the library, I worked on a draft of the report I would be turning in on the Amorous Litigator. Finally, I wandered over to the reference desk. There I asked the librarian to help me get some information on the Harzine Institute. She took me to a deserted stack where we found an old paperbound collection of scholarly articles about the Institute.

"What are you looking for?" she asked as she handed it to me.

"I'm not sure, just curious about the past, I guess." Though I was born curious, there was more to my interest in finding out about the Harzine than mere nosiness. Sure, the dump job was O'Dell's case, not mine. But I couldn't stop thinking about that young girl and the mystery of her death. Though there was no logical reason, other than location, to link her murder with Alice's, the two kept getting mixed up in my imagination. And I was taking Alice's death personally.

After spending a few minutes trying to make my aching eyes wade through the book's dense print, I checked it out. I had to have the thing at home where I could take my time.

Ten minutes later, I stopped at Mount Vernon Square where Randall lives.

"Your timing is excellent," he said when he opened the door to me. "I've cooked for two, but Johnathan just called to say he won't be home for dinner. You might as well supply an alternate mouth and gastrointestinal tract."

"Since you put it so graciously, don't mind if I do. What's on the menu?" I asked as I followed him past Tiffany lamps, oriental rugs and a velvet-covered empire-style sofa.

"*Filet de boeuf Richelieu* with braised lettuce and baked tomatoes. Meet with your approval?"

"Sounds like heaven. I've been eating peanut butter all week."

Surrounded by big antique copper cook pots and heat from his precision-made German restaurant-grade stove, we sat down to a cozy dinner. He added a fine red burgundy to the meal, and as I sipped it and forked up the delicious food, I basked.

It didn't bother me that I was taking Johnathan's spot. I've never been comfortable with the guy. Perhaps it's his unearthly blond beauty. Or maybe I'm just jealous and want Randall all to myself. Yet I know Randall and I can never be anything but friends. That's part of why I feel so comfortable with him.

"How's the decorating going?" he asked.

"Lousy. I haven't had a decent job in days."

"Well, if a customer turns up in need of good antiques, I know where some can be had cheap. Remember Chad Kerr?" he asked, referring to an artist friend of Johnathan's who also lived in the Mount Vernon area.

"Sure. Nice guy."

"His lover died of AIDS, so he's selling his stuff and moving to a commune in Sedona."

"I'm sorry to hear that."

We talked about old friends, city politics, the weather and the latest political scandal in the city.

Finally, I asked, "So, how's the Jerome Robinson case going?"

"I was wondering when you'd get around to that." Randall reached for the wine bottle. He'd shed his suit jacket and tie. Against his smooth, ebony skin, his crisp shirt gleamed all the whiter. A pair of chunky gold cufflinks lay on the Italian tile cooking island where he'd removed them so he could roll up his sleeves. His dark forearms were long and sculpted with muscle. "Is that why you came around, to weasel out of being a witness? Forget it, Toni."

"I came because I wanted to see you. You're the best friend I've ever had."

"Too true, and at the risk of sounding crass, you owe me. Has O'Dell been crying on your shoulder?

"O'Dell isn't exactly the weepy type."

"No? Wait until I get through with him." Randall swirled the ruby liquid in the deep bowl of his wine glass.

"You are really on his case, aren't you?"

"You got it, Babe."

"Why? What's he ever done to you?"

"To me personally, nothing. He messed up Jerome Robinson pretty good, though. You know how old Jerome is? He's fourteen."

"He looks older, and he was smashing other people's windows."

"You'd be out smashing windows, too, if you had his life. Raised in the projects, no father, mother on crack. That kid has so many needs, so many needs." Randall grimaced. "Being slammed around by a vindictive cop isn't one of them."

"O'Dell hasn't had such an easy life either. His parents were alcoholics. He was raised by a redneck uncle who only treated him decently when he learned to use a gun and started bringing rabbits home for the cookpot."

"What has O'Dell's shooting bunny rabbits got to do with anything?"

"Only that he and Jerome have more in common than you might think. The anger that set Jerome to breaking windshields isn't so different from what O'Dell bottles up. When he caught Jerome it was at just exactly the wrong time." I reminded Randall about O'Dell's dump job, and then told Randall about Alice. While he listened in stolid silence, I fished out my book on the Harzine Institute and told him the little I'd managed to glean from it.

"It was privately owned and operated until it was donated to the state in the early fifties. It was connected with all the colleges and universities around here which gave degrees in psychology. The librarian said I might be able to find out more about it from the medical records library at Hopkins. Do you think they'd let me in there?"

"Not unless you're studying to be a doctor at Hopkins, which so far as I know, you aren't. You could try UMAB," he added, referring to the University of Maryland medical school. "What's your interest in this, anyway?"

I toyed with my own wine glass. "I can't stop thinking about that girl's body buried there all those years. Sandy and I must have walked right over it when we were kids."

Randall sighed. "What is it with you, Toni? You imagine that because you shot your no-good husband you're obligated to seek justice for the rest of this sorry world by poking your nose into every wrong you come across?"

"Look who's talking. Four years ago you took my case and didn't charge me a cent?"

"And don't you forget it. Speaking of favors I've done you, I hear you're working for Angus Maloney now. How's it going?"

"Fine, except now I have a problem in diplomacy to work out. Maybe you can advise me." I told him about Brockloff and Maloney's wife.

Randall shook his head. "Poor Angus. He's really hung up on that woman."

"You know her?"

"I've worked with Karla Maloney on several personal injury cases. It's common knowledge that Brooks Brockloff's sex life would make Clinton look like a slacker. Take my advice for a change, Toni. Don't say anything about Brockloff and Karla to Angus Maloney. Believe me, he won't thank you for it."

Chapter 7

SATURDAY MORNING I biked to Baltimore Martial Arts.
Maloney's dojo was in the old warehouse complex on the Jones Falls
in Hampden. At one time Hampden was a mill village. Now the big
old brick buildings at what used to be its industrial heart have been
abandoned or turned over to impecunious theater companies and
starving artists.

"Says something for your ingenuity that you found the place,"
Maloney remarked after I threaded my way through the maze of
crumbling tunnels and dank abandoned spaces that led to his cave. It
featured a dozen royal blue mats laid on the floor of what looked to
have been an old stable.

The make-do facilities didn't seem to bother the four barefooted
men rolling around on mats. They all wore white karate outfits with
different colored belts. Maloney, too, wore the traditional pajama-
style white. A loosely knotted black belt girdled his middle.

I wondered why he and Karla had run into trouble. He seemed
like a nice guy. Of course, in the final years of our marriage, Nick had
seemed like a nice guy—to everyone but me.

"Got the report for Brockloff's missus?" Maloney asked.

I handed him a brown envelope with two neatly typed pages.
Randall, bless his heart, had shown me how to type my scrawl into his
computer and use it to correct my spelling and punctuation.

"Neat place you've got here."

"It's a dump, but it's all I can afford." Maloney glanced over the
report. "You don't identify the last female that Brockloff met at the
Mariott.

"A classy looking blond, but nobody I'd know," I lied.
"Brockloff was the first to come down, so I decided to follow him
back to the office."

"Hmmm, okay. You certainly ought to have more than enough
other names here to satisfy our client. Good work, Toni."

"Thanks." I stood there glowing. For a stupid moment, I almost felt like crying. That's how much simple praise means to me. For so many years Nick made me believe I was the dumbest, most incompetent person in the world.

Maloney patted my shoulder. The gesture hung a necklace of guilt around my neck. I'd lied to him. The man had a right to be told the truth of who Brockloff was bedding, even if it hurt. Nevertheless, I took Randall's advice and kept my mouth shut.

"Okay," said Maloney, "so far, so good. "Got an hour to spare?"

"That's why I'm here. I thought you wanted to show me some self-defense. Maybe you're too busy."

We both looked at the guys going at each other a few feet away. From time to time one would glance our way. Mostly, they concentrated on each other, their thuds and grunts echoing off the scarred wooden rafters.

"They can take care of each other for a while," Maloney said. "Take off your shoes, and I'll get you started."

While I unlaced my thrift shop Nike's, I noticed my hands felt like Popsicles. The place had no heat, but the icy hands were from nerves. I'm strong, but Maloney had to be close to twice my size. He intended to teach me, not hurt me, but I remembered all too vividly how it had felt when he'd grabbed me in his apartment. It had felt as if he could break me in half. And that was before I'd read he was a martial arts super jock.

But it was more than fear of pain turning my hands blue. Let's be honest. Since what happened with Nick, I'm still not normal about sex. The idea of a man touching me, holding me—any man—makes me feel skittish and faintly sick. When I stepped onto the mat where Maloney stood waiting patiently, my heart was drilling a hole in my ribs.

"Ready?"

"As I'll ever be."

"It's etiquette to bow before stepping onto the mat, by the way."

I bowed.

"I'm going to teach you some traditional Tomiki style Aikido. That's the best unarmed self-defense for a woman. In Aikido, you blend with the power of the attack. You redirect the aggression against the opponent."

"Sounds good to me."

"First, you should learn about falling. Pretend I'm your mirror and do what I do." He dropped into a crouch position, then rolled back on the mat, slapped it loud with the flats of his hands and sprang back up.

Awkwardly, I mimicked him. My slap felt and sounded a hundred times weaker than his.

"Slap off to the side thirty degrees. That's what takes the impact. Straighten the legs as you roll back and shift the weight. Reach out as you slap so you can bounce back. Keep doing it until it starts to feel more comfortable. In Aikido you practice the moves so often that you don't have to think. You just react. Slap the mat harder, Toni."

"I'm doing it as hard as I can."

While I rolled around on the floor, Maloney watched. "Okay. Stand up and I'll explain something."

When I'd struggled to my feet and we faced each other, he put his palm low on his belly against the knot on his black belt. "In oriental thinking, this is your center."

"I know Tai Chi. A long time ago a friend taught me the short form."

"Okay, then you understand about bringing your mind to your physical center of balance. You don't block an attack. You don't stop it. You blend with the motion and all from your center of balance. The idea is to break the balance of your opponent and make him vulnerable.

"Gotcha."

"Sean." He called over a well built youngster with tight curls and a handsome mahogany face sheened with sweat. "We're going to show Toni here a couple of release techniques. Try grabbing me."

As I watched the two move in against each other in a kind of slow motion ballet of violence, I was amazed by Maloney's delicacy. Despite his size he danced lightly around the mat. After he'd demonstrated several throws and evasive techniques, he turned me over to Sean. As Maloney walked away to join his other students, I surprised myself by feeling a twinge of disappointment. During the whole learning session, he hadn't even laid a hand on me.

WHEN I GOT back to my place, I found my sister parked in front. "Where are the kids?" I asked after I got over my surprise and peered in at her.

Though she didn't unlock the doors, she rolled down her

window a couple of inches. "With Mom. Get in, I'll take you to lunch."

I'd just peddled all the way from Hampden and would have liked to shower. But desperation glinted from Sandy's eyes. I slid into the passenger seat, and she gunned the motor and pulled away from the curb as if she were the getaway driver on a bank heist.

"Where are we going?"

"The harbor."

"We could have walked. It's only a couple of blocks."

"If I left my car in your neighborhood, I'd worry about someone breaking into it."

"Sandy, for that you'd have to leave an ingot of gold in plain view on the passenger seat of this heap."

Ten minutes later we'd shed seven bucks to park in a downtown garage and walked across the bridge over Light Street to the Chinese restaurant that looks out over the harbor.

"What's this all about?" I asked after we ordered. "Al getting on your nerves again?"

Sandy glared. "You always have to say something smart, don't you? You were always like that, even when we were kids—always mouthing off."

"Hey, I'm your sweet little kid sister, remember?" I took the book on the Harzine Institute out of my jacket pocket where it had been rubbing against my side and placed it on the table. Since checking it out of the library I'd carried it with me everywhere, trying to read it whenever I could."

"What's that book?"

"Just some research I'm doing."

"You, doing research?" She picked the book up and riffled through the pages. "It's some kind of fancy gibberish about psychological experiments. Why would that interest you?"

"Remember Alice Ritco, the woman you turned away from my place? She was murdered that same night. I think this book might have something in it that would help solve the crime."

Sandy stared at me. "Are you saying I'm responsible because that homeless drunk got herself killed?"

"I'm not trying to say that, Sandy."

"But you're thinking it. You brought that up because you want me to feel guilty. You know, whenever Al calls you a murdering bitch who blew away his best friend, I defend you. But, honest to God, Toni, there are times when I can see why Nick might have wanted to knock you around."

My throat closed. Of all the people who'd dumped on me after the accident with Nick, my own family had been the worst. My father had thrown me out, and my mother hadn't stood up for me. Al had tried to get Sandy to stop speaking to me. I'd thought we'd made up and she'd come around to seeing things my way a little bit. "Spoken like a true servile Italian bride. Al took up your training where Dad left off, didn't he?"

"It has nothing to do with being an Italian wife. Besides, Al is Polish."

"And he's got a joke for a brain, too."

Across the table we bristled at each other. I was on the point of getting up and stalking away when I noticed how lousy Sandy looked. At her best, she looks like me twenty pounds heavier, dressed frumpy and gone to seed. But now her eyes were sunken and framed with shadow. A crease bisected her forehead, and her mouth under the lipstick was pinched.

"Before we cut each other up, what's this all about Sandy? Something's really wrong, isn't it?"

She hid her face behind her hands. "I hate my life," she whispered through her fingers. "My life is shit."

"It's Al, isn't it? What's he done?"

"Oh God, Toni, you won't believe the latest. He's quit his job—just handed in his badge and walked off. He's no longer a cop."

I gaped. Al no longer making life hell for teenage runaways, homeless panhandlers and harmless gays—I couldn't picture it. "Then how does he propose to make a living, for crying out loud? Theoretical physics?"

"He's going to sell sno cones."

"Would you care to repeat that?"

"I'm not joking, Toni. He's taking all his retirement money out and using it to buy a van. He plans on driving around to construction sites selling sandwiches, cold drinks and sno cones. According to Al, Baltimore is the second biggest sno cone city in the country, the first being New Orleans. There are a dozen bottles of strawberry, cherry and grape syrup sitting in cartons in our basement right now."

Sandy massaged her forehead. "Between you and me, one of the reasons I married Al was to get away from Mom and Dad and the restaurant. I was sick of scraping other people's dishes and smelling other people's food. I guess that had something to do with why you married Nick, too."

I didn't argue. Sandy and I had both seen wedding bells as a way out from under Pop's thumb and the kitchen at Credella's. So we'd convinced ourselves we were madly in love.

"Now Al is trying to talk me into spending my evenings slapping together ham and cheese sandwiches. I feel sick."

"I don't blame you. Al's a stubborn guy. If he's determined to operate a roach coach, how are you going to stop him?"

My sister gazed at me with naked despair. "That's just it. I can't."

"Then relax. See what happens. Who knows, maybe Al will become Baltimore's Sno Cone mogul."

SANDY AND I parted on a doleful note. She drove away to rescue mom from my nephews and I set off for home.

It had turned into a beautiful autumn afternoon. People jammed the harbor's brick promenade. Young mothers from the suburbs pushed strollers. Harried teachers and parents shepherded rowdy school groups who eddied and flowed around rubbernecking conventioneers and photo-snapping Japanese tourists. CEO types in business suits strolled back to their offices at a brisk pace while they talked money and power.

As I watched the multitude flow by, I spotted a familiar looking old woman in a fur coat. She was being dragged to the water's edge by a ratty genetic error on a leash. Mrs. Meyer and Fluffy.

Around the performance space between the Pratt and Light street pavilions, a crowd listened to an acapella singing group perform R&B favorites. Nearby, I spotted Harmony juggling yellow tennis balls and Jimmy rattling a paper cup at passing tourists. As I approached, a woman dropped a couple of quarters into Jimmy's cup.

"How's business?" I asked as I did the same.

Jimmy gave me a startled look.

"Hi Toni." Harmony dropped one of his tennis balls. It rolled toward the promenade's edge where a water taxi was taking on passengers. With an anguished squeak, Harmony went after the ball, dodging through a gaggle of black teenagers from the projects. He careened off a pair of muscular youths wearing leather jackets and knit caps pulled down low over their foreheads.

"Hey man," one said, grabbing Harmony by his skinny shoulder, "watch where the fuck you be going."

Like a stunned rabbit, Harmony stared up at his captor. "I got to get my ball."

"Leave go Dontay," the other youth told his infuriated companion. "The little creep's elevator don't go all the way to the top."

"Yeah, well..." A cop on a bike peddled past and the angered youth's grip loosened. Harmony wriggled free and sprinted after his ball which was now bobbing in the drink next to the water taxi.

"Close call," I said to Jimmy.

He shrugged. "If that hoodlum hadn't backed off, I would have gone in."

"Could you have scared them off?"

"Not me, my wheelchair. When this motorized chariot is in gear, it's a tank."

He had a point. But the wheelchair wasn't Jimmy's only tactical advantage, I thought. The Vietnam vet's legs might be useless, but his shoulders were wide under his flak jacket and his blocky hands looked powerful.

"You have to come to Harmony's rescue often?"

"That's how we got together in the first place." Jimmy smiled grimly. "People like to pick on the weak. A gang of kids had Harmony cornered in an alley. They were beating the shit out of him. That's what life was like for him before I came along. Now that he and I are a team, things are different. We look out for each other."

Harmony skipped back to us clutching the tennis ball, his expression agonized. "It's wet, Jimmy. I can't juggle it wet."

Jimmy gestured at the Pavilion behind us. "Take it to the men's room and dry it off in the hand blower."

Harmony's face lit like a neon sign. "That's really smart. I'll do that. Back in a sec."

We watched him dash inside the sprawling glass and steel building. I commented, "He's a nice kid."

"Yeah, long as he's got me to make sure he takes his medicine, he's okay." Jimmy looked up at me. "I suppose you're wondering why I'm out here with a paper cup when I'm already getting government handouts for my disability."

"I wasn't wondering that."

"I'll tell you anyway. I'm here because it gives me something to do. It's no damn good sitting by yourself in an apartment. This way I get some sun, see people, shoot the breeze a little bit. You know, I never thought I liked Alice hanging around. She was such a loony old bat. She never hurt anybody, though. Harmony and me, we miss the old girl."

"I miss her, too," I said. And it was true. The harbor was such a favorite haunt of hers that I kept expecting to see her.

Jimmy's big hands squeezed around his plastic cup until it crumpled. "If I ever run into the creep who killed her, he'll be in big trouble."

Chapter 8

MALONEY SHOWED up at my door that night. As I stared at him in surprise, he shifted from big foot to big foot. "I've been thinking about what you said. You know, about my place."

"What did I say?" I stared at him, drawing a blank.

"You know, maybe I should try to do more with it, make it homier. Well, I was wondering...you're in the decorating business. Got any suggestions?"

I remembered his bristling reaction to the way I'd criticized his decor. Why the change of heart, I wondered. I invited him in and fixed him a cup of tea.

"If you'd be interested in picking up some furniture, I know a friend of Randall's who's selling really nice antiques cheap."

Maloney frowned. "I don't want anything too fancy."

"This is stuff that would look great in your place, honest. Listen, why don't I give Chad a call? If he's home, we can go over right now and take a look."

"You'll tell me what you think I should get?" Maloney peered at me from under his bushy brows. His uncertainty made him almost cute.

"Sure I will."

Chad was home, so we headed out for Mount Vernon in Maloney's aging Chevette.

"I suppose this guy is gay," Maloney said as we cruised down Howard.

"Yes. Does that bother you?"

"Why should it? Randall's been a friend for years and he's gay."

"Well, Chad's sort of more in-your-face about it."

"Earrings, pastel clothes, dyed hair?"

"The whole bit. He's an artist. He doesn't just wear earrings in his ears, either. He's got them in his nose and, I suspect, other parts of his body."

Maloney rolled his eyes. "One time I might have been threatened by something like that. These days the only thing threatening me is the fear my ex will marry another guy and take my kid away from me."

I wondered how to respond. It turned out I didn't need to. Howard at night is kind of a scary street. What used to be Baltimore's busiest shopping district is now a ghost area. The storefronts that aren't boarded up look seedy. Trash and broken bottles are the landscaping of choice. Derelicts haunt shadowy corners.

A couple of blocks east, transvestites hang out under streetlights, hawking their wares in wigs, high heels and mini-skirts. Drunken hooligans from north of the city sometimes invade the locale in their good-old-boy pickups. They come in gangs, bent on finding themselves a victim on one of the less well-lit cross streets where the gay community has staked out its territory.

Maloney swung his Chevette east on Monument where Chad had a lovely apartment in a townhouse across from the Historical Society. I had just noticed there was some kind of a ruckus going on when Maloney slammed on the brakes. Only my seatbelt kept me from merging with the dashboard.

Cursing, Maloney leaped out of the driver's seat. After disentangling myself, I followed. A gang of young white guys wearing tee shirts and backward baseball caps were circled up like coyotes closing in on a wounded dogie. Two of them carried baseball bats.

"Okay, what's going on here. Break it up!" Maloney shouted, barreling toward them.

When they turned to look at him, I could see they'd captured a short little guy with a shaved head. He was cowering with his hands raised protectively. Though I didn't know him by name, I'd seen him wait tables at Louie's. Either he'd been coming home from a costume party or he'd wandered into his mother's closet by mistake. He was wearing a strapless evening gown and a diamond tiara.

"Okay, you've had your fun. Now go home," Maloney insisted, confronting the group.

He looked formidable with his broad shoulders and bear-like head. But he was only one and there were five of them. Not only that, they were drunk and egging each other on. Testosterone poisoned the night air.

"Fuck off!"

"Go home and fuck your broad. Don't stick your big ugly nose in where it doesn't belong!"

"Get the hell out of here, creep!"

One of the guys carrying a baseball bat leaped forward and swung, smashing at Maloney's left knee. Maloney stepped to his right and backhanded the kid. I saw blood spurt from his nose.

Two of his pals charged, swinging with both fists. Maloney did something swift with his leg, cracking them both in the knees so they fell like toppled trees. Another kid threw his bat at Maloney, but he ducked it easily. He charged, scattering the remaining two assailants. They fled down the street followed by their cohorts who could still limp. Their intended victim ran in the opposite direction, his high heels clacking on the sidewalk.

A moment later only the boy with the bleeding nose remained. He lay moaning on the sidewalk, doubled up in a fetal position. Maloney grabbed his arm and jerked him to his feet. "Which car is yours?"

"The pickup. Ow, man, watch it! You smashed my nose."

"Get your pals to take you to an emergency room." Maloney thrust the kid into his truck. "Now don't come back."

The truck went weaving down the street. When it was gone, I stared at Maloney in awe. "Wow, you don't kid around, do you?"

He looked puzzled. "What?"

"You were outnumbered five-to-one."

"By a bunch of shit-for-brains kids."

"Mean kids with baseball bats. They would have hurt you if they could."

He shrugged. "Where's this guy with the furniture live?"

"A couple houses down from here. You still want to look at his stuff?"

"Sure. That's what we came for, isn't it?"

THAT NIGHT I woke up, a cry jammed in my chest. I knew somebody was standing over me, watching me and thinking about doing me harm. Before I could open my eyes and when my cry was only half out of my throat, something soft came down over my face and smothered me.

I fought, but the hands pressing me down were too strong and the thing over my face was like a lead weight. I couldn't breathe. My head pounded and my lungs burned. My heart felt as if it was going to burst from my chest. I grew weaker.

THE SUN COMING through the window next to the bed burned my eyelids. When I lifted them, I had a jackhammer headache.

I lay there blinking and hurting. My pillows were scattered and the bedclothes were tangled. Sometimes I'm a restless sleeper, but not that restless. The memory of being smothered hit me. While my eyes remained fixed on the pillows, I pressed my hand against my mouth.

Downstairs, I discovered the kitchen window smashed. Somebody had broken into my house. I ran my finger along the jagged edge of the glass. Horribly vivid before my mind's eye, I saw the hands holding me down, felt the weight over my face. While I lay unconscious in my bedroom someone had been standing over me and trying to kill me.

But that made no sense. If an assailant had been in my bedroom last night, why was I walking around this morning? Why hadn't he tried to rape me? I would certainly have made easy pickings

Was burglary the only motive? After a careful search, I didn't find much missing. A couple of cans of diet coke from the refrigerator and a box of graham crackers were gone. A fancy Italian leather card box and a pair of silver candlesticks that I inherited from my grandmother had disappeared from the dining room. Oh, and one other thing—the book on the Harzine Institute was gone, too.

Was it possible that somebody had broken into my house and come close to smothering me to death because they wanted the book? Who would even know that I had it? Sure, I'd told Randall about it, but I didn't suspect him.

I knew better than to bother calling the police—who, since I shot Nick, haven't exactly been my biggest fans. With so little missing from my house, they wouldn't take much interest in my broken window. And since I still looked healthy, they'd only sneer at my claim of having been smothered. They'd tell me I'd had a nightmare, and maybe they'd be right. Maybe while I'd slept I'd heard the burglar downstairs and translated that into an attempt at murder. But I knew in my gut that wasn't so.

The split second the hardware store opened I made arrangements to have my glass replaced. After I installed shutters and locks for my back windows and blocked the broken ones with plywood, I went to the medical library at UMAB. If there was some connection between

Alice's murder, O'Dell's mysterious dump job and my burglar, I wanted to know.

Anyhow, with the book gone, I was even more curious about the building which had occupied the site of both murders.

Lucky for me, it was slow the Sunday afternoon I asked about Harzine. The librarian found several newspaper articles on microfilm, which I then spent a couple of hours deciphering.

I learned the Harzine building had been standing virtually empty for almost five years before it was demolished. At the time it was being used only for meetings, and occasional special academic projects.

"What kind of projects?" I asked the librarian.

She shrugged. "I suggest you try the psychology departments at the institutions that were affiliated with Harzine. UMAB wasn't one of them, so Hopkins would be your best bet. Talk to someone on the faculty who was around in that era."

IT WAS LATE afternoon when I got out of the library. I peddled to Sip & Bite where I treated myself to a couple of their crab cakes. Then I wandered over to Fells Point and Bertha's to listen to zydeco.

I left Bertha's around ten, humming under my breath. Since darkness had descended on the Point's scruffy streets, I would have been wise to take the most direct route home. I guess all the time I'd been nursing a beer and listening to music, I'd also been thinking about the Harzine Institute. I selected the winding waterfront route which would lead me past the Harzine's old location.

The city had been enjoying a spell of Indian summer. It was a windless night with a full moon tracking a silver ladder on the glassy black skin of the water. Many of the waterfront's rotted piers were still abandoned. But here and there sailboats bobbed in new marinas that had replaced crumbling pilings, some of them probably left from the last century.

My bike tires bounced and rattled over scarred blacktop speckled with broken glass and belted by abandoned trolley tracks.

Along the lonely stretch that ran parallel to a brackish canal, I spotted the profile of an earthmoving machine behind chain link fencing. A four-door Chevette squatted outside it.

I cruised up alongside, braked and peered in. Crammed into the driver's seat, Maloney sat talking on a car phone. His eyes met mine and he cranked the window. I heard him say, "Love you, too," to whomever was on the other end of the airwaves. "Be good, and I'll see you next Saturday. Okay, pal?"

Maloney replaced the receiver, then propped his arm on the window ledge. Like me, he wore jeans and a sweatshirt. "That was my son, Andy."

"I figured it wasn't a girlfriend. Men don't usually call their girlfriends 'pal.'"

"Is that so? Wish I'd heard that sooner. Could be I called my wife 'pal' just before she threw me out. Maybe that's why she dumped me. What are you doing here this time of night with nothing but a bicycle between you and trouble? This place isn't safe for a pretty girl alone. Hell, it's not safe for an ugly guy alone."

"You're not ugly."

"I'm not?"

"Ruggedly individualistic would be more like it."

"That sounds like another way of saying ugly. Long as you're here, got a minute? I got a couple of questions about your report."

My heart started hammering. Had I made some terrible mistake in spelling or grammar that gave away my dyslexia? Reluctantly, I propped my bike against a telephone pole and slid into the Chevette's passenger seat.

Maloney did such a good job of filling up his side that I felt as if I'd been wedged into a sardine can packed with a great white shark.

"How do you manage to spend the night in this little car?"

"It's amazing what a bill collector can persuade a guy to do. Mrs. Brockloff's reaction to your report was generally favorable."

You mean she liked hearing that her husband is a letch?"

Maloney blew out his lips. "I didn't get the impression this information about her husband's amorous activities came as a shock to the lady. Let's just say, she appreciated getting the specifics. Speaking of which, she wants a name on the mystery blond."

"You mean Brockloff's wife wants me to keep on watching her husband?"

"That's it. Seems she thinks the blond you couldn't identify might be her sister, who she's suspected of cheating with hubby for a long time. She wants to know for sure before tossing out accusations that might spoil the next family picnic."

Squirming, I reviewed my options. Of course, I could say

nothing and go on following Lover-Boy Brockloff. Maloney had already written me a nice check for my work. If I kept my mouth shut, I could collect another. But that would be cheating both him and his client.

"The blond wasn't Mrs. Brockloff's sister."

"How do you know?"

"Because I recognized the blond."

"You said you didn't know her."

"I lied, sort of. Maloney, I didn't want to upset you. The blond was your ex-wife."

An ominous silence filled the car.

"Let's get this straight. You're telling me Brockloff is boinking Karla?"

"I don't know that for sure. Maybe they were just going over briefs or something." Honest, the double meaning didn't hit me until the words had left my mouth. Though it was too dark to see Maloney's color, I knew from the set of his jaw that his thin Irish skin had turned dark red with rage.

"Listen, Miss Credella. Sparing my feelings was not part of your job description. I don't pay people to leave important information out of reports."

"I know and I'm sorry. Honest, it was just that ..."

"Forget the apologies."

"Do you want me to talk to the client?"

"I'll handle relations with the client."

"You're not going to let me work for you again, are you?"

"What do you think?"

"I think you're truly pissed," I said and climbed out of the car. He didn't try to stop me and he didn't follow me home to make sure I arrived safely.

Chapter 9

AS I PEDDLED home through Baltimore's dark streets I felt lower than dirt. When I braked at my place, Gus O'Dell had his rusty Pinto parked in front. He slouched toward me, one hand rubbing the back of his neck. His eyes were smudges of shadow in his high-boned face. He wore an Orioles jacket and sweatpants that had seen better days.

"Don't ask me what I'm doing here," he said. "Damned if I know myself. I went out for a six-pack. Instead of the liquor store, this is where I lit."

We stood gazing at each other, both of us tired, lonely and beat up. "All I've got inside is coffee, tea and a half empty bottle of diet coke. You're welcome to any of those."

"Coffee sound great. Thanks, Toni."

I had my doubts about inviting O'Dell into my house at this time of night. But he looked as down as I felt.

Inside, I flicked on the hall light and led him back to the kitchen. "You've done a lot of work," he said. "I haven't seen this place since you moved in. It was a real shithole then."

"Watch your language. It's my private castle you're insulting."

"Yeah, well I can see that, Princess. You're doing a good job." He stood in the entry, a hand cupped around the freshly painted woodwork.

Pleased to see that I'd left the kitchen clean, I ran water for coffee. "I could use something hot myself," I said, flicking a glance over my shoulder. O'Dell was just straddling a chair. He let his head slump back so far he was almost staring at the ceiling. One foot tapped the floor like a metronome. "What's going on with your dump job?" I asked.

"The bones were sent to the Smithsonian for a facial reconstruction. I hear it might be ready the end of next week."

I'd seen a TV show on the forensic reconstruction work at the Smithsonian, so I knew what he was talking about. Even on the oldest skulls, specially trained artists could mold faces startlingly like that of the original. Many missing persons cases had been solved because of such work.

"What about Alice Ritco's murder?" I asked. "Anything new on that?"

"If there is, I wouldn't know."

"Aren't you working it anymore?"

"Toni, I'm not working, period. I'm suspended from active duty pending the outcome of this lawsuit your friend Randall has slapped on me."

"Gus, I'm sorry. Honest. But maybe it's not so bad. You need a rest."

"Sure." He snorted. "You know how I've spent the last two days? Sacked out in front of my TV watching ESPN. It's made one fact crystal clear. Outside of my work, I have no life. This is the first I've left the house in forty-eight hours."

"I'm flattered you gave up basketball to come see me."

"You're the only person I wanted to see." He pushed off the chair. A split second later he had his hands on my shoulders. "Toni, I shouldn't have come. I'm ready to explode."

Before I could answer, he dragged me closer, cupped the back of my head with one palm and kissed me hard. I hadn't been expecting it, and it took my breath away.

Though there had been something simmering between O'Dell and me for months, this was the first time we'd kissed. He hadn't laid a hand on me before, and I hadn't wanted him to. Or maybe I had. Maybe I'd been wanting this for a long time. Certainly it had been too long since a man had made love to me, or even touched me with tenderness.

Not that O'Dell's kiss was tender. If I had to analyze it, and for sure I wasn't doing any analyzing at the time, I'd put it at sixty percent bottled up hunger and forty percent raw male frustration.

It must have been a persuasive mix. A couple of minutes later we were on the kitchen floor with our sweatshirts off groping each other like overheated teenagers. Except that neither O'Dell nor I were kids. We both had long, sad histories. As he produced a condom from his pocket and then unsnapped my jeans and dropped hot kisses on my breasts and belly, I flashed back to scenes like this between Nick and me.

Sometimes after he'd roughed me up, he'd come back with flowers and candy and literally beg me to forgive me. "Oh Toni, I'm crazy about you. It'll never happen again," he'd vow. At the sight of the tears in his eyes, I'd melt. Soon, we'd be tearing the clothes off each other. It kills me to admit it, but the sex was never better between Nick and me than during those times.

The memories made me want to stop O'Dell, to say "No, I didn't mean this to happen! Not with you. I'm not ready!" But it was too late. His hard mouth sealed the words in my throat and his body thrust into mine as if he were proving something to me and the rest of the world.

As he worked for his own satisfaction, I tried to hold back. He wouldn't let me. His body insisted and at last I gave way and heard myself gasp and felt myself shudder. A moment later he went still, breathing heavily while his damp, hot weight welded my backside to the tiles.

Finally, he propped himself on his elbows and looked into my face. At first his features were soft, his expression tender. Then his brows drew together and his mouth firmed. "You don't look like a satisfied customer."

"I guess I just wasn't ready for this yet."

"God," he said and rolled off me.

After he rearranged his clothes and I did mine, we lay next to each other in silence, gazing up at the neon tubing fixture on the ceiling. I reflected that neon was a very unflattering after-sex light.

"How did that happen?" O'Dell said.

"I don't know. You tell me."

"Okay. Stuck home like I've been, I've been thinking about you a lot. Imagining us together. Truth is, I wanted to have sex with you the minute I met you. Wasn't mutual, was it?"

"No. At least, I don't think so. Where sex is concerned, I don't have too firm a grasp on my own feelings."

"But you wanted it then. At least, while we were kissing it felt as if you did. Then at the last minute you seemed to change. But I couldn't stop. I just couldn't. I didn't hurt you, did I? Hurting you is the last thing I want, Toni."

"You didn't hurt me."

"Then why..."

"Why did I change? I started thinking about Nick."

"Oh, jeez!" Gus made a rude noise. "Talk about going to bed with a fucking ghost! Is he always going to be there?"

"I hope not. Eventually, I hope I'll get over this. But in some ways, Gus, you're a lot like him. In some ways, what attracted me to Nick is what I find attractive in you."

"What's that?"

I turned my head. He was still staring up at the ceiling. "You're tough. You're unpredictable. It only takes one look at you to know you're nobody to push around."

"In other words, I'm a mean s.o.b." O'Dell jumped up off the floor.

Though I felt drained and immensely weary, I pushed myself up.

When we stood facing each other, Gus said, "I am not like your husband. I have never in my life hit a woman. I would never hurt you."

I stuck my hands into my waistband and took a deep breath. "Don't take this wrong, Gus. It's not that I don't believe you. And it's not that I don't sympathize. I appreciate that you're bored and lonely right now."

"Without my work I have no life."

"Then maybe you need to work on getting yourself one. But it can't involve me. I shouldn't see you for a while. I mean, if Randall is going to call me as a witness, what we did just now is probably not too ethical."

His face hardened. "So, you're giving me my walking papers."

"For a while."

The stark silence in the room made me aware that the coffee pot had stopped burbling on the stove.

"Coffee smells good," O'Dell said. "I guess I'd better pass, though. See you in court, Toni."

THE NEXT afternoon I went to Alice's sparsely attended memorial service. Jimmy and Harmony were there along with three of Alice's other street friends. Doris Ritco, pretty in a gauzy dress and jacket printed with oriental symbols, came in. She stopped and said a few words to Jimmy. I figured Alice had probably introduced them. The music started and Doris hurried to the front of the church.

I thought Reverend Mike did a good job with the sermon. He talked about how difficult life is and how important it is to have compassion, not only for others, but for ourselves.

It wasn't hard to apply all this to Alice's sorry life and death. I pictured her as a bright-eyed little girl playing with dolls or jumping rope. Somehow, between bad luck and bad choices, she'd wound up a pathetic, drunken old woman. Maybe Alice hadn't done smart things with her life. But she hadn't deserved to be strangled on a dirt heap. Her murderer shouldn't be able to just walk away.

After the service, I caught up with Jimmy and Harmony outside the church. As Harmony guided Jimmy's wheelchair over a curb, I fell into step alongside. "It was nice of you two guys to come."

Jimmy grimaced. "We could afford the time."

"Jimmy, I heard you say you've lived around Baltimore most of your life. Do you remember an old building called the Harzine Institute? It used to be down on the waterfront between the Inner Harbor and Fells Point?"

"Used to be all kinds of buildings down there. You talking about a building on the site where they found Alice?"

When I nodded, he looked thoughtful. "I do remember a big old place down there. I never knew what it was, though. They blew it up when I was in college and that land hasn't been anything but a brick pile since."

It shook me to hear that Jimmy had gone to college. Even a college education hadn't protected him from the kind of life he had now. That was really scary.

"Ball game should be letting out pretty soon." Harmony squinted up at the sky where puffy white clouds rode the breeze. "Crowds ought to be good down at the harbor."

"Yeah, I guess." Jimmy sounded glum. "Poor old Alice. She's just one more dead pal in a long line for me, you know."

Harmony said, "Tell Toni about what happened in the war." His sunlit curls glistened beneath his knit tam and his Adam's apple danced. His skinny arms angled out of a shapeless gray tee shirt, their long fingers looking strong and agile beneath his knobby wrists. His ever present harmonica poked from the back pocket of threadbare jeans.

"Know how I was crippled?" Jimmy shot me a dour look.

"He got his legs blasted out in Nam, rescuing his buddy, Todd. Jimmy was a hero!" Harmony exclaimed.

Jimmy snorted. "I'd be more of a hero if I'd managed to save my buddy. But the gooks got him along with my legs."

"Jimmy really is a hero," Harmony insisted. "He shoulda' got the Purple Heart."

"Point is," Jimmy interjected morosely, "Alice is just another friend lost in the wars. It's a war around here, too, in case you haven't noticed. Harmony and me, we're survivors. You, too, I guess, Toni. Is that right?"

I nodded, thinking about all the bad stuff that had gone on recently, about Maloney firing me and my having sex with O'Dell and it turning out all wrong. It seemed like every day was a battle against extinction. Right now I literally didn't know how I was going to pay next month's heat bill. "Yeah," I said, "I'm a survivor."

"You want to go with us to the harbor?" Harmony asked. "I can teach you how to make balloon animals. You're a nice looking chick with big knockers, so people would like watching you. You can do balloons while I juggle."

I patted Harmony's skinny shoulder and shook my head. "Thanks for the compliment, but I'm not quite ready for that yet."

BACK HOME I was working on one of the ceilings upstairs when my front doorbell rang. I came down the stairs struggling to strip off sweaty rubber gloves. My hair and clothes were full of chalky paint chips.

I had a horrible feeling I was going to find Gus O'Dell on the other side of the door. It wasn't Gus, but Angus Maloney.

"Hi."

"Hi."

"Can I come in?"

I stood aside and watched in amazement as Maloney ambled past me. "Looks as if you're busy," he said, taking in my disheveled state. "Maybe I should come back another time."

"No. I've been scraping old paint off the ceiling upstairs. I'm due for a break. Can I fix you something? Tea, coffee?"

"Got any beer?"

"Sorry." This was how last night's conversation with O'Dell had started.

"Water will be fine," he said.

As he followed me down the hall, an image of O'Dell and me rolling around on the kitchen floor flashed before me. There was no way Angus Maloney could know about that. Nevertheless, as I crossed to the sink, I felt the back of my neck go red.

"So what are you doing in this neck of the woods?" I said as I handed Maloney a glass of ice water.

"I took my boy to the game at Camden Yards. I just dropped him off. His mother lives at Harborcourt," he added, naming a nearby luxury condominium.

"I'm here to apologize to you for what happened last night," he went on. "You were out of line not making a complete report. But maybe I overreacted, firing you and all."

"Maybe?" I felt a rush of anger. Dammit, I was tired of being dumped on by bad-tempered men. First Nick, then O'Dell, now this guy.

Maloney's big jaw clenched and unclenched.

"Look, let's just say that my personal life hasn't been the best lately and I'm tense. You want to forget all this and go on as before?"

"Sure." I took a swig of ice water. Did he mean he wanted me to go on working with him? I was about to take another drink when a paint chip fell out of my hair, slid down my nose and plopped into my water glass.

"Better not drink that," Maloney said. "Likely, it's full of lead. I hope you're working with a facemask. Scraping paint in one of these old places and breathing in all that lead dust could make you sick."

"Yeah, I know. It's probably lowered my IQ by ten or twenty points already, and God knows I didn't start out with a big number.

"Oh, I wouldn't say that." For the first time since he'd come in, Maloney smiled at me. He can put a beguiling smile on his homely Irish mug. It starts at his mouth, flares his nostrils and then lights his eyes. "You seem like a pretty smart lady to me. Good taste, too. That chair you talked me into buying from Chad the other night looks great in my apartment. Andy's crazy about it."

"Yeah? Then he's the one with the great taste."

"That makes two of you. A gal with your brains can probably afford to lose an IQ point or two."

"Ha! If you only knew!" Suddenly I found myself spilling my guts about my dyslexia.

"You mean you can't read at all?" He stared.

"I can read some. I'm working on it. I'm just very slow."

"But that report you turned in looked terrific."

"I got help from a friend with a computer," I admitted.

Maloney frowned. "That's not good. A client's business is

confidential."

I was glad I hadn't mentioned that the friend was Randall, although he hadn't read the report. He'd only shown me how to use his computer to put the report into decent shape.

Maloney paced between the stove and refrigerator. "In the future you should just give your reports to me, no matter what condition they're in."

"Does that mean there's going to be a future?"

"Do you want to go on working with me?"

"Sure. I like getting paid for being nosy. Only, there's something more you should know about the dyslexia. I don't drive, and I don't own a car. That's why I was riding a bike last night. I get around the city on a bike. I followed Brockloff on a bike."

Maloney threw up his hands. "Well, I'll be damned. Now, I've heard everything."

"It's not so strange," I defended myself. "Actually, as long as I stay in the city, I can get around pretty well—better than if I had a car when the traffic's thick downtown."

"Now let me get this straight." He rubbed his forehead. "You're illiterate. You can't drive and don't own a car. You have no police experience and don't know how to defend yourself, and because of what happened with your husband you've got a bad rep with the local authorities. All that, and I'm paying you to be an assistant private investigator?"

Put like that, it did sound crazy. Convinced I'd sent my chance of Maloney re-hiring me down the tubes, I said, "Look, thanks for coming around. I appreciate the apology. You're a nice guy, and I enjoyed having you for a boss, even if it didn't last long."

"Did I say I was going to back out of our arrangement? I was just marveling at the weirdness of it all."

"You mean I'm still hired?" I caught a reflection of my hopeful face in his green eyes.

"You can go on working for me on a trial basis, okay? But for it to make any sense at all, you need to make some changes."

"Like what?"

"You'll have to learn how to defend yourself, so you'll need to keep on with the Aikido. I'd like you to look around for an old computer with a spell check to help with the reports."

"I can't afford..."

"We'll worry about that later. The main thing is you've got to learn to drive. There's no reason why you can't do it, Toni. I know lots of truck drivers who can't get through the alphabet. It's just a matter of learning the rules and memorizing all the important signs. A smart cookie like you should be able to do that, easy. I'll help you."

Overwhelmed by his kindness, I felt my throat thicken up. "Why are you doing all this for me?"

He jammed his hands into his pockets and walked to the door. "I'm not so sure myself." When he turned around, he looked amused. "You did a good job with Brockloff. You're smart and gutsy, and I admire that. Also, you're not bad looking. I've been pretty lonely and it's nice to have someone like you to talk to."

I grew wary. "I'm not about to have a sexual relationship with my boss."

"Who said anything about sex? Look Toni, I still have feelings for my wife. I'm crazy about my kid. I want the three of us to be a family again, and I still hope that might happen. In the meantime, the life I'm leading is lonely. I like you. As long as it doesn't cost me anything, I'm willing to help you out. Let's not make more of it, okay?"

"Okay by me."

Chapter 10

AFTER MALONEY left, I kicked myself for not telling him about my break-in. I hadn't mentioned it to O'Dell, either. We'd been distracted by other matters, and now it was too late.

I told myself the burglar had just been a kid on drugs looking for a TV to rip off. When he hadn't found what he wanted, he'd grabbed whatever looked portable and taken the book on impulse. Yet, I couldn't shake the feeling that stealing the Harzine book hadn't been a random act.

And what about his attempt at smothering me? A sensible person would just drop the whole Harzine thing. After all, the place didn't exist anymore. But I guess when they built me they left out sense. All my instincts told me there was something here I needed to find out about.

THAT NIGHT I called Don Parham. Don is an English professor at Johns Hopkins. A few months back there had been a mild attraction between us. Nothing had developed from that, possibly because of all my hang ups. But we remained on friendly terms.

"I don't know, Toni," Don said after I explained that I wanted to find out about the Harzine building. "That's way out of my bailiwick. I never even saw the place. I was still in high school in Pittsburgh when it was demolished."

"There's got to be somebody on campus who had some connection with it. What about the people in the psychology department?"

Long silence. "Well, actually, a couple of those guys are pretty old," he finally allowed. "Give me a chance to ask around and I'll get back to you, okay?"

"Great!"

That afternoon Don called back. "I've got your man. He's Professor Harold McDaniel. He's been a tenured Associate professor of Psychology at Hopkins for the last thirty years, and he has office hours Monday, Wednesday and Friday from 3-4."

"Perfect!"

Five minutes later I was grabbing my jacket and getting ready to take off for the Hopkins campus when the phone rang again. Wondering how come I was suddenly so popular, I picked it up. Sandy's frantic voice drilled into my ear.

"He's done it!"

"Done what?" For a minute I didn't remember Sandy's latest problem with Al.

"He's resigned and taken out a second mortgage on our house to buy a fancy truck. Tomorrow he's going out to a bunch of construction sites to sell sandwiches. Oh God, Toni, I feel like I'm losing my mind!"

"Sandy, calm down! Maybe it's not as bad as you think."

"It's worse. My life is hell. When Al tried to talk me into making sandwiches, we had another fight and he went stomping out. I can't stand it around here. I'm eating dinner at Mom and Pop's tonight. I want you to come, too."

"Why is that?" When she isn't doing her damndest to make me feel bad about my life, Sandy is promoting family solidarity. In our family this makes about as much sense as rooting for the Celtics at an Orioles game. My father is never going to stop disapproving of me, and my mother is never going to gaze at me from her soulful Madonna eyes with anything but grief and disappointment.

"Because you're my sister, and I need your support," Sandy said.

"All right. I'll come." After I hung up, I figured I still had time to get over to Hopkins and catch McDaniel.

Traffic was thick downtown. I almost got clipped by a fire engine clanging up Charles. Still, as I wheeled my bike along the path that winds through the museum's sculpture garden, it was only 3:30.

The Baltimore Museum of Art's sculpture garden borders the southern end of the Hopkins campus. The afternoon had turned blustery, and a chill damp slicked the statues that dotted the stone paths of the garden.

At the end of the path I crossed a service road into the brick tranquility of the JHU inner sanctum. Bordered by neighborhoods threatened by urban flight, JHU is an academic fantasy island afloat in a gritty urban sea. There are kidnappings at nearby ATM machines and guards patrol the school's parking lots.

Still, when you trudge JHU's gravel paths past the stately brick and mortar federal architecture and students playing touch football, all's right with the world.

I found Harold McDaniel's office in Gilman hall, a mellow old structure at the north end of a grassy rectangle. Its tile floors were skating rinks of thick wax. Its long, quiet corridors seemed to rustle with the hushed whisper of generations of students asking for an extension on their term papers.

"Professor McDaniel?"

He was a painfully thin older man with wisps of gray hair brushed back over a shiny pate. Behind his horn rim spectacles, his eyes were earnest and brown. Liver spots mottled his hands. He wore a threadbare tweedy jacket. Coffee spots decorated his red bow tie. He was alone, whiling away his office hour with a thick book.

"McDaniel is certainly my moniker. What can I do for you, young lady?"

"My name is Antoinette Credella. Professor Parham recommended that I come see you. He thought you might be able to answer a question for me."

"What question is that? Don't just hover there in the doorway, Antoinette. Enter my sanctum and sit down. Are you a student of mine?"

"No sir." I pulled out a chair on the opposite side of his desk and slid into it.

"I thought not." He eyed me. "If you were a student of mine, I would have noticed you. Well, what is it you wanted to ask me about?"

I told him about the Harzine Building.

"Of course, I remember it. Marvelous old place with walls a foot thick and ceilings high enough to give a person some breathing space. It was with a tear in my sentimental old eye that I watched the Philistines take it down."

"In the years before it was leveled, how was it used?"

"Oh, the use was careless and random. Neglect is the lot of aging dinosaurs, no matter how worthy of veneration. Occasionally, conferences were held at the Harzine. Various institutions conducted weekend seminars. As I recall, our department made use of the facility on several occasions."

"For what purpose?"

Behind his glasses, his sharp eyes narrowed. "What is the exact nature of your inquiry, Antoinette?"

I figured that if I just told him I was curious he wouldn't help me. So, I lied. "I'm working on a history of the waterfront. I thought I'd like to write about some of the old buildings that have disappeared and talk about their history."

Professor McDaniel rose and turned to the solidly packed bookcases which lined two walls of his office. One shelf contained a row of black and white speckled composition notebooks, each with a date written in white tape on its black spine.

"These are my journals. I've maintained them throughout most of my academic career."

"Are they like diaries?"

"You might say that." He gave a small, dry smile. "However, they do not chronicle my personal history. Instead, they are observations about circumstances around me. They contain jottings about current events, agendas at department meetings, that sort of thing."

It sounded boring, but possibly also helpful. I waited expectantly.

Let me see," he muttered, reaching up and running an exploratory hand along the dusty spines. "Harzine was taken down in the mid-sixties, so we're talking about the decade before that. Here's 1959 to 1964."

He pulled out five notebooks and sat back down with them. As he riffled through each one, I prayed he wouldn't offer to show them to me. From what I could glimpse, tiny handwriting in faded ballpoint ink covered their yellowed pages. No way would I be able to make sense of it.

As he continued flipping through, he pulled out a scratch pad. From time to time, he jotted a note in tiny script. Marked only by the soft rustle of turning pages, the minutes ticked by. I watched dust motes swim like microscopic fish. They were caught in the slanting net of a late afternoon sunbeam filtering through the window at the back of Professor McDaniel's head. I listened to the solemn ticks of a clock somewhere in the hall close by.

"There." He tore the sheet off the notepad and slid it at me. "There were a half dozen projects conducted at the Harzine Institute in the years immediately before it was demolished. Not all were conducted by Hopkins' Department of Psychology. In some cases members of the department merely cooperated with independently funded researchers. Do you want to expand your interrogation to specifics?"

Of course, I did. But as I stared at the marks he'd scratched on the paper, they might as well have been ancient Babylonian hieroglyphics. I wanted to cry with frustration.

When I was a little girl, the teacher sometimes forced me to the front of the class to read something in a book.

Remembering still makes my palms clammy. I would stand there terrified, unable to make anything of the black marks on the page. In my panic, my skin would turn icy and my insides would roil. At first the other kids in the class would only titter behind their hands. Before long, they'd be laughing out loud. Finally, the teacher would send me back to my desk quivering with shame.

Gradually, I learned to copy from the person in front of me or get Sandy to help me memorize test questions. Of course, none of that really worked, so I dropped out of school and went to work in my parents' restaurant. I never got over the fear and panic. Now, despite all the questions bubbling in my head and McDaniel's apparent willingness to answer them, the fear seized me.

"Thank you," I said. Rising to my feet, I folded the paper and stuck it in my pocket. "I appreciate your help."

"Any time. Come back and brighten my lonely office hour again."

OUTSIDE, I marched down the marble steps to my bike. My eyes were wet. The wind whipped my hair across my face, and I brushed it back with clenched fists. My bike was in sight when I turned on my heel and marched back. This time I headed for Don Parham's office.

Don is a tall man with a long angular body and sandy hair brushed back over a high forehead. Though he specializes in Victorian poetry, he could pass for an ivy league basketball player.

He smiled and leapt out of his chair when I knocked, but some of his pleasure diminished when I handed him the list McDaniel had written and begged him to research the names on it for me.

"Why can't you do this yourself?" His sharp hazel eyes challenged me.

"Don, I can't even read McDaniel's handwriting."

"Okay, okay, I'll print them out. Roth's sleep deprivation study,

Cunningham and Fisher's memory transference workshop, the Margraf experiment, Neff and Roth's group therapy weekend and Ridge and Fisher's preschool cognition weekend."

"They all sound pretty weird to me."

"No more weird than some of the experiments I hear about today. I'm sure there are records on each of these in the Hopkins Medical library."

"Don, I'm neither a student nor faculty here. They wouldn't let me into that library. Even if they did, it would take me forever to read through that material, and I wouldn't understand it when I was finished.

"Don't always sell yourself short, Toni. Your reading skills have improved a lot in the last few months."

"Not that much. Don, please, please help me with this."

"What's so important here?"

"Maybe nothing, but I won't know that until I've got more information."

Don sighed. "When you smile at me like that with those big brown eyes, how can I refuse?"

WHEN I LEFT the Hopkins campus I headed for Little Italy and my parents' place. Sandy was already there with her kids and Mom was taking a huge pan of Chicken Cacciatore out of the oven. The chicken was delicious, but that's about the only positive comment I can make about the evening.

We sat around the kitchen table listening to Sandy moan about Al quitting the perks and security of the BPD and going into the roach coach business. Mom and I tried to cheer her up, but she wouldn't be cheered. "He'll never make a go of this," Sandy protested. "We'll be ruined."

To make the evening worse, as I peddled home on my bike, I had a prickly feeling in the back of my neck. I kept looking over my shoulder, flinching at odd sounds. It's just your nerves, I told myself.

Yet, as I neared my street, I put my head down and peddled like a mad woman. A couple of minutes later I was bolting my doors. I even stacked soup cans under first floor windows as a makeshift burglar alarm.

Alone in my empty bed, I slept uneasily. Often, I awoke to the wail of ambulances and police sirens and the occasional tinkling of breaking glass somewhere out in the alley. Toward morning I thought I heard Harmony's harmonica playing a mournful version of "Camptown Races." I pictured him wandering the streets, his impish face with its ruddy cheeks and slanted brows at rest as he listened to his own music.

Maybe that's why he plays his harmonica, I thought. Maybe the world doesn't bewilder and pain him quite so much. For a brief instant before falling back into the deep well of sleep, I envied Harmony that solace.

When I woke up, I had a call from Maloney. "The job I had lined up for today didn't pan out. Want to learn how to drive?"

"Ahhh, sure." What else was I going to say? He'd made it clear my continued employment depended on driving.

"Okay, first you need a learner's permit. I'll pick you up and take you to the DMV for it. I'll coach you on the way down. You haven't got a thing to worry about. It'll be a snap."

Sure, I thought. A half hour later I was pacing in front of the living room window waiting for Maloney to show. When the phone rang, I raced for it, half hoping it was him calling to cancel.

It was Don Parham. "This is your obedient servant, eager to lay the his research gems at your dainty feet."

"What?"

He chuckled. "I looked up the items on McDaniel's list at the Medical Library. Don described the projects on the list. None of them sounded interesting. Until he came to the Margraf Experiment.

Chapter 11

"OKAY, HERE'S what I've got on the Margraf Experiment," Don said. "It's named after a pair of independent researchers. For their experiments, conducted in the spring break of 1964, they recruited students from several colleges and universities in the area."

"Is that unusual?"

"Not at all. Most students are hard up. They're a lot more likely to sell their time and body fluids cheap than working adults. Besides, at that age you think you're immortal. You're more open to new experiences."

"Okay, so why was this thing called the Margraf Experiment?"

"Margraf was the brainchild of Dr's. Norma and Robert Margraf, a husband and wife team of independent researchers. They weren't actually affiliated with Hopkins, only using some of the facilities on a pay as you go basis. They're not around anymore."

"Where'd they go?"

"Both dead in a plane crash. That's all I could find out. Why don't you go back and talk to McDaniel again? He'll probably remember the Margrafs."

"Maybe I'll do that." I heard a horn beep outside. Maloney, at last. My nerves started jumping like Mexican beans. "Listen, I've gotta' go."

"Think nothing of it. How about lunch at Louie's on the 16th? I need your advice on something."

"Sure. But what could I advise a smart guy like you on?"

"Love, Toni. I've found the woman of my dreams, but I'm not sure how to make her mine."

I laughed. "Well, neither am I, Don, but if you're paying for lunch, I'll be happy to let you pick my brains." And with that, I was out the door.

OUTSIDE IN Maloney's car I asked, "What's this?"

"Copy of the Maryland State Driver's Test. By the time we get to the DMV you'll have it cold."

When you're dyslexic, you develop a pretty sharp memory.

Maloney was as good a teacher of driving regulations as he was of Aikido. When he pulled into the Motor Vehicle Administration's giant Glen Burnie parking lot, I had a good grasp of the questions. Besides, I already knew most of the rules of the road from biking around Baltimore.

"Relax," Maloney said as he took my arm and steered me to the entrance, "nobody wants you to fail this test. Being able to drive a car is an American birthright. I can't believe your parents didn't do this for you as soon as you hit sixteen."

I thought about myself at sixteen—a high school dropout, filled with self-doubt, slaving away in the Credella kitchen for less than minimum wage. "My parents don't do much driving themselves. Cars in the city are mostly a nuisance. Finding a husband was the only skill my folks considered indispensable for a girl my age. They were glad I didn't push them about driving."

Maloney gazed at me curiously. "What about later, after you were married?

"At first I tried to hide my reading problems from Nick. When he asked me about driving, I said I wasn't interested. Later, he did try to teach me. My husband wasn't a patient person. After one disastrous session in the car with him, I never brought the subject up again."

"You gave in too easily, Toni."

"I didn't have the money to buy myself a car, so what was the point?" I felt defensive and would have refused to take another step if I'd thought there was any way I could go on working for Maloney without my driver's license.

An hour later I emerged from the DMV with a learner's permit.

"See. Didn't I say you could do it?" Maloney grinned at me.

My eyes felt damp. "Thanks. You're a nice guy, you know that?" I wanted to give him a sloppy kiss on the cheek, but I restrained myself.

"Of course I know that. Now, if only I could get my wife to notice."

"How'd a sweet guy like you get into police work in the first place?"

"Watched too many cops and robbers shows on TV. Grew up with a white knight complex. Wanted to save the world." Maloney shook his head.

Why had he left the police department, I wondered. Had Maloney given up the regular pay, pension and medical benefits because of some personal dispute?

"Of course," I said as he opened the passenger door for me, "this little piece of paper doesn't mean I can drive. I don't even have a car."

"That's why you're so lucky I'm your boss." Maloney pulled out of the parking space and nosed the Chevette back onto the road. "I'm going to give you a driving lesson. Hey, don't look so scared," he added after shooting me an amused glance. "I'm the soul of patience."

As Maloney guided his car back to the city, I told him about my break-in. He seemed truly concerned and gave me detailed advice on making my house secure.

When we arrived at the construction site where Alice's body had been found, workmen swarmed around the giant cavity hollowed by earthmovers. Cement trucks trundled around the edges of the hole like giant overladen worker bees.

"Once you start pouring a foundation that size, you can't stop until the job's done. They'll be there until midnight," Maloney commented after we parked and walked over to take a look. He pointed at the newly created roads surrounding the construction fencing. They were all but deserted and, I had to agree, made as good a place as any to practice driving.

"Besides," Maloney explained to me as we traded seats in his car and I slid reluctantly behind the driver's wheel, "I don't have to start watching the site for a couple of hours, so that leaves plenty of time for me to get you started driving."

"Sure."

Peddling a bike and driving a car are two very different skills. Maloney's car was a stick shift.

"You're releasing the clutch too fast," he warned after I'd stalled the car half a dozen times trying to get it moving. Underneath the deadly calm of his voice, I knew he was counting up what it was going to cost to get his burned-out clutch repaired. I was counting, too. If I damaged Angus Maloney's precious car, how would I pay for it?

"Listen, Angus, maybe this isn't such a good idea. You've got to work tonight, and I'm tired." I was still emotional jelly from the stress of taking a written test. My shoulders were up around my ears, and my sweaty hands slipped on the steering wheel like downhill skiers.

"Don't chicken out now, Toni. I want you to drive down this road, turn right and then come around back the other way. Now, let that clutch out slow and easy."

One look at Maloney's clenched jaw persuaded me not to rebel. When Nick had seen me burn out his clutch, the lesson had ended in bruises—mine. I tried starting up the Chevette again. The car jerked into motion like one of those old-fashioned mechanical penny banks.

"Good," Maloney exclaimed.

I hung onto the steering wheel as if it were the saddle horn on a bucking bronco.

"Relax, Toni."

My eyes never wavered from the road. "I'm concentrating."

"This isn't the Indy 500. Hardly anyone makes it down here. You're perfectly safe."

"There's someone coming now." I tried to keep the panic out of my voice. A blue sedan eased around the curve where I'd just swung to the right. As it passed me, I caught a glimpse of an older couple rubbernecking at the empty marina.

"Tourists," Maloney commented. "Bet they don't know that people are still getting murdered down here."

"Did you know the woman who was killed?" I continued staring at the road as if it might go up in smoke.

"No. Did you?"

"She hung around my neighborhood. Harmless old girl. I can't imagine why anybody would hurt her."

"Maybe she was in the wrong place at the wrong time. Never underestimate the power of bad luck and plain meanness." Maloney sighed.

"Another woman got killed in almost the same spot. They found what was left of the body when they were excavating the site."

"You don't say."

"Funny coincidence, isn't it." I chanced a split-second glance at Maloney.

"You trying to scare me about spending the night parked out here all by my lonely?"

"Of course no..." We were headed back to the spot where we'd started. A cement truck trundled out of the construction site. As it cut directly across my path, I gasped.

"Brake!" Maloney yelled.

My feet scrabbled for the mysterious peddles beneath them, Right or left, which was I supposed to push first?

"Hit the brake!" Unsnapping his seat belt so he could throw his leg over the shift, Maloney tried to hit the brake for me. But I'd already found it. The car stopped like a rocket slamming into an invisible Klingon shield. I went flying forward, but my seatbelt kept me from hitting the windshield. Maloney wasn't so lucky.

When I managed to peel my chest off the steering wheel and look at him, he was slumped over the dashboard. "Maloney?"

Nothing.

"Oh, God! Are you okay?"

Groan.

"Can I help you?" I tried pulling him back into the seat. It was like manhandling an inert punching bag filled with lead weights.

"Ouch! Hands off!" Slowly, he straightened. His hand went to the back of his neck and he fell heavily against the head rest. "Jesus!"

"What is it? What's wrong?"

"I can't turn my head."

"What?" My heart beat like the wings of a hysterical canary.

"I can't turn my head. See?" He made an effort to look my way and yelled. "Ah! Dammit to hell!"

"Oh God, Angus, what do you want me to do?"

"Well, I sure as hell don't want you to drive me to the hospital. Can you get the car out of the middle of the road?"

The truck had long since lumbered off. With my nerves jumping, I restarted the car. After several bad tries letting out the clutch, during which Maloney remained grimly silent, I managed to guide it to the curb.

"Now use my car phone to call a cab," he told me gruffly.

TWO HOURS later Maloney walked out of the Emergency room at Mercy with a thick white collar around his neck and an unhappy expression on his face. He was too groggy from painkillers to do anything but hit the sack, so we caught a taxi to his place. After he stepped out, I directed the cab to the construction site and Maloney's beached car. I'd talked him into letting me fill in for him watching the site that night. I figured it was the least I could do.

As I settled behind the wheel, I noted that Maloney had been right about the cement job. The fenced-in area was still livelier than an ant hill under a melted chocolate bar. Two cement trucks were queued up to dump their load. While the hard hats yelled down to the men at the bottom of the pit, they directed a spray of gray goo through a hose attached to the body of the first truck in line. I suppose that if I'd been a guy I might have been entertained by all this.

I leaned back and closed my eyes. It was going to be a long night. At least it would be a safe one. Nobody was going to hassle me with all these trucks and hard hats on the scene.

Sourly, I reflected on the day's events. What is it with me and the opposite sex? Why does everything always get so messed up? Not only had I killed my husband, I was about to testify against a man with whom I'd all-too-recently had consenting sex. If that weren't bad enough, I had just put my brand new boss in the hospital—worse yet, my brand new boss had been trying to do me a big favor. Racking up quite a score there, Credella.

I sat dozing and reflecting in a dreamy way on what a nice guy Maloney truly was. Once again Angus Maloney had demonstrated that no matter how sorely tested, he only lost his temper at the right people. Why couldn't I find a man like that? What would happen if I did?

As the hands on the car clock crept toward seven, the rumblings of my empty stomach turned my thoughts to more practical matters. Answering my prayers, a blue van pulled into the site. I didn't pay much attention until I saw a group of hard hats walk away from it toting wrapped sandwiches, bags of chips and Styrofoam cups.

Oh boy, food! Scrambling out of the Chevette, I rushed through the unguarded entrance. That's when I saw Al—and he saw me.

"Well, if it isn't the city's new challenge to public health."

His face turned red and his tiny pig eyes narrowed. "What rock did you crawl out from under?"

"Is that any way to greet your favorite sister-in-law? Al, I think Sandy's wrong about your new calling in life. You look a lot cuter in that little white paper hat then you ever did with a nightstick. What's the specialty *du jour*? Bacteria on rye?"

"What makes you think I'm going to feed you, you mouthy little bitch?"

"Come on, Al, I bet my sister made those sandwiches you're

overcharging for."

"Your hoity toity sister thinks she's too good to help me feed her family. I made these sandwiches with my own hands."

"You've just lost my appetite. I think I'll have a couple packages of peanut butter crackers and a sno cone." I pointed at the array of labeled flavorings in plastic containers on a shelf behind him. "I'll try raspberry."

"I'd rather sell my children for dog meat than make you a sno cone. I'd see you starve before I'd offer you a crumb off the floor of this truck."

"Is there some problem here?" The deep voice came from behind me. I turned my head and saw a tall, curly headed guy with eyes the color of freshly brewed coffee. Though he was dressed in dusty blue jeans and a work shirt no different than what the other construction workers wore, he had an air of authority. I knew him.

"Mario?"

"Toni? Is that you?" His eyes lit. He beamed down at me and suddenly I was thirteen years old all over again. In those days, Mario Caprini had been the smartest kid in the class. Unfortunately, I had been the dumbest.

"It's me all right. My mother told me you were back in town."

"I'm back, all right. Chief engineer on this project, as a matter of fact."

"Chief engineer, no kidding! I'm impressed. That makes you the man in charge, doesn't it."

"It does." He squinted at Al. "You're the new food service we're trying out? Is there some problem here?"

Al had been staring at the two of us with his mouth open. Now, like a frustrated turtle, he snapped it shut. "No problem." Muttering, he tossed a couple packages of crackers on the counter and set about making my sno cone.

Keeping an eye on him to make sure he didn't spit in the flavored ice, I explained to Mario what I was doing there. He appeared both impressed and amused that I was working for a detective agency and that I was guarding his construction site.

After I paid for my food, he walked me closer to the scene of activity. I said, "My mother told me you're divorced. I'm sorry to hear that."

He grimaced. "Yeah, well, guess I'm not lucky in love. My

mother told me about your troubles."

"I bet she did. The grandmothers in the neighborhood still cross themselves and dig out their rosaries when they catch sight of me. In Little Italy, I'm considered the bad seed."

He smiled at me oddly. "You don't look bad to me, Toni. You never could. I'll tell you something else. I never liked Nick. When I heard you married him, I got drunk."

I laughed and shook my head. Mario was exaggerating, of course. He'd always been a straight arrow—not the type to go on a binge. While I ate my crackers and nibbled my sno-cone, he filled me in on what had been going on with him the last few years and then explained about the job he was supervising. "We'll probably be here well past midnight."

"That's a lot of gray goop you're pouring."

"You got that right."

I gazed down at the bottom of the excavation where men in rubber boots smoothed gelatinous cement. I couldn't help thinking about the girl whose body they'd found while digging that hole. Now Mario's workers were sealing it, perhaps burying the secrets of her and Alice's murders forever.

"What next?" I asked Mario.

"Once this foundation is in place, we'll begin actual construction. Soon we'll start assembling the big crane." He pointed at a stack of white metal framework pieces that looked like parts of a giant's erector set.

"How tall is that thing going to be when it's all together?"

"It's a hundred and fifty-footer."

"Really? How do you put together something so tall?"

"We have a team of guys who specialize in crane assembly. They're fearless. If you have time, you should come around and watch their show. It's better than a high wire act at a circus."

I told Mario I might take him up on that, then carried what was left of my cone and my second package of crackers back to the Chevette.

A couple of minutes later Al's blue van came barreling out the entrance. A second before he turned right, he glared and gave me the finger. I would have laughed if I weren't feeling sort of tired and depressed. I was still hungry.

To take my mind off my stomach, I turned on the radio. It

crackled to life on the tail end of a local news report about a fire. Then the announcer started in on something that made my eyes fly open.

"The Charles Village community is shocked by the latest violent crime in its neighborhood. Hopkins professor George McDaniel was found beaten to death outside his Charles Village apartment. Presumably the motive was robbery, but the assailant is still unknown."

Chapter 12

"MY DAD IS an Aikido champ. People come from all over to get him for a teacher."

Maloney, sporting a padded collar around his neck, patted his son on the rump. "That's right, stick up for your old man. Remember, he wasn't always the broken wreck you see before you."

I'd found Maloney at his Aikido studio. His faithful students had delivered him there and propped him up on an old mattress.

"Dad, you didn't have anything wrong with you until you gave that lady a driving lesson."

Catching Maloney's eye, I choked. We both grinned at Andy. He was a smaller version of his father. I guessed the rat-tail of white-blond hair trailing down the back of his neck was his mother's idea. "Hey, I said I was sorry."

"Where's your manners?" Maloney asked his son. "Get out there and take a couple of falls with Bruce. Show me you've learned something."

Tightening the green belt around his middle, Andy trotted out to the mats.

"Cute kid." I squatted on the mattress a couple of feet from where Maloney lounged on his nest of pillows. "You must be pretty proud of him."

"Sure I'm proud of Andy. Since Karla and I split, I only get to see him every other weekend." Maloney's rough features settled into sad lines. "I always try to make some plans for us doing something together. This afternoon I was going to take him to the Aquarium. The way my neck feels, I don't think I can make it. I've got the mother of all headaches. Every time I tip my head I worry it's going to fall off and split open like a ripe pumpkin."

"What does the doctor say?"

"Says to wear the collar and take it easy. Says I've got whiplash. Don't put any strain on the neck."

"Do you want the name of a chiropractor? I know a good one."

"If I don't start feeling better soon, maybe I'll give that a try."

I hated knowing that Maloney's pain was my doing. "Is there anything else I can do to help?"

"How about you taking Andy to the Aquarium this afternoon?"

He'd caught me off guard with that. I opened my mouth to make an excuse. I'm not that fond of kids. On the rare occasions when I've babysat my hyperactive nephews, I've come away overjoyed that I'm childless. What's more, I had planned to spend the afternoon checking on what had happened to Professor McDaniel. But I owed Maloney too much to refuse. "Sure. I'd love to."

He looked amused. "It'll be good for you, Credella. Don't worry about money. I'll spring for lunch and the tickets."

I spent the rest of the morning at the studio, working out with Tyler, a muscular African American bike courier who was also one of Maloney's most advanced students. Tyler had agreed to watch the construction site for Maloney over the weekend. Maloney hoped that by Monday he'd be able to take up where he'd left off.

From the look of him, I doubted that.

When the time came for Andy and me to leave, I could see he had as many doubts about spending the afternoon together as I did. We took the light rail up to the harbor. There I used part of the fifty bucks Maloney had stuffed into my pocket to buy us crab cakes and fries at one of the stands in the Light Street Pavilion. We were lucky and found a table on the balcony outside.

It wasn't all that hard to engage Andy in conversation. He spent most of his time talking about his dad. He told me about the Orioles games they'd attended and the baseball he had enshrined in his bedroom. Angus had caught one of Cal Ripken's homeruns and then taken Andy down to get it signed. Obviously, Andy and his dad had a mutual admiration society going.

"You must be pretty proud of your mom, too. It's not that easy to be a lawyer." I knew I was probing and should be ashamed of myself. But hey, I've never claimed to be a flawless human being. I was curious about Karla Maloney. From the outside, she looked like everything I could never be—blond, gorgeous, rich and well-educated. If it weren't for her rendezvous with Brockloff, I'd think she had good taste, too, since she'd married Maloney.

"Yeah, my mom makes a lot of money for us—a lot more than my dad, she says." Andy picked at a burnt spot on one of his fries. "I don't think money's so important."

"What would you say is important?"

He cocked his blond head. Afternoon sunshine washed his green eyes. They were so like his dad's. They made me think of river water, moving slow and reflecting golden light off a floor so deep you could only guess at it. "I think it's important to not be mean and to have some fun," he said.

"You're a wise person."

If Andy heard my compliment, he didn't react. Activity on the promenade below us had distracted his attention.

"Wow, look at that guy!"

I peered over the edge of the balcony railing and spotted Harmony. He was performing a circle of cartwheels, his skinny body flipping in smooth, continuous arcs, hands-feet, hands-feet. When he bounced upright, the crowd clapped and whistled. He'd left his knit tam upended on the pavement. Several people dropped change and dollar bills into it.

Eyes bright, he looked past his audience to Jimmy, who sat a little way to one side. Their special relationship was so clear in that glance. I could almost feel the father-son emotion between them. It was as strong as that between Andy and Maloney—stronger even. Harmony was more like a loving son to Jimmy than a real son is to most parents these days. How lucky those two were to have found each other, I mused. Harmony's guileless good cheer brightened Jimmy's gloomy outlook and Jimmy gave Harmony stability. They complemented each other perfectly.

Andy and I spent the next couple of hours in the National Aquarium. Seeing the sharks and the tropical coral reef was as much a treat for me as it was for Andy.

When we left the building, we headed back across the harbor to Harborcourt, the fancy condominium building where Andy lived with his mother. Inside the lobby, the man at the reception desk called up to let her know we were there. When he put the phone down, he asked us to wait a few minutes. I wondered why until the elevator doors shooshed open and Brooks Brockloff strolled out.

I glanced at Andy who apparently didn't recognize the man. "I wonder what's wrong with mom," he said.

"I bet we'll be able to go up in another minute," I said. It turned out I was right.

When Karla Maloney opened the door on her twelfth floor unit, I

could see why Angus Maloney still pined for her. Tailored white
slacks clung to her slim, curvy form like a second skin. The deep vee
of her fawn silk blouse showed a tantalizing glimpse of cleavage and
her hair swept her shoulders in deep honey waves. Her perfume
smelled expensive, and her flushed skin looked healthy and poreless.
She was as cool and creamy as a butterscotch sundae.

"Hiya, hon!" She bent to give Andy a hug.

He wriggled free. "Can I show Toni my baseball collection?"

"Who's Toni?" She looked up and seemed to see me for the first
time. "Oh. Oh, sure. But you better not take her to that mess you call
a room. Bring the baseballs out here."

Andy scampered off and Karla and I were left staring at each
other in the hall. In my jeans and tee shirt, and with my hair a
windblown mess, I felt like a squishy gray caterpillar meeting a
Monarch butterfly. It was hard to believe we even belonged to the
same species.

"Miss a ... ?"

"Credella, Toni Credella. I'm Angus' assistant. He's not feeling
so good, so he asked me to help him out with Andy."

"Yes, he called to let me know that. You look familiar, Miss
Credella. Have we met before?"

"I live near the harbor. You've probably seen me around."

"Won't you wait in the living room? Can I offer you something?
A coke, a glass of wine?"

"No thanks. Hey, this is really something."

The hall opened out onto a gray and maroon living room with
the most spectacular view I'd ever seen. Below us, the crumpled blue
silk of the harbor glittered and undulated. Tiny sailboats glided on its
surface.

"So, how do you like working for Angus?" Karla stood behind
me, lounging in a hipshot model's pose. One manicured hand lightly
caressed the back of a gray velvet wing chair.

"I like it fine. He's a nice guy."

"Oh sure." She continued to study me, her eyes narrowed and
speculative. "You two dating, by any chance?"

I swung around and assessed the muted hostility in her glance.
I'd known other women like this. Even when they'd kicked a man out
of their lives, they didn't like the idea of another woman having him.
I said, "I'm just an employee, that's all. Angus is a great boss, and I

admire him."

She didn't look as if she believed me, but her laughter came out light and amused. "Angus has always been a nice guy. Even when he's up to the gills in the booze, which he claims he isn't these days. Tell me Miss Credella, is it really true he's not drinking?"

"Are you saying that Angus is an alcoholic?"

"With a capital A. When he's on one of his benders, he positively sloshes."

"I wouldn't have known if you hadn't told me." I wasn't surprised. There had to be a reason why Maloney's marriage had fallen apart and why he was scratching out a living as a freelance law man instead of rising through the ranks in the BPD. Still, I hated the scorn dripping from Karla's voice, and I knew she'd told me only to dim any romantic interest I might have in him. I wanted to tell her that whatever weaknesses Angus Maloney might be nursing, he was ten times a better man than a creep like Brockloff. Andy came in with his baseballs at that moment, so I was saved from making a scene and a fool of myself.

Still, I left Karla Maloney's building angry.

PROFESSOR MCDANIEL had lived within walking distance of the Hopkins campus in one of the classic old townhouses that line St. Paul. He'd rented the upstairs apartment. His landlady occupied the first floor of the building.

"Mrs. Imhoff?"

She peered out at me. The chain on her door bisected her face just below her chin. At her back the light made a halo of her white curls. "Oh my," she chirped. "Who are you?"

"My name is Toni Credella. I'm investigating the death of Professor Harold McDaniel, and I wondered if I could ask you a few questions?"

"You don't look like police. Can I see your badge?"

"Actually, I'm a private investigator." That was true, sort of. "Can I come in? I'd just like to ask you a few questions and then I'll be on my way."

At her feet, a Siamese cat wound itself between her ankles and stared at me with slanted sapphire eyes. "Oh well, I guess it can't do any harm. Come in. I was just about to eat dinner and watch one of my shows."

I followed her into the living room and noticed two other Siamese cats. One reclined atop the arm of the flowered couch while the other lay curled on a perch that had been fixed to the windowsill. Both animals eyed me regally. Mrs. Imhoff herself, bent by a pronounced widow's hump, was anything but regal. She wore a pink and blue flowered housecoat with scalloped, tea-stained lace trim on the sleeves. She'd jammed her large, square feet into royal blue satin mules. Though they were frayed at the toe, fake diamonds still twinkled in the satin rosettes decorating their heels.

Overstuffed furniture from a former life crammed her living room. Everywhere it was possible to stick a pin, she'd affixed lace doilies to chair backs. A bookcase under the window overflowed with vintage framed photographs—grandchildren, a balding bespectacled husband, a daughter in a white mortarboard. A shiny cherry coffee table in front of a flowery couch held many copies of GLAMOUR, MODERN MATURITY, and CROSSTITCH COMPANION. It also held a microwaved Healthy Choice chicken-rice dinner. Somewhere in the background I sniffed the distinctive fragrance of well-used kitty litter.

"Sit down, sit down." She waved me at an orange tweed chair with a box-pleated skirt, then returned to the couch and retrieved her fork.

"Did you know Professor McDaniel, Mrs. Imhoff?"

"Oh my, yes. Such a tragedy. You don't mind if I finish, do you? These microwave dinners get gluey if you don't eat them right away."

"Not at all. How well did you know the professor?" Gingerly, I settled into the chair.

"Not that well, considering he rented his place from me for more than ten years. He was quiet. A courtly gentleman. Such fine manners and so well educated." She sighed. "Mr. Imhoff, now he owned a furniture store. Never read a book in his life. I like to read, myself." She pointed at a row of romance paperbacks in her bookcase.

"Did Professor McDaniel have any particular friends or enemies in the neighborhood?"

"Not that I know of. He kept to himself. Always polite, but not a joiner. It's terrible what happened to him. They say he was hit over the head so hard it broke his skull. Whoever did it used a brick. Can you imagine that?" She shivered. "I don't know what the neighborhood is coming to. Poor old fellow never harmed anybody."

She flicked a button on her remote control, and raucous laughter from the TV exploded into the stale little room.

WHAT I DID next surprised even me. When I left Mrs. Imhoff's, it was dusk—a softly grayed purpling that seemed to come as much from the exhaust of homebound autos as from the waning light. I crossed University Parkway and peddled my bike through the hallowed grounds of the Johns Hopkins campus.

South of Homewood field, students wandered the paths. Despite their tattered jeans and long hair, they all looked bound for success. Some day they would be chemists, doctors, and computer scientists and rule the world. On one of the lawns a bespectacled young girl played with her Golden Retriever.

I thought of McDaniel taking this same route home year after year. If you lived and worked on a campus like this for most of your life, a walk across it at the end of the day would be like flipping through an album filled with memories.

I thought of Alice. She and McDaniel had been about the same age. Yet they might as well have lived on separate planets. How different Alice's memories must have been as she made her nightly circuit of street corners and trash bins. As I pictured her, an early night wind blew sadly through the oaks.

And what about the girl entombed so long and forgotten beneath those bricks? Was there any chance either McDaniel or Alice had known her? Was their any possibility those three dead people hadn't lived on such separate and distinct planets, after all? It was a crazy idea, I knew. Yet, I couldn't seem to lose it.

I circled around the Hopkins Club to the back of Gilman hall. Figuring McDaniel's office would be locked tight, I didn't even bother going inside the building. The cleaning crew would be around by this time. Best not to be seen by them, I thought.

Luckily, the office was on a ground floor. An overgrown clump of yew screened the window. Once I'd slipped behind it, I felt a bit safer. A passing student heading across to the Greenhouse for dinner couldn't easily see me.

I peered through the window. By now it was pretty dark, but so far as I could tell, nothing inside McDaniel's office had been disturbed. Considering what I wanted to do, I marveled at my audacity. No way would the old Toni have even considered breaking and entering. Right now I was more than considering it, though the thought scared me silly.

I looked around the window frame for burglar alarm wires. I didn't see any, which didn't surprise me. Gilman hall is so ancient it doesn't even have air conditioning. When I tried lifting the window, I was surprised. I'd expected I'd have to break some glass, but the window rattled right up. Climbing through was a bit of a struggle.

Once I stood up on the other side of McDaniel's desk, my heart raced with pride as well as terror. Maybe I'd missed my calling. Maybe I was meant to be a cat burglar.

I scanned McDaniel's bookshelves. The row of black and white notebooks he'd referred to during our conversation was apparently undisturbed. I took a step toward them, then froze. My ears had picked up the scrape of a key in the lock.

Chapter 13

AFTER DIVING for the desk, I took about two seconds to scuttle between the shelter of its pedestals. I was just dragging McDaniel's swivel chair back into place behind me when the door squawked open.

The overhead light flicked on. Listless feet shuffled over the wood floor. The wastepaper basket scraped. A sigh. The feet shuffled closer, came around to my side of the desk and paused in front of the window. I'd left it open. A light breeze and the rush and retreat of traffic on Charles wafted through it.

I peered around the pedestal of McDaniel's chair at the stockinged legs of a cleaning woman. She was looking directly at my bike leaning against the yew outside.

"Oh, my," she whispered and hurried from the room, doubtless to call Security.

I scrambled out from under the desk, tugged a half dozen of McDaniel's notebooks off his shelf and threw myself out the window. Five seconds later I was peddling off the campus with imaginary sirens screeching in my ears.

DON AND I smiled at each other. We were seated at a table at Louie's Bookstore Cafe and Don was telling me about the new woman in his life. She was a colleague, a professor of History at Hopkins. "It just feels right with Clea," he said.

"That's great. I'm really happy for you. Listen, try a weekend on the Eastern Shore, just the two of you. I'll bet that will put a ribbon on what already sounds like a great package."

After we finished our salads, I hauled out one of the notebooks I'd been pouring over during most of that day. Making sense of McDaniel's script was an almost impossible challenge. Still, I thought I might have found something interesting.

"Don, is this a name you recognize?"

In the faint light from Louie's ancient overhead fixtures, Don peered at the spot on the notebook page where I'd placed my finger.

"What's this?"

"It's a description of the Margraf Experiment."

Don took the notebook out of my hands and, holding the place, flipped through it. "This is one of Harold McDaniel's notebooks. What in God's name are you doing with it? Did he give it to you before he was killed?"

"Not exactly, but he showed it to me."

"Then how do you happen to have it in your possession?"

"Well..."

"I heard a rumor about his office having been broken into last night. Was that you?"

"The window was unlocked, so I didn't actually break in. I just climbed in."

"My God, Toni, and you stole his notebooks?"

"I didn't steal them. I just borrowed them. I wanted to find out more about the Margraf Experiment."

"Did you?"

"Not really. As far as I can tell, McDaniel didn't have much to say about it. There's only this sentence and this name, and the writing is so smudgy I'm not really sure what it says."

"It says a student named Bill Bodner monitored the experiment. B-i-l-l B-o-d-n-e-r." Don printed the name out on a napkin and pushed it to my side of the table. Then he snapped the notebook closed. "How many of these did you take?" The camaraderie had evaporated from our table. His tone was the kind you use when you're addressing a lower form of life.

"A half dozen."

"Where are the others?"

"At my place."

"Let's go get them."

"Now?"

"Now."

Don drove me home in silence and waited woodenly in my front hall while I went upstairs to collect the notebooks. After I handed them over, he said, "I can't imagine breaking into a dead man's office and stealing his private notebooks just out of idle curiosity."

"My curiosity isn't idle, and since Professor McDaniel is dead, I don't think he would care about me taking his notebooks for a good purpose."

"We have a very different view of these things, Toni."

"I guess we do. Does this mean we're not friends anymore?"

Don sighed and shook his head. "Sometimes you don't make it easy, Toni, but we're still friends if you want it that way. I've got to return these notebooks to McDaniel's office, though. I just hope to hell I can do it without anyone being the wiser."

THE NEXT morning I peddled down to the construction site. Maloney's car was still parked in front. I tried the Chevette's door and was pleased that Tyler, Maloney's Aikido student, had locked it after filling in as watchman last night. On the other hand, the car still being here meant Maloney wasn't up to driving it, which worried me.

A major production was underway on the other side of the fence. I remembered Mario's invitation and ambled over to watch the construction guys assemble the big crane. Smaller cranes stacked the pieces atop each other, pausing long enough for hardhatted men in jeans to scramble over it like monkeys on a Jungle Jim making sure the joints were secure.

I heard a lot of yelling punctuated by the roar of revving engines and the metallic squeak and groan of levers and wires. Up and up the vertical shaft went, until it seemed it would sway and then topple in a high wind. Only the giant slabs of concrete weighting its base would keep it from doing exactly that.

The real excitement came when the horizontal boom had to be hoisted and attached. On fragile looking cables it trembled and lurched in mid-air. As the web of pulleys and motors worked, I thought of a spider hoisting a twig fifty times its length.

"Something, huh?" Mario said. He'd noticed me gawking outside the fence and had come over to say hello.

"Amazing!" The back of my head was practically on my shoulder blades as I shaded my eyes and peered up. "Those men weren't born with nerves. They're not even using safety belts. What's their life expectancy?"

He laughed. "There aren't as many accidents as you'd think. Crane mechanics are a special breed. Believe me, they're well paid for what they do."

"They deserve to be. The thought of being up there with them gives my stomach the sick flutters. What's that little blue box inside the vertical part?"

"You mean the cab where the crane operator sits?"

I studied the glassed-in box. How would it be to sit in a thing like that all day long? Hot in summer, I bet. Yet, what a feeling of power the operator must have, high above the world like an eagle in his own private nest and lifting weights mere mortals couldn't even consider. "How many guys have the key to the engine?"

"Cranes don't have keys, just switches. There's only one crane operator insured to use it, though."

"You don't ever have to warn guys off it?"

"Not if they work for me, I don't. As for anybody else, that's what we have somebody watching the property at night for—to keep that from happening."

"Actually, I'm here because your workmen found an old woman murdered where that crane is standing now. And that was after they dug a skeleton out of what's going to be the foundation of your condo."

Mario nodded. "I wasn't here when they dug up the skeleton. But I was on the job just before Alice Ritco was murdered. You know what one of my men told me? Alice Ritco was standing right there where you are when they uncovered that skeleton."

"She was?" A shiver rippled down my spine.

As I peddled back downtown, images of Alice watching bones being unearthed filled my head. The irony was too much. Alice sees a young girl's bones, and only a few hours later Alice is dead in the same spot herself. I looked back over my shoulder and saw the crane's boom swinging in the air like the club of an invisible giant.

My next stop was Randall's office. His sleek young receptionist made me wait for almost an hour before she let me see him.

"You're lucky you're in here at all," he informed me. "Most people make an appointment."

"I know, oh high-priced one, and I'm sorry. I tried to call you last night but you were out. I did leave a message on your answering machine."

"I got in late last night."

He looked it. Randall, as always, was immaculately dressed. His collar and cuffs were snowy against his dark skin and his short hair was cut so close to his strongly shaped skull that it needed no brush. But his eyes looked tired. I detected an edge of irritation in his voice.

"If you're here to put in more good words for O'Dell, save your breath. It looks as if my client may settle out of court on that one."

"You mean I won't have to testify?"

"If O'Dell is willing to eat enough humble pie, maybe not." Randall didn't exactly look pleased about letting me off the hook. In fact, he looked as if he might like to put a fist through a door.

"Are you mad at me, Randall?"

"No, Babe." He passed a hand over his forehead, as if trying to smooth out the grooves between his eyebrows. "I love you and I'm always glad to see you. Now, what's up?"

I told Randall about my lunch with Don. He shook his head. "He's right about those notebooks. Are you crazy? Breaking and entering is a felony. I wish you hadn't told me. Now my ethics are compromised."

"Are you going to turn me in?"

He leaned forward, folded his hands in front of him and looked at me seriously. "I'm going to give you a lecture. Toni, you're on the edge. You've already been tried for murder once. You can't afford any more trouble. Nosing into this homeless woman's death isn't part of your job with Maloney. Why are you doing these stupid things?"

"Oh Randall, I should have let Alice in that night. If I had, she wouldn't have wound up with her head bashed in."

"Maybe, maybe not. My college roommate told me Jews were the ones raised on guilt. Italians must come a close second."

He had that right, I thought. Growing up in the Credella household, I'd inhaled guilt and duty-until-death right along with the oregano and garlic.

"Listen, I did come here to ask a favor. I dug the name Bill Bodner out of McDaniel's notebooks. He was the graduate student in charge of the Margraf Experiment. I hoped with all the fancy computer search programs you've got, you could help me track him down."

"Have you tried the phone book?"

"Uh, no, I never thought of that."

Randall reached into a bottom drawer on his massive desk. He fished out the Baltimore directory, flipped through it and then spun it around and shoved it in my direction. "William R. Bodner, psychotherapist," he said, tapping a spot on the page.

BACK AT MY place I found a message from Angus Maloney on my

answering machine. His voice sounded strained. "I'm not going to be able to make it down to the construction site tonight, after all, and Tyler has to work his other job. I hate asking you, Toni, but could you take over for me?"

I dialed Maloney and he told me his neck was paining him so bad he could barely roll over to pick up the phone. No way could he sit up all night in a car.

"Why don't you try that chiropractor I mentioned?" I gave him Doris Ritco's name and number.

"Thanks, maybe I'll call her."

"Do you need the car to get out there?"

"I can't drive. If I decide to try Dr. Ritco, I'll get a cab. You use the car at the construction site. Listen, Toni, thanks."

"I'll be glad to be your stand in."

Since I needed the money, this was true. I packed a brown bag with a diet Coke, an apple and plenty of peanut butter and crackers. If Al was there again, I didn't want to have to wheedle food out of him.

This turned out to be a needless worry. When I arrived, the construction crew was just getting off work. As I unlocked Maloney's car and climbed in, a couple of them waved at me. One gave me a wolf whistle and some of the others laughed and shot flirtatious looks. I didn't mind. Actually, it felt sort of good.

However, once the workers were all gone, I began to feel lonely and unsafe. Though close to downtown, the stretch of empty property outside the car was oddly silent. In the distance, the buzz of evening traffic was only a faint drone.

The sinking sun sent spectral shadows crawling over the empty roads and made monsters of the earthmoving equipment abandoned on the gravel. The big swinging boom on the new crane hung over the darkening skyline like an executioner's ax.

I locked the doors and opened my dinner bag. I'd finished off the peanut butter and was munching the apple when I spotted Jimmy and Harmony coming down the road.

They were far away when I first saw them, but their figures were distinctive—Jimmy, stolid and square, rolling along in his motorized chariot. Harmony skipping around him like an overgrown ten-year-old. Now and then he'd play riffs on his harmonica.

I rolled down my window and pretty soon the breeze off the water carried the sound of his music. He was playing *Camptown*

Races. The sprightly tinkle made me feel less lonely and frightened. The corners of my mouth turned up.

"Hey, lookee here." Harmony's eyes rounded as he recognized me inside Maloney's car. "It's Toni. What are you doing out here, Toni? Is that your car?"

"Not mine. Belongs to a friend. I'm just using it to guard the place."

"You're guarding the place?" Harmony stared at me, then at the construction behind me. "You mean, you're guarding all those big machines? Hey, Jimmy, did you hear what she said?"

Behind him, Jimmy said, "Women are doing just about anything you can name, nowadays, Harmony. It's no big deal that Toni's got herself a job as a guard."

Harmony pocketed his instrument. He tilted his scraggly head back and gaped at the boom on the new crane. The wind that had come up off the water had set it to quivering. Slight shivers of motion vibrated down its vertical spine and from time to time it creaked. It was as if it were alive and trying to say something.

"I bet it's fun to stand on the top of that thing," Harmony remarked. "Did you ever do it, Toni?"

I shook my head. "Not allowed. Only the crane operator is allowed up there."

"Who's he? Is he someone special, like God?"

"He's just a guy with a license," Jimmy said.

A sly grin crept across Harmony's elfin features. "A license is only a piece of paper."

Before I could even think of a response, he'd scrambled around the car and flung himself at the chain link fence. For a split second he clung like a squirrel. Then, with a whoop, he was up and over the fence and jumping lightly down on the other side.

Jimmy and I both yelled at him. I dropped my apple and scrambled out of the car. Harmony sprinted over to the base of the crane some fifty yards off.

"Stop him!" Jimmy yelled. "Oh, Christ!" Jimmy's balled fists hammered the arms of his wheelchair in frustration. "He'll do something stupid!"

I was already scaling the fence. I didn't go up it anywhere near as fast as Harmony. There was no barbed wire at the top, so when I threw one leg over I could pause long enough to scope out what he was doing.

"Oh Jeez!" I screeched when I saw him start to climb up the ladder to the blue cab. The damn thing wasn't locked.

I fell onto the gravel. Half-limping, I ran to the crane. "Don't do that! For God's sake!"

But Harmony was already halfway up to the cab. I climbed after him, but he was twice as fast as me. I'd only made twenty feet when I looked up and glimpsed Harmony staring out at me from the cab's glass door. He looked like a demented leprechaun. I figured he must be playing with the controls. The cab swayed sickeningly. He gave me the high sign.

"Oh, God!" I started to climb faster. I was yelling my throat raw. "Harmony, stop! Stop!"

The cab teetered, pausing drunkenly, and then the vertical arm started to shift. I felt nauseous. I kept climbing, hauling myself up on the metal ladder. The iron cut into my hands. My muscles throbbed. My neck, thrust back so I could see the cab above me, began to feel as if it would snap off.

All at once, my arms and legs turned to cooked spaghetti. It was all I could do to hang on. When I looked down, I saw that I was almost fifty feet off the ground. My stomach lurched.

Above me, the vertical arm stopped swinging. The cab's door opened and Harmony poked his head out. "What's wrong, Toni? You look funny."

"I can't climb any further."

"Then you better go back."

"I can't do that, either. I'm stuck. I'm afraid I'm going to fall."

Chapter 14

"GET OUT OF that damn box and help her!" Jimmy's voice exploded from the other side of the fence. He'd rolled his wheelchair right up to it. His hands clutched the wire as if they wanted to rip it apart.

Obediently, Harmony climbed out of the cab. It shimmied and danced with each shift of his weight. Seizing a metal brace, he stepped lightly onto the top of the ladder above my head.

"The view is great up here," he commented, pausing to look around like a tourist on the roof of the World Trade Center. I could see the view reflected in his eyes. The sun was a blood red gob of flame on the horizon. The fiery fingers of its dying rays stretched in all directions.

"If you say so."

He laughed. "Scared to look? Don't worry, Toni. I won't let you fall. Just hold tight."

It was the only thing I could do. My muscles had frozen into place.

Dropping down the ladder four and five rungs at a time and landing with catlike grace, Harmony perched on an angled piece of iron next to mine.

Smiling, he reached out and took my arm. I was surprised by the strength of his grip. Frail though he looked, he had steely muscles.

"Put your foot there," he urged. "Don't worry, I'm holding you. I won't let go. Toni, I'm sorry if I scared you. I didn't mean to scare you."

"Well, you did. It's my job to guard this place, Harmony. I'm not supposed to let people climb on the crane."

"I just wanted to have some fun."

"Well, don't do it again."

"I won't. I promise. There, see, we're almost back on the ground."

Seconds later, I tumbled onto the pile of cement slabs weighting the crane. Moaning with relief, I curled up and put my head in my hands. My calves trembled. My stomach felt like a pudding in an earthquake. "Ohhhh ..."

"You okay?"

"Just great." Looking up, I found Harmony's face thrust close to mine. His teeth needed some work. A couple of them were missing and one was chipped. I noticed a bump on his nose where it had been broken. No wonder, I thought. If he'd been like he is now when he was a little kid, he must have been falling out of trees daily.

Then I remembered what Jimmy had told me about saving Harmony from getting beat up. Probably, that's where he got his broken nose and chipped teeth. He was too surefooted to fall out of trees.

"I'm okay," I said. I put my head between my knees.

Harmony crowed in my ear. "See. Everything's okay now. They'll never know."

"Sure."

"Give me your hand, Toni. I'll help you over the fence."

Somehow, I managed to climb back outside. After a few more apologetic words from Harmony, he and Jimmy left. Over the whirr of his wheelchair, I could hear Jimmy lecturing his impetuous young sidekick. "When are you going to stop acting like a two-year-old? What if you'd got stuck up there or Toni had fallen?"

Gradually, their voices faded and I was alone again. I glanced at the crane and shuddered.

Harmony and Jimmy weren't my only visitors. A couple of hours later the headlights of a car appeared at the end of the street. My drooping eyelids lifted and I stiffened.

The car's headlamps pressed cool fingers of white light on the pavement. It slowed, drew up alongside and braked, the motor growling like a cat with a mouse between its paws. The driver rolled the window and stuck his head out. It was O'Dell.

"What the hell are you doing here?" he demanded.

"I might ask you the same."

"I'm a cop, remember? This happens to be the scene of a murder I'm handling."

"You're not driving your cop car. I thought you were retired from active duty."

"That doesn't mean I can't still take an interest in my cases. I thought you couldn't drive. Whose car is that? What are you doing sitting behind the driver's wheel out here?"

When I explained, the scowl on O'Dell's lean face deepened. "Maloney should know better than to let you take over for him out here. It's dangerous. I never did trust that guy's brains."

"You don't trust anybody, and I sure as heck don't trust you."

His expression shifted. He searched my face, which I thought must look pale as a boiled egg in the light streaming from his headlights.

"I've been thinking about you a lot, about what happened between us the other night at your place."

"Well, stop thinking about it, O'Dell. It was a mistake."

He tapped his steering wheel. I noticed he was wearing a leather jacket. His hair had been cut recently. A scabbed-over nick creased his left ear. What barber did he patronize, Jack the Ripper?

"I have a proposition for you. How'd you like to go down to the Smithsonian with me tomorrow morning?"

"Are you inviting me to go see the First Ladies Inaugural Ball gowns with you?"

"We'll be looking at bones, not ball gowns. Remember, I told you we'd sent that dump job's bones to the Smithsonian?"

I nodded.

"The forensic anthropologist down there has been working on the bones. I'm driving down to take a look at his results. If you want, you can come along. It might be interesting."

He needn't have bothered to throw in that last because I didn't require persuading. "What time will you pick me up?"

AT DAWN'S early light, I peddled home. I'd had all of three hours sleep and was just downing my second cup of instant coffee when O'Dell tooted his horn outside my door.

"Don't you think it's about time you got a newer car?" I remarked after I climbed into his 1967 Pinto. I cast a quick glance over him. Freshly shaved and showered and wearing a new three-piece suit, he looked unusually well dressed. Despite his sartorial splendor, however, his lean face appeared drawn and discontented.

"Why so glum?" I asked.

"I've just come from a conference with Internal Affairs. They've worked out a deal with your pal, Randall. Instead of ruining my joke of a career completely and smirching the whole department, he's going to be content to just watch me writhe in hell for six months."

"What does that mean?"

"He's agreed to drop the charges against me. In return, I have to pay Jerome Robinson's medical bills and make a cash settlement of a thousand dollars to help provide for his future education."

"Do you have the money?"

"Is Elvis Presley alive and well on the moon!" O'Dell exclaimed irritably. "The department is going to take it out of my paychecks for the next twenty years or so. But wait, there's more. Not only does your lawyer friend wants to make a pauper out of me—which should be no trouble at all since I'm already there—he's demanding that I and every other cop in Homicide go through sensitivity training. On top of that, I'm supposed to perform 100 hours of community service in Jerome Robinson's neighborhood and personally mentor Jerome for half a year."

"Mentor?"

"Check his homework. Take him to basketball games and neighborhood picnics. All of it under the supervision of a counselor."

"What kind of counselor?"

"Some bleeding heart who majored in psychology because he belonged in a loony bin himself. That ought to be a barrel of fun, huh?"

"Did Jerome ask for any of this?"

"Are you out of your gourd? Of course not! He'd like to line my jockey shorts with ground glass. The mentor thing was strictly Randall's cockamamie idea. Apparently he's chairman of some committee that got the department a private grant for trying experimental programs with at-risk youth 'to create better communication between the police and the community.'" O'Dell sneered as he mouthed the quoted phrase. "They're going to use Jerome and me as guinea pigs."

"Well, maybe it's not such a bad idea," I ventured.

O'Dell snorted. "I need to go for counseling with Jerome Robinson like I need an extra head. The first time I try taking the kid to a basketball game he'll probably slip rat poison into my beer. Some fun year I have to look forward to!"

I slanted a covert look at O'Dell. I thought I could guess what Randall had had in mind when he negotiated the counseling/mentor experiment. He'd figured it might do a guy like O'Dell some good to get to know one of the kids he now regarded merely as the enemy. Who knew? Getting to know O'Dell better, with the supervision of a specially trained counselor, might not be bad for a rudderless kid like Jerome, either. However, I was diplomat enough not to say this to O'Dell who looked mad enough to spit tacks.

"So you won't get to testify against me, after all. Disappointed?"

"I never wanted to testify against you, Gus."

As we pulled up to a red light, he appraised me. "You're looking mighty fine this morning. You should wear your hair like that more often. Suits you."

I'd dug out my best tweed blazer and good wool slacks. My hair I'd drawn up into a topknot. At my ears I wore a pair of silver earrings Randall had given me. Randall's taste is impeccable.

"It's not often I get to visit the Smithsonian, even to look at bones. Tell me about this forensic anthropologist. What will he show us?"

"The guy's name is Tomlinson, Doug Tomlinson. Most of his cases are FBI, but occasionally he'll take a case like this one of mine. He can look at a bone and practically recite the life history of the person it came from. The hope is he'll be able to give us information on the girl's bones that might help us identify her."

"What can he tell from a bone?"

O'Dell whistled. "You'd be amazed. Once, he looked at a thigh bone and told me the owner was six feet tall. Doug knew his sex, age at death, ethnic origin, body weight, the way he'd walked. He even had clues about diseases and how the victim had earned his living. If Doug can give us any information like that on this dump job, we may be able to get a line on her. But it gets better. Sometimes Doug does facial reconstructions. I've seen him sculpt the face right over a model of the skull. He can do that with computer imaging, too."

I stared out the window. We were on 95, headed south. O'Dell pulled out into the fast lane and urged his creaky Pinto past a behemoth of an oil tanker. As we settled back into the middle lane in front of the tanker, I thought about seeing a dead girl's face. A queasy feeling spread in my belly.

"You probably already know this," I said, "but I'll mention it anyway. Mario Caprini, the foreman over at the condo construction, told me that a woman matching Alice Ritco's description was hanging around the site the day they found that girl's bones."

O'Dell took his eyes off the road long enough to pin me with a sharp glance. "When did he tell you this?"

"Yesterday. He said one of his men told him. You mean you didn't know it?"

"Never said a word about it to me, and I questioned everyone who works on that site pretty closely."

"Maybe I'm better at asking questions than you are."

"Or possibly this Caprini would rather talk to you than me, though I can't imagine why." O'Dell smirked.

"So, what do you make of that? Alice sees a girl's body unearthed and twenty-four hours later she's dead. Quite a coincidence, isn't it?"

"That's probably all it is, Toni. Until we know who those bones belonged to, there's nothing to indicate a connection between them and Alice Ritco."

I didn't argue. But I couldn't get the notion out of my head that the two murders were intertwined.

When we walked into the National Museum of Natural History, the queasiness in my stomach had come to life and sprouted wings.

Tomlinson was a middle-aged guy with a short pepper and salt beard and the air of a kindly uncle. After O'Dell introduced me to him, he walked us along a corridor lined with large green drawers which rose in stacks some sixteen feet from floor to ceiling. The drawers, he told us, stretched in an immense labyrinth through the museum's third floor and held one of the world's largest collections of human bones.

"We've got the skeletal remains of some 33,000 individuals of all races, shapes and sizes."

He slid open a draw filled with skulls, and then one with what looked like leg bones. "It's the other army of the Potomac," he mused.

"Is our girl in one of these drawers?" O'Dell asked. He looked impatient.

Tomlinson shook his head. "Come with me."

He led us into a small room. Gray metal shelving lining the walls held books, stacks of paper, and a variety of other objects including bones, small microscopes, tools and a few loose skulls. Their eyeless sockets looked down on desks with computers and several narrow examining tables. Tomlinson pointed at one. "That's yours."

An almost complete human skeleton lay on the table. Quickly, Tomlinson and O'Dell walked to it. I moved less eagerly. In my mind, this murdered girl had become almost legendary. Now I was seeing her for the first time.

"My findings are not greatly different from your ME's," Tomlinson said. "The remains are those of a female, somewhere between sixteen and twenty, Caucasian, 5'5", dead as much as twenty to thirty years. The trauma to the head is this jagged crack at the junction of the right occipital and temporal bones. But that may not have been what killed her. In my judgment, she was slammed violently against a wall or some other solid object and then most likely strangled. She was strongly built, probably athletic, so she would have put up a good fight. Whoever killed her must have been pretty strong, himself."

We gazed at the quiet bones, each of us silent as we imagined the horrid scene Tomlinson had just described so clinically. Somewhere inside my head I heard screams and curses. Fists flailed and pummeled as a girl's strong young body fought vainly to live. I tasted blood and felt the crack of bones, and then the final choking darkness.

Her killer had entombed her in a mountain of rubble where she had lain hidden for over a quarter of a century. Now no one knew her name. What monster had snuffed out her life so meanly and why?

The men moved away from the table. "Want to see what she looked like, Toni?" O'Dell asked over his shoulder.

"Sure, sure." I hurried to join them and stepped next to O'Dell just as Tomlinson reached for a head covered with cheesecloth. It stood on a shelf with a row of several others in various stages of preparation, some with pins set in layers of clay, others nothing more than skulls with glass eyes glued into the eye sockets.

"Before I unveil this, keep in mind that it can't be anything more than an approximation of the victim's appearance. Let me explain the technique," Tomlinson said. "After I set tissue thickness markers in place, I use clay to fill in the intervening spaces. There are clues in the bones about noses and lips and chin types. Still, putting it all together is as much an art as it is a science. Sometimes there's enough hair left with a body to judge coloring. Not with this young woman though, so hair is strictly a guess."

"Okay, let's see our girl," O'Dell said.

I wondered if his stomach felt as tight as mine. As Tomlinson lifted the cheesecloth, my mouth tasted like the chalky inside of a kiln.

The cloth fell away and we stared in silence. If Tomlinson was right, she had been neither pretty nor delicate. Hers had been a strong face with a prominent nose and a square jaw.

"Why did you make her eyes blue?" O'Dell asked.

"Just a guess. That's a Nordic cheek structure. If I were to put hair on her I'd make it short and blond."

Again, we were all silent, staring at what had once been a living woman and was now only bone and imagination. I stole a glance at Tomlinson. He gazed at the head somberly. As its creator, he knew more of its secrets than either O'Dell or I ever would, I thought. In a way, he had brought a girl back to life. He glanced up and caught my eye.

"You really believe this is how she looked, don't you?" I said.

"Yes, I do. There's a strange thing that happens when you're working with bones. Some religions believe that part of the spirit stays with the bones, and sometimes I believe that, too. Occasionally, especially when I'm working with victims of violent trauma, I get the feeling the person is telling me about himself or herself. It's almost as if they're guiding my fingers and my inner eye as I try to recreate a semblance of what they were in life." He laughed self-consciously. "Yes, I think this is how your girl really looked."

Returning my gaze to the head, I locked my cold hands behind my back. "I think you're right," I said. "I think this is her."

MOST OF THE way home from the Smithsonian, O'Dell and I discussed the dump job case and Alice's case. Again, he laughed at my notion that the two might be linked. Nevertheless, when I told him about Bill Bodner, he got interested. "I'll look him up tomorrow. You can come along if you want."

"Thanks a lot, since I'm the one who came up with the name."

"It's probably going to be a waste of time, Toni. Listen, it's past noon. How about stopping for lunch?"

At the mention of food, my stomach felt like a moon crater. I yearned for a bacon, lettuce and tomato sandwich. I shook my head.

"Why not? I'm buying."

"That's why, Gus. I don't want this to turn into anything but business."

"Oh, for Pete's sake." He sighed. "Toni, I'm not a bad guy. Honest. I know the sex the other night was kind of rough and ready. That was because I didn't know it was going to happen. I'd been craving you for so damn long. If you'd give me a chance, I'd please you. I'd be the lover you want."

I turned my head away and pretended to look out the side window. "I don't know what kind of lover I want."

"Then let me try to show you."

I shook my head. "Please, Gus, drop it. Just be my friend. That's all I need right now, and that's all I want."

"What about me? Friendship isn't all I need and want."

"I can't fill up the empty spaces in your life, Gus. You have to do that for yourself. You have to find something or somebody besides your work."

"And you're telling me flat out that something or somebody isn't going to be you."

"No, it's not."

Chapter 15

WHEN O'DELL dropped me off, neither of us had much to say. The little red light on my answering machine flashed like a beacon on an ambulance. Normally, I pounce on it, hoping for an income-producing job. This time I felt so hollow that I headed for the kitchen and opened a can of chicken soup. While I waited for it to heat, I stuffed myself with a bagel slathered with cream cheese.

Full, I stripped off my fancy duds and let my hair down. Then I collapsed into bed and a marathon afternoon siesta. My dreams were of accusing bodiless heads, of screams and the sound of bricks falling into place over a nameless tomb. I woke up to evening shadows. After my break-in, I'd been keeping all my windows locked. The room felt as airless as a burial chamber.

After stepping into jeans and a tee shirt, I headed for the phone and pressed "play."

"Toni, this is Angus. Thanks for taking over on the site last night. The check is in the mail, as they say. I'll be back on the job tonight, so you can get your beauty sleep. Take care."

I played the message again. Maloney sounded tired. I glanced at the digital clock. Too late for me to call and try to convince the big lug to stay home and get himself well. I grabbed my jacket, another bagel, and rolled my bike out onto the street.

By the time I reached the construction site, the sun floated on the harbor's dark water like a giant incandescent beach ball. Scarves of pink and scarlet draped the lavender sky.

I peered into the driver side window of Maloney's car. He was resting his head against the seat, his aggressive nose and solid Irish jaw thrust out. A big white foam collar encased his neck.

He opened one eye and looked at me. Though I hadn't seen Maloney's hand move, the window cranked down.

"Why aren't you home watching TV?"

"I've heard enough bad news today."

"You're not going to hear any good news from me."

I walked around to the passenger seat and tried the handle. With an obvious effort, Maloney reached over and unlocked it.

At that moment a black guy wearing a dark uniform emerged from the shadows on the other side of the fence and shone a flashlight on us. "Everything okay here, Mr. Maloney?"

"Fine. Mr. George Parsons, meet Miss Toni Credella. She's a colleague of mine."

"How do you do, Mr. Parsons. Please call me Toni." I shaded my eyes against the glare of the flashlight.

"And you can call me George." He snapped the light off. "If everything's okay here, I'll go on with my rounds. You take care, now."

"Who's that?" I asked when he'd merged with the darkness again.

"Night watchman. The chief engineer on the job, a guy named Cabrini, says they found signs somebody had been fooling around with the cab on the crane. You know anything about that?"

Should I tell Maloney about what happened with Harmony and Jimmy? Lying to Maloney hadn't done much for me in the past. When the story was out, Maloney shook his head.

"What is it about you, Credella? Trouble homes in on you like a hungry mosquito on a hot summer night."

"Ain't it the truth." I opened the car door and slid in. "Honest, I'm sorry, but it wasn't my fault. Does this mean I've made trouble for you? Now that they've hired a night watchman, are you out of a job?"

"No. Just to make sure everything stays copasetic, they're keeping me on."

"You should be home in bed."

"Bed is boring when I'm the only one in it." Maloney replaced his head against the seat. His lids slipped down over his eyes. Even in the uncertain light I could see new brackets of strain around his mouth.

"Angus, you're just not up to this. I can see you're in pain."

"I'm fine."

"Oh sure. What does the chiropractor say?"

"I don't see her until tomorrow."

"How about the doctor?"

"Says I should be more careful about who I let drive my car."

I crossed my hands over my chest. "You don't have to remind

me this is all my fault. I know. You're still mad at me, aren't you?"

His eyes popped open. Deliberately, he waggled his big head back and forth, as if testing the range of his discomfort. "Toni, I'm mad at me. This is just a piece with every other damn thing in my life. My mother used to say I was born under a lucky star. The woman was cracked. Some lucky star. Since the day I was born I've stumbled over every rock in the road."

"I'm sorry."

"So am I, darlin'. But it's hard to sound like Little Mary Sunshine when you've got a wife who's cheating on you, a son you see only once a week, a business that's touch-and-go only on good days and a neck that feels like Captain-fucking Hook-sank his steel claw into it. Such conditions might almost drive a man back to drink."

"You aren't going to do that, are you?" More anxiety laced my voice than I'd intended to put there.

Maloney looked at me. "So you know about the drinking, do you? Who told you? Your playmate O'Dell?"

"Actually, it was Karla."

"Ah, my loving helpmate strikes again. Well, she told the truth. I used to be a souse. Resigning from the BPD wasn't my idea. I was invited. But those days are over. I know what it's like to grow up with a dad who spends his waking hours as waxed fruit. I don't want Andy to have the same memories. Karla just won't believe me."

"Is that why she kicked you out?"

"That and other reasons. The lady says she fell out of love with me."

"But you're still in love with her, aren't you."

"In love...I don't know. A man needs a woman. It's a cliché and a song title, but so is God Bless America. A man needs a woman. I'd take her back in a minute if she'd have me."

"There are other women in the world."

"Yeah, I know, but none of them know me the way Karla knows me, and none are the mother of my son."

I wanted to yell at him, "Your Karla is a bleached bitch. She isn't half good enough for you."

I didn't say a word. Just sat there like a lump with the twilight clotting into night around us and the wind a half-hearted sigh through the open crack of the window.

The car phone jangled, shocking us and the stillness. With a groan, Maloney leaned forward and took it out of its holster. "Yes?" he said, holding it well away from his ear.

"Dad?"

I could hear Andy's voice, reedy and frightened.

Maloney pressed the receiver closer. "What is it? What's wrong?" A moment later he whispered urgently, "I'm coming. Just hold tight." Maloney turned to me. "That was Andy. He says there's a woman in the living room holding a gun on Karla."

THE DESK clerk at Karla's condominium knew Maloney. He let us go up without a problem.

"What now?" I whispered when we arrived at her door. I was still having a hard time believing this was happening. I wondered if maybe Andy had been having a bad dream or playing a prank.

Maloney pressed his ear against the door. He listened, then drew back. "Nothing," he whispered and took out a ring of keys. He looked pale, but his hands were steady. "I'm going in. You stay here."

For a crazy instant, I almost grabbed his elbow to hold him back. I was afraid of what Angus would find. Despite the collar girdling his neck, Maloney was a big, healthy guy and I wanted him to stay that way.

I stepped to one side as he softly turned the key in the lock. Fortunately the door's well-oiled hinges slid open silently.

Maloney slipped inside. A half minute later the buzz of angry voices filtered back to me. My stomach knotted, anticipating a scream or the crack of a gun. A couple of minutes later my feet decided to follow Maloney's. Inside, light from an overhead fixture flooded the marble entry.

I paused, trying to make out words and meaning from the rise and fall of emotional voices in the living room. Snatches of high-pitched phrases from a woman flew back to me: "Two-timing bastard, bleached blond slut, doesn't care who she hurts." Below this hysterical litany, I could hear the rumble of Maloney's deep baritone.

To my right, another hall led to what I presumed were bedrooms. Though it was dark, a slight movement drew my attention. Andy crouched in the shadows. He wore pajamas, and his arms were wrapped around his knees which were drawn up tight to his chest. Gliding over to him, I whispered, "What's going on?"

"There's a crazy lady in the living room holding a gun on my mom," he whispered back. "Now she's holding it on my dad, too."

"Who is she?"

"Dunno. I was asleep when I heard her yelling, so I sneaked out. I saw her and the gun and heard all the crazy stuff she was saying, so I called Dad's car phone."

"That was good, Andy. Did you call anybody else? Did you dial 911?"

He shook his head. "'Fraid to. My dad can take care of her. I know he can. He just needs to get that gun away."

I patted Andy's head and squeezed his cold hand. He was trembling. "Stay put."

I tiptoed back into the main hall and began inching down it, plastering my body flat to the wall. The hall opened directly onto the living room. A few more feet and I had a clear view of the scene. Fortunately, the three people in it were too busy with each other to notice me.

Karla huddled in a maroon chair next to the window. Her hair looked as if she'd been twisting it into strings. Maloney stood with his broad back to me. With the exaggerated calm of a shrink trying to talk a nutcase off a ledge, he was reasoning with the other woman in the room. She was thin, wore a green trench coat and had short dark hair which fitted her small head like a shoe polish cap.

Strong emotion pinched her face. She either grimaced or whinnied nervy laughs. Her gaze, glassy with unnatural excitement, swung like a metronome between Karla and Maloney. She clutched a revolver aimed squarely at Karla.

"You lied to me," she accused Maloney in a voice that trembled on the breathless edge of hysteria. "You never told me it was her he was seeing. After all the money I paid you, I had to find out about her by following the big creep myself. And that's exactly what I did, oh yes!"

"Believe me, Mrs. Brockloff..."

"Why should I? You cheated and lied just the way he's been cheating and lying. I saw them...oh God, I saw them...and when I think of all the promises he made me. The shit, the dirty shit!"

"Mrs. Brockloff, Marnie, I know you're very upset. But you need to think about what you're doing here. Is that husband of yours really worth going to jail for?"

"The world is pigshit! Men, men like you and Brooks are turds!"

"I know it's tough to learn your husband has been unfaithful..."

"This...this woman is a whore. It's cunts like her who ruin marriages. She doesn't deserve to live. She should die in the street like a dog!"

"Marnie, that's not for you to say."

"Oh yes it is! I'm the one with the power. I'm the one!" She waved the gun as if it were a magic wand and she intended changing the world with it.

I recognized in Marnie Brockloff's rage and paranoia some of what had made a crazy person out of me the night I shot Nick. What if that gun went off in Mrs. Brockloff's hand the way it had in mine? What if this time the bleeding body on the floor were Angus Maloney's?

I rushed in to the right of Maloney. "Mrs. Brockloff, it's all my fault. Let me explain."

Her head jerked and swung. Her bruised, flaring eyes stared at me, and she screeched. As her cry cut the air, Maloney sprang forward and twisted her arm behind her back. The gun thunked on Karla's thick white carpet. Mrs. Brockloff screamed and screamed.

Over her shoulder, Maloney glared at me. "I thought I told you to stay put, Credella."

"I THOUGHT I told you to stay put," Maloney said again a couple of hours later. We were driving back from the emergency room where Marnie Brockloff had been sedated while her husband and the police sorted out her custody.

"How could I stay put when the woman was about to shoot you? I was going to tell her that I was the one who left Karla's name off your report."

"No kidding. And what difference would that have made?"

"It made a hell of a difference. You got the gun away from her, didn't you?"

Maloney snorted. "She could just as easily have shot all of us. If you want to work for me, Credella, you have to do what you're told. Next time when I say stay put, stay put."

"Right."

We drove through the dark streets in mutually resentful silence. Maloney headed his car toward South Baltimore and my row house. "My bike is still at the construction site," I pointed out.

"Yeah, right. If it hasn't already been ripped off, I'll pick it up and get it to you on my way home tomorrow morning."

I squirmed behind my seatbelt. "I suppose after you drop me off, you're going back to see Karla."

"I think I should, don't you?"

"Sure."

"I need to make sure Andy's okay with this."

"Of course you do."

We drove some more. Outside, the streets looked deserted and threatening. Inside the car the silence was thick.

"I need to make sure Andy's okay," Maloney said again.

"He seemed okay when we left." After Mrs. Brockloff had been disarmed, Andy had strolled in. He'd taken a scornful look at her twisted, tear-blotched face and then gone back to bed as if the whole thing had just been an episode on the Saturday morning comics. I figured it was Karla that Maloney intended to comfort, not Andy.

Maloney pulled up to the curb and killed the engine. By the time I'd climbed out he was already standing on the sidewalk.

"You don't have to see me to the door."

"Getting you safe home is the least I can do. After all, you may have saved my life."

"I thought you were mad at me about that."

We stood on the stoop in front of my door, me on the first step and Maloney on the ground, which brought our faces about even. The light from the streetlamp on the corner emphasized the prow of his jaw.

Maloney sighed. "Toni, you're a funny girl."

"Yeah, I'm a laugh riot."

He touched my shoulder lightly with his palm. "What you did tonight was foolish, but brave. You're smart and gutsy and you deserve better than a penny ante job with a basket case like me."

"My life story isn't exactly a string of successes." I shrugged. "If you're a basket case, Maloney, we're two of a kind."

He gave me a long, slow smile. "I'm thinking being a matched pair with someone like you wouldn't be such a bad deal."

"Oh yeah?" I couldn't take my eyes off him. I felt as if my heart had stopped beating.

He leaned forward and kissed me lightly. His lips against mine were warm and firm. He smelled of sweat and coffee and big strong male. I breathed in deeply and liked it.

He pulled back again and shook his head. "Sorry about that."

"It's okay. No harm done."

"No. I had no business touching you. You can't work for a boss who's trying to put the make on you. Sexual harassment and all that. Chalk it up to a long night, okay?"

"Sure."

"Won't happen again. You've got my word."

"No problem."

He left then. I stood on the porch until he drove away. When he was gone, I unlocked my door, undressed and fell into bed. Sleep didn't come, though. The room was stuffy, so I got up and cracked the window. The minute I opened it the faint strains of a plaintive tune drifted through. *Home On the Range*.

Somewhere out there Harmony was playing his harmonica. I lay down and wondered if he felt as lonely tonight as I did. My eyes closed, and I dreamed of Alice.

In my dream, I was caught in a rushing river. All around me the water churned and frothed, dashing me against the rocks, filling my nose and mouth. On the bank close by, Alice held out a rope to drag me to safety. But though I tried and tried, I couldn't grab it.

Chapter 16

EARLY THE next morning, the doorbell rang. I looked out and saw my bike on the stoop and Maloney pulling away from the curb. He still wore his neck brace, and he looked like hell. I surmised that Karla hadn't invited him to spend the night. That cheered me up.

"What's got you so chipper?" O'Dell asked when he came by a little later to take me to see Bill Bodner. He was dressed in a suit again and carried a briefcase. He looked like the hard-nosed professional cop that he was. I recalled our most recent parting and felt discomfort. So much had been going on with Maloney in the few hours since then that I hadn't given my brush-off to O'Dell a thought. From the way his cold gaze slid over me, however, I felt certain he'd been giving it a lot of thought.

"What's up with Jerome Robinson?" I asked, wanting to get a less personal conversation going.

"We've had our first counseling session together. I'm spending the weekend with him."

"So, what are you going to do?"

"I don't have a clue. What do you suggest?"

"There's a walking tour of historic Mount Vernon this Saturday. If the weather's good, you could take him on that."

"Yeah, and if he doesn't steal a piece of marble off a fountain or spray paint a monument, we'll have a nifty time discussing Baltimore's neo-classic period. Got any other suggestions?"

"What about Maloney's dojo?"

"What about it?"

"You practice there, don't you? Why don't you take Jerome along? He might like to learn some Aikido, too."

"All the better to smash my head in when I'm not looking?"

"Having the ability to defend yourself builds self-esteem. Self-esteem makes you into a better person." I should know. It was a lesson I was still learning.

O'Dell gestured impatiently. "Let's talk about something else. I heard you and Angus Maloney were involved in a ruckus last night."

When I told O'Dell about Marnie Brockloff terrorizing Karla, he whistled. "Domestic disputes, they're the worst. There's more blood, violence and pure mean hatred in the bedroom and kitchen than anywhere else."

"I ought to know," I said.

"Sorry. I forgot. Let's try another subject. How's your sister?"

"Interesting that we should be discussing domestic violence. She's furious with her husband."

We discussed Al quitting the force. The idea of Al making sno-cones for kids and construction workers amused O'Dell. I found less to chortle about. I kept picturing Al's expression the night he'd given me the finger at the construction site.

"The man's never going to forgive me for what happened to Nick," I muttered.

O'Dell shot me a curious look. "Does it matter so much?"

"Al's family."

"So? I could care less what my family thinks."

"You told me everybody in your family was dead."

"Maybe that explains it."

I sighed. "It's hard to explain about Italian families. Even when we're not speaking, we care about each other. It's a terrible feeling when your family rejects you."

"Al isn't even Italian. He's Polish, right?"

"That doesn't change his being married to my sister and the father of my nephews. He's convinced Nick never really beat me and that I shot him deliberately. It's not true."

"I know it's not true."

He sounded so sincere. "You can't really know it. You can only take my word."

"That's good enough for me, Toni."

"I appreciate that, but it makes you unusual. Most would rather believe the worst. I hate the thought of people pointing their finger at me, whispering, saying I'm bad. A second before he turned his attention back to traffic, I caught O'Dell's eye. Something in his expression made me ask, "Do you ever hear people talk about me at work?"

"Nothing you need to worry about."

"That means they do." I locked my arms across my chest. "What do they say?"

"I don't know. Cops have a lot of other things to talk about besides you, believe me."

"I was married to a cop. I know what they're like. Do they say things to you because you're friends with me?"

"You're a sexy woman, Toni, and I'm not Mr. Sociability. Whether he's a cop or not, another man is going to know my interest in you isn't purely platonic. So, yeah, they make remarks."

"Like warning you about hanging around with a man killer?"

"Yeah, like that. Doesn't bother me. I like my women dangerous."

He was trying to make a joke, but I wasn't amused. "I'm not your woman, O'Dell. I'm not anybody's."

"You already made that crystal clear."

While he concentrated on his driving, I stared ahead. No matter what I did, I would never be able to put what happened to Nick behind me. As long as I lived in this city my past would affect everyone I met and everything I did.

I'd thought about moving away, about getting on a bus and letting it carry me to the other side of the continent. But Baltimore was all I'd ever known. Its streets and buildings, houses and harbor were as familiar to me as my own skin and bones. My family and the few friends I'd made were all that stood between me and the abyss of the unknown. No, I'd never leave Baltimore. Which meant I'd never be able to escape my past. I'd just have to live with it and try, somehow, to make up for it. But what can a person like me do to make up for killing her husband?

DR. WILLIAM Bodner was a psychotherapist practicing from an office in an affluent northern suburb of Baltimore. He'd agreed to talk to O'Dell and me on his lunch hour at a Chinese restaurant on York Road. When O'Dell and I arrived, the restaurant was almost deserted. A few minutes after we were seated, Bodner joined us.

He was a youngish, balding guy with a fringe of reddish hair over his ears and the clear eyes of a well-disposed baby. He dressed nicely in tan twill pants and a tweed sport coat. I was glad I'd worn slacks instead of jeans.

After we all shook hands and ordered, O'Dell explained about finding an unidentified body on the site of the old Harzine building. He talked briefly about our interest in the Margraf Experiment.

Bodner nodded warily. "That was a long time ago."

"We understand that," O'Dell said, "and there's probably no connection between Margraf and this case. We're just trying to learn whatever we can about what went on in that building in the years before it was demolished. Whatever you can tell us, we'd appreciate."

Bodner cleared his throat. "Well, I can tell you about Margraf because I was the experiment's student coordinator."

"What exactly does that mean?"

"At the time I was a graduate assistant working with the Margrafs as a facilitator for their projects."

"Did you get money for this?"

"They paid me a small salary with funds they'd received out of a private grant."

O'Dell turned a fork over and pressed the tines lightly into the tablecloth. "The Margrafs were a husband and wife team, both PhD's?

"Yes, they were a remarkable couple—attractive, brilliant, dynamic, and very innovative in their thinking. That's not just my opinion. Anyone who knew them would say the same. Graduate students flocked to them as if they were gods. We all accepted whatever they had to say as gospel. I felt truly blessed to be able to work with them. Those were exciting days." He sighed. "I enjoy my work now, of course, but it doesn't have that same exhilaration that was part of my student days."

"The Margrafs are both dead now?" O'Dell asked.

"Killed in a plane crash. It happened very soon after the Margraf experiment and was a terrible loss. They were a brilliant pair of researchers."

Bodner had certainly made it clear he was an admirer of the Margrafs, I thought.

"Tell me about the Margraf experiment. What exactly was it?" O'Dell inquired.

The waiter brought our meals and the conversation stopped while he arranged the dishes in front of us. I dug into my shrimp fried rice and listened.

"I'll be glad to tell you what I know," Bodner answered O'Dell, "but before I begin I need to explain something about the academic research climate during that period. It was much more freewheeling. A lot of social experiments were conducted in those days that would be tightly regulated now. Some of them might not be conducted at all."

"Why is that?"

"Well, because they might pose some risk to the subjects—not just physical risk, but emotional, too. We're much more conscious of ethical issues now than we were in those days."

"I take it you're talking about the students who let themselves be guinea pigs?" O'Dell questioned.

When Bodner nodded, I chimed in, "All kinds of weird things were happening at universities then. Wasn't it around that time when Timothy Leary was feeding LSD to himself and some of his graduate students?"

O'Dell shot me a cold stare. I shut up and returned my outward attention to my fried rice.

"Miss Credella is right," Bodner said, "the research climate in the universities and the attitude toward using willing students for experiments was much looser. I point that out to account for the somewhat unusual nature of the Margraf Experiment."

"Which was?"

Bodner washed down a forkful of Szechuan Lo Mein with tea. "Norma and Robert Margraf recruited 20 area college students to partake in a controlled experiment on the sexual dynamics of authority."

"Wait a minute. Let's take this a step at a time. Did they do the actual recruiting, or did you?"

"As their student facilitator, it was part of my job to visit psychology departments in the area and recruit willing participants."

"Did you tell these participants what the nature of the experiment would be?"

"In part. I was instructed to tell them only that it was a social experiment involving sexual dynamics."

"I bet that brought them flocking in like pigeons to a peanut spill," O'Dell muttered.

"It wasn't difficult to find twenty willing subjects," Bodner agreed, "especially among the young men. They might not have been so eager if they'd known what was in store for them."

"Which was?"

"The Margrafs set up a mock prison situation in which female students supervised males who had to perform menial and meaningless tasks."

"Such as?"

"Such as scrubbing floors which were immediately dirtied again, washing windows which the females then rubbed with grease so they needed to be cleaned again. The idea was to force males into the roles they'd been conditioned to expect of females, and to give females the kind of power over the opposite sex that males, at that time, had over females. We wanted to see if the role reversals would bring about corresponding changes in personality and attitude."

My fork clattered against the edge of my plate. "I can just imagine how that went down with the guys!"

Bodner gazed into his teacup. "At first, the students were amused. After two or three days, that changed. You have to understand, it was a real prison situation in that we were cut off from the outside world. Nobody could leave. The students had signed a contract to live in the Harzine building for two weeks while I and a couple of other graduate students observed the dynamics between them."

"But the students who signed that contract didn't know what they were letting themselves in for," O'Dell said. "Were the Margrafs there to keep an eye on things?"

"They were busy with other projects. I reported to them on the telephone from time to time. Otherwise, we were on our own and completely isolated."

"My God," I muttered. Even I could tell that locking a bunch of college kids up together with a potentially explosive agenda and then just backing off and waiting to see what happened was criminal.

"So, what happened?" O'Dell asked.

Bodner's gaze looked faraway. "The experiment started out friendly and fun. Though the women were in charge, they were aided by a team of five male enforcers who were rewarded with special privileges."

"What kind of privileges?"

"Better food, better mattresses, the right to push the other males around."

"Who were the women in charge?"

"Third-year psychology students named Beth, Heidi, Liz, Connie and Margie. I can remember them so clearly, as if they're standing right in front of me. Of the five, Connie quickly emerged as dominant. From the first it was obvious that the other women were conflicted. Not Connie. She took to pushing men around like a duck to water."

Bodner's suddenly bitter tone made me stare. Obviously, this Connie had not been his favorite person.

"As the days went by tensions between the male 'prisoners' and 'enforcers' and the females in authority quickly grew. Late in the last week they exploded."

"What do you mean, 'exploded?'" O'Dell leaned forward.

"There was a riot, and unfortunately it ended in violence. Beth Shane died of a blow to the head in the melee. It was ironic, because of all the women she was most hesitant about her leadership role and most conflicted about giving orders and meting out punishment."

"How did this happen? Who killed her?" I asked.

Bodner shrugged. "I wasn't actually there at the time the disturbance broke out. I didn't get there until it was all over. Apparently, Connie had ordered the young men to stack bricks. When they'd finished stacking them, she'd knock them down. Some of the young men started throwing bricks. A student named Todd Lawrence threw the brick that killed Beth. It was just an unfortunate accident, and later on that's how it was judged.

"You mean Todd never received any punishment?"

"No. It was never brought to trial."

"Weren't you supposed to be supervising what went on between the students?" I demanded. How could intelligent people, people with Ph.D's, dream up and take part in such a stupid thing?

Bodner shook his head. "My role was strictly that of observer. If I'd interfered, it would have ruined the experiment."

"But didn't you realize that things were going wrong before the violence broke out?"

Bodner's skin reddened. He stammered slightly. "I-I realized, of course, that some ugly emotions were running high, and I reported that fact to the Margrafs. But we were so close to the end of the experiment and getting such interesting data. They thought we'd get through it without any serious trouble. They thought it was just...interesting."

"So you let them persuade you not to do anything, even though you were on the scene and they weren't?"

"As I said, what happened to Beth was just a terrible misfortune.

It was no one's fault, really, just an accident. The Margrafs paid a price for it, though. The experiment was dropped, and they left the area under a cloud." Bodner reached into his pocket and withdrew a folded sheet of paper. "I've taken the time to dig back into my student notes and prepare a list of the students who participated in the experiment."

Mistakenly, he handed the list to me. I gave it a cursory glance and passed it along to O'Dell.

He stuck it into his jacket pocket. "Before we wind this up, Dr. Bodner, I have something I'd like you to look at." O'Dell produced the computer enhanced image of the reconstruction of the girl's face that Doug Tomlinson had done for us at the Smithsonian.

"Does that young woman look at all familiar to you?" O'Dell queried.

Bodner stared down at the image. "I think I know who she is."

"Was," O'Dell corrected. "This girl has been dead for many years. Now, who do you think she was?"

"Dead? My God!" Bodner shook his head. "It's Connie Swenson," he said. "I'd know that chin anywhere."

Chapter 17

"TONI, HELP!"

My sister's urgent voice jerked me from my early morning torpor. Clutching the telephone receiver, I glanced at the clock on the stove. It was eight A.M.

"I just brought Al back from the hospital."

"The hospital! What happened?" I couldn't even imagine Al in the hospital. As far as I knew, outside of his obligatory police physicals, he'd never seen a doctor in his life.

"He had an accident in his van."

"What kind of accident? Anything serious?"

"It's just a sprain. I'll tell you the rest later. I'm driving into the city to leave the kids with Mom. Can I pick you up and bring you back to the house with me?"

"Sure. I guess. But if Mom's going to be taking care of the kids, what do you want me to do?"

"I don't have time now. I'll tell you on the way."

I fixed myself a second cup of coffee and sat down to wait for Sandy. I didn't blame her for not wanting to be alone with her husband. Al with a hurt body part was going to be about as much fun as wall-to-wall rattlesnakes. But having me around would only add to his irritation.

Sandy arrived wearing a wrinkled denim jumper over a shapeless sweater. The socks she wore with her sneakers were different shades of blue. Gray showed in her roots and her eyes looked wild.

"If I'm not completely nuts by the end of this day, it will be a miracle," she declared as she dragged me out to her car. Once we were in it, she set her face to the west and drove as if she were battling for the title of the Indy 500.

"How's Al?" I asked when we exited 95 still intact.

"Picture King Kong with the top of the Empire State Building up his ass."

I replied after a moment's thought. "It's amazing how far a

person's imagination will stretch when put to the test."

"Yeah, well unappealing as Al's state of mind is at the moment, mine is worse."

"Why is that?"

"You'll see when we get there."

Ten minutes later Sandy pulled in front of her house and turned off the ignition. She couldn't put her station wagon in the driveway because it was full of Al's van. As I gazed at it I began to understand what was bugging her.

Sandy lives with Al in a three-bedroom split level tract house in suburbia. As they point out, their kids are safer in suburbia and have plenty of other children like themselves to play with. Right now, a gang of those tots were gawking at Al's van. And with good reason, for it was a sight to behold.

"It doesn't look badly damaged," I said after I got out of the car.

"No. Al did most of the damage to himself and the neighbor's car he backed into. The van's only got a dinged up cargo door. It's the mess, the godawful mess! And the bees! Oh Toni, what am I going to do about the bees?"

We were having a spell of Indian summer in the height of sweat bee season in Maryland. Bees, flies, ants, and every insect which could fly, creep, crawl or inch to the smell and taste of sticky sweet syrup swarmed around Al's van.

"It's the sno cone stuff, huh?"

Sandy whimpered. "Cherry, strawberry, orange, lime, blueberry, root beer and banana-papaya—they all fell over and trickled out when Al had his accident."

"It's dripping out from under the door," I said.

A river of glutinous purple and red prime matter oozed down the lower right hand side of the van and onto the driveway. A mass of ants so solid that they looked like a carpet creature wallowed in the dissolved sugar.

Frenzied sweat bees dive bombed them. Clouds of flies performed aerial acrobatics. The neighborhood kids and their pals pointed and squealed.

"You go on home!" Sandy shouted. "You'll get stung."

They ignored her.

"I guess you brought me out here to help you with this," I remarked.

"Oh God, Toni, I don't know what to do. The van has to be cleaned up, but I don't even know how to get at it without being stung to death."

I caught a flicker of the curtain on Sandy's picture window. "Where's Al?"

"On the couch in the living room. "He's not supposed to walk. The doctor put his ankle in a cast. He's in no shape to help."

Strangely, I felt stirrings of sympathy. It must be hard on Al, seeing me out here with Sandy surveying his disaster. Al might not be a whiz kid, but he had his pride.

"How's the garage?" I asked Sandy. "Any goop spilled in there?"

"As far as I know, it's goop free."

"Then it's probably relatively bug-free, too. Okay, this is my suggestion. First, you get on your bathing suit. Then I use your garden hose to blast the right side of the van. That ought to disrupt the bug attack long enough for you to run through the water and drive the van into the garage."

She stared at me. "Supposing I'm not felled by the bees first, then what?"

"Then we clean the sucker out."

"All right, but I catch cold easily. You're going to be the one in the bathing suit, and I'm going to be the one with the hose."

I threw up my hands. "You know how poor my driving skills are. What if I drive Al's van through your garage instead of into it?"

"I'll risk it."

After I changed into one of my sister's old bathing suits, which hung on me so badly I was barely decent, we tried out the scheme. Surprisingly, it worked pretty well. Sandy handled the hose like a fireman on amphetamines. I managed to get the van into the garage with a merely manageable number of bees and flies.

Sandy rejoined me, and we went after the critters with a pair of flyswatters. After flailing away as if we were dancing the Tarantella, broken insect bodies littered the cement floor.

The van's inside was a sugary, Technicolor nightmare.

"I'll never eat another sno-cone again as long as I live," Sandy moaned as we surveyed the damage.

"Or pancakes, either," I said. I emptied the bottle of detergent she'd carted out of the house and then dumped a pail full of warm water on it.

"That's not going to do a hell of a lot of good."

"We have to start somewhere."

We set to work.

Many bottles of detergent later, we sat back on our tired haunches and mopped our sweaty brows. "I think it's about as good as it's going to get for now," Sandy said.

After the first fruitless minutes, we'd decided not to waste our energy on the carpet. Al might have loved it once, but nobody would ever love it again. We'd ripped it out. I ran a finger along the van's bare metal floor and sniffed. "It doesn't feel sticky, but I can still smell raspberry and orange."

"I don't care if it smells like dinosaur shit. I'm done." Sandy glanced at her watch. "God, we've been at this for four hours. Come on in and have some lunch."

"Um, I don't know. I'm not really hungry." Actually, I was so starved I felt faint.

Sandy surveyed me. "If you're trying to avoid a scene with Al, I promise right now he's harmless. In fact, he's probably not even conscious. They gave him a bunch of codeine which, last time I looked, he was eating like M&M's." Inside the kitchen, Sandy hauled out a bag of sandwiches." Hope the construction guys don't starve," she said as she dumped it on the table. I sorted through egg salad, ham and cheese, chicken salad and bologna. By the time she found us a couple of cans of diet soda, I'd wolfed half a ham and cheese.

"No, you weren't hungry," she said as she watched me cram food into my mouth. She picked out an egg salad and unwrapped it. "Know what this reminds me of?" she added a few minutes later.

"No, what?"

"Remember that time Mom left us alone in the restaurant while she went to a funeral? The Rosica kids came over and we got into a napkin fight. We knocked over a pot of marinara sauce and had to get it cleaned up before Mom got back."

I giggled. "What a mess! God, that was a long time ago!"

A plaintive voice wafted in from the living room. "Sandy."

She crossed her eyes and got up. "Yeah, hon?"

"What's going on in there?"

"Toni and me are just having some lunch."

"What about me?"

"I thought you were asleep. You want me to fix you something?"

"A beer and a couple of bologna sandwiches."

I rose to my feet. "Guess this is my cue to be on my way."

"How are you going to be on your way without me? I have to drive you, and I can't do that until Al is fed. Why don't you go in with me and say hello?" she asked when she had assembled a tray.

"You're kidding, right?"

"I'm not. You just did Al and me a big favor. He should thank you."

"Fat chance of that."

"Maybe. Maybe not. Al and I talked about you last night, about his attitude. I told him you're my sister and it's about time he stopped treating you so bad. Come on into the living room with me, Toni."

"Sandy..."

"Please. C'mon."

Reluctantly, I trailed her through the dining room. It surprised me how hard my heart was thumping.

Al was definitely the centerpiece in the living room. Wearing a navy tee shirt and torn jeans, he was propped on the couch in a nest of pillows. A blue and white cast swathed his left ankle. At his left hand next to the couch a snack table held water glasses and brown vials of pills with white plastic caps. Sandy pushed some of this to one side so she could set the tray down.

"There you go, hon. How's that?"

Al gazed discontentedly at the wrapped sandwiches and beer. "That's almost seven dollars in lost revenue, right there."

"No point in thinking about that now, hon."

"What else is there to think about? We got a mortgage payment coming up. How'm I going to make it?"

"Forget about that and say hello to my sister. She gave me a lot of help this morning. The syrup's all cleaned out of the bottom of the van. Without her, I couldn't have done it."

Al caught my eye and stared at me fixedly while he went through an internal struggle. I could just imagine what was going through his mind. *I hate her, but she's a relative and she just helped me out. My wife will make my life even more miserable if I don't watch myself.*

"Hello," he said.

"Hi, Al. How's the leg?"

"Feels like shit. I saw you out there. That was a neat trick with the hose."

"Yeah, worked pretty good, too. The van ought to be nearly tolerable when you're up and around again."

"Yeah, in about a million years."

"It's not going to be that bad," Sandy said. "You're healthy. You'll heal quick."

Al popped the tab on his beer and took a long pull. He looked from Sandy to me and back. "I wish your sister weren't standing there to hear me eat crow, but so be it. You were right."

"What?" Sandy looked blank.

"The van, quitting the department, it was a mistake. Tomorrow I'm going to ask if they'll take me back."

"Al, you don't have to do that. The van's not badly damaged. It's not going to take much to get it rolling again."

"I don't want to get it rolling again. I hate it. I hate selling sandwiches. I hate making sno-cones. It's not for me. Now, I don't want to hear anymore about it, okay?"

"Okay," Sandy said.

"I guess I don't feel like eating anything, after all. I'm going to take another codeine and go back to sleep."

"Sure. I'll take the food away. You can have it later."

Al took another pill with his beer and then settled back into the pillows and closed his eyes.

Two minutes later, Sandy and I were back in the kitchen. "Thank God," she said and fell into my arms. Tears squeezed out of her eyes and she shook with suppressed giggles. "Don't let Al hear, but thank God," she whispered into my ear.

BACK AT MY place that afternoon, I phoned O'Dell at work. To my surprise, I got through to him. "I've been thinking," I said.

"Uh-oh."

"You know that list of names Bodner gave you?"

"Of course I know. I'm going to work on it when I get the chance. The way things are going today, that won't be for a while. We just had another multiple shooting in the Pimlico area."

"Well, it just occurred to me. Alice has a daughter named Doris. I wonder if Doris Ritco's name is on that list."

"No, it's not. You still trying to put Connie Swenson's murder together with Alice Ritco's?"

"I just wondered, that's all. Would you read me the list?"

"There's no connection between these two murders, Toni. But just to make you happy, I'll read you the list—provided, you do a favor for me."

O'Dell's wheedling tone set off warning bells. "What kind of favor? I told you we weren't going to have a relationship."

"Relax. The counselor says I'm supposed to do something with Jerome again this Saturday. When I asked the kid for a suggestion, he said he'd like to go to a wrestling match."

"So?"

"So, I wondered if you'd go with us."

"Why?"

"To take some of the edge off, Toni. The kid hates me. I'm not his biggest fan, either. The counselor keeps talking about common ground, but I have nothing in common with that kid. Maybe if you're there the time will go by faster."

"Faster for you, maybe."

"Please, Toni."

"Why should I?"

"So you can hear the names on Bodner's list?"

"Cute, O'Dell."

Chapter 18

THE HODEN River Democratic Club held a roulette wheel. At a table next to it, you could buy canned sodas, keg Bud or pizza at two bucks a slice. The Club also held about four hundred people who'd paid nine bucks each to be here

O'Dell, Jerome Robinson and I were among those people and, like them, we were sitting on folding chairs. O'Dell had placed me between him and Jerome. This meant I got the full effect of Jerome's reaction as we watched Axl Rotten and Doink the Clown.

Rotten, a bleached blond, 265-pound wrestler, was a baby-faced twenty-three. He had strutted into the ring to the sound of the Beastie Boys' "Fight for Your Right (to Party)." He wore a denim jacket with a ragged British flag pinned to the back. After he looked around, he made an enraged face and then banged his head off the ropes a half dozen times. His fans roared.

"I hear he's a local boy made good," O'Dell remarked.

"Man, what a fool," Jerome said loudly. "This place sucks. Everybody here be low class redneck honkies."

The Democratic Club was in the heart of Essex, a white working class enclave which wouldn't appreciate Jerome's fashion statement of black knit cap pulled so low it covered his eyebrows, oversize jeans clinging—just barely—to the tops of his thighs, multiple gold chains and clenched fist sweatshirt.

He was a skinny kid with an attitude. I couldn't blame him. It was no more his idea to spend the evening with us than it was O'Dell's.

Jerome's was, in fact, the only black face in the crowd. And since he wasn't exactly keeping his insulting remarks to himself, he was beginning to draw some negative attention.

"That Doink ain't nothin but a fat, middle-aged white man," he said disgustedly.

"They've got a right to live, too," I muttered.

On the other hand, Doink with his green hair, blue-and-orange-striped suit, purple tights, Day-Glo lime green tie and beer belly, wasn't exactly your average middle-aged white man. Pluckily, he was now mocking Rotten's every move—bending over to display his sizable rear end and looking backwards through his legs, sticking his tongue out and waggling his fingers in his ears. The crowd loved it.

Rotten jumped Doink, pinned him to the floor and loudly threatened to kill him. Doink responded by tickling Rotten until Rotten lost his grip. While Doink's fans cheered, Rotten complained bitterly to the referee.

"Oh man!" Jerome muttered. "This be the stupidest motherfuckin' shit."

More dirty looks from the crowd flew our way. I was beginning to get nervous. Beneath the jeers and laughter in the group, I smelled violence.

"Listen, I don't think this was such a hot idea," I whispered to O'Dell. "Maybe we should go."

"Why? Morgan the Maniac is coming up next." O'Dell actually seemed to be enjoying himself. He offered me his bag of popcorn and, when I refused, stretched it over to Jerome who grabbed an oversize handful, half of which scattered like Styrofoam chips off a Van de Graff generator.

Some flew into the collar of the thick-necked guy in front of us and slipped down his back. He whirled around and glared at us. "Watch it, buddy." He picked popcorn out of his collar, glowered at it, then hurled it on the floor.

"Sorry," O'Dell said.

"I don't think Jerome is having a good time," I whispered when the guy turned to the front again.

"This was his idea."

"He didn't know it was going to be all white and in Essex."

O'Dell leaned across me and spoke directly to Jerome. "You want to split?"

"Yeah," he said.

"Okay, we're outta' here."

Outside in the back seat of O'Dell's car, I heaved a sigh of relief. Sitting between O'Dell and Jerome, I had felt like a rabbit separating a pair of edgy jungle cats.

"You know we're missing Luna the Moon Goddess versus Tiger Woman, don't you?" O'Dell commented. "They were coming up after Morgan the Maniac."

"I think Jerome and I can live with that."

Jerome, his face turned away as he gazed sullenly out the window, didn't comment.

"Where to now?" O'Dell said after he pulled out of the lot.

"Man, I got things to do. Take me home."

For the next five minutes brooding silence filled the car. O'Dell swerved off the road and into a liquor store parking lot. It was one of those good old boy places. Day-Glo posters advertising special prices on jug wine, cheap whiskey and six packs plastered its storefront windows.

"Outta' beer at home," O'Dell explained tersely. Back in a couple of secs."

When he was gone, I flipped the driver's seat forward, yanked the door handle and started to climb out. "Legs feel cramped," I told Jerome. "Think I'll stretch them a minute or two."

"Cool by me," he said, then added as my feet hit the blacktop, "you afraid, alone in a car with me?"

"Why would I be afraid to be alone in the car with you?"

"Don't know. Sometimes white women they act like they're afraid, you know, when they're in an elevator with me or something. You got nothin' to worry about. I ain't no rapist. I got nothin' against you."

"I've got nothing against you, either, Jerome—though I was there the night you smashed O'Dell's window."

"Yeah? Then you saw what that motherfuck did to me." He pointed at his shoulder and grimaced. "Mean son of a bitch." Scornfully, he surveyed the interior of O'Dell's car. "Figures he'd drive shit like this. I wouldn't bother to smash no window on this junk heap."

Ignoring the accurate assessment of O'Dell's car, I said, "Well, it isn't as if you didn't give him some cause to be upset that night. Why were you doing it, anyway?" I got out, rolled down the Pinto's window and leaned over the ledge so I could look inside.

"Doing what?"

"C'mon, you know what I'm asking. Why were you breaking the windows on people's cars? That late at night a boy your age should have been home in bed."

"I ain't so young."

"You're young enough you should be doing your homework, not

vandalizing cars."

In the shadowy interior of the Pinto, Jerome ducked his head. The gesture emphasized his youth. Despite his nearly adult size, he was just a kid, really not that much older than my own nephews. "Couldn't go home," he said.

"Why not?"

"My mama, she entertainin' her boyfriend, that's why."

"Oh." I took a moment to chew on this. "You don't get along with your mother's boyfriend?"

"I hate his black ass and he hates mine. What you want to know for, anyway? What's it to you?"

"Believe it or not, O'Dell wants to help you. I'm his friend, so I want to help you, too."

"Yeah. They makin' him help me. He don't want to."

"In his heart, he does. And so do I, Jerome."

"You his chick?"

"No, I'm just his friend. What about your father, Jerome?"

"What about him?"

"Do you ever see him?"

"I don't know nothin' about my father. I don't even know who he be. Neither do my mama. Or if she do, she ain't sayin'."

"Listen, Jerome, it sounds to me as if you could use a friend. I know you've got good reason not to like O'Dell, but why don't you give him a chance? Honest, once you get to know him, he's not so bad."

His eyes opened wide. "Now you sound like that fancy ass counselor they stuck us with. You got to be a crazy lady. That honky cop beat me half to death."

"He's sorry for what he did to you, Jerome. He'd like to get along with you. He just doesn't know how."

"That makes two of us. "Cause I sure don't see gettin' along with no cop."

Wondering what was taking O'Dell so long to buy beer, I glanced over my shoulder. A trio of young guys in tight jeans and denim jackets came out of the store. Even as the door banged shut behind them, I could tell they were half bombed. They were laughing that pack-male laugh that always sounds like the back end of a dirty joke. One popped the tab on his Bud and took a long swig.

Another, a muscular blond with a handlebar moustache, caught my eye. Stopping dead in his tracks, he let his mouth drop in an exaggerated expression of drunken awe. Then he slapped his knee and pointed. "Will you look at the rear on that little gal. Man, that is the sweetest ass I've seen all day."

While the others guffawed, I felt my face turn red. I turned my head away and pretended I hadn't heard.

Egged on by the others, the one with the blond curls veered closer. "Not only do you have one fine ass, little lady," he slurred, "but you also got a find lookin' face. How'd you like to get better acquainted?"

"I wouldn't like that at all," I snapped. "Now go find yourself another playmate."

The others howled and pushed their pal at me. "Watch it, watch it," he cried as he stumbled forward. "The little lady ain't as friendly as she looks. She might bite."

The car door opened on the other side and Jerome came hurtling out. "You heard what she said, cracker. Go fuck yourself!"

It was not the most diplomatic comment for the time and place. Blondie stared, taking in Jerome's clenched fist sweatshirt and black face. His beery grin vanished. He looked at me sternly. "You saying you prefer a black man to a white man? What's wrong with you, girl? You blind and crazy?"

That was enough for Jerome. He came barreling around the front of the car. I grabbed him just as he started to take a swing.

Blondie upended the bottle in the brown paper bag like a club. Shouting racial epithets, his pals made to back him up.

"What the hell's going on here?" O'Dell's voice rang out from behind them. Before they'd assimilated his presence, he grabbed the collars on Blondie's friends and jerked so hard he sent them sprawling backward.

Brandishing his whiskey bottle, Blondie whirled. With a downward cut of his fist, O'Dell sent the bottle spinning across the parking lot. It crashed into the side of the low concrete building, spraying alcohol and broken glass.

A gun materialized from O'Dell's shoulder holster and with his free hand he flashed his badge. "I'm a Baltimore City Detective. Any of you want to go on making trouble, be my guest.

As quickly as it had erupted, the problem melted away. The three drunks backed off and then disappeared into the night. When they were gone, O'Dell scowled at Jerome and me.

"You're as bad as he is," he said. "Every time I turn around, you're getting yourself into trouble."

"Too true," I admitted. I caught Jerome's eye.

He was breathing hard, strung as tight as piano wire. His hands were clenched, mirroring the image on his sweatshirt. But when we looked at each other, he cracked a tense smile and unballed a fist to point at O'Dell's gun. "Man, did you see the way those honky drunks run off when he flashed that piece?"

"Sure did," I said. "Now, admit it, Jerome. There are times when it's not such a bad deal to have a guy like O'Dell around."

O'DELL TOOK Jerome home first. When he pulled up in front of my house, I said, "Forget it. I'm not inviting you in."

"Did I ask?"

"No, which was smart of you. But there's a question I want to ask you. You said Doris Ritco isn't on that list Bodner handed over. What if she knew someone who was? Have you interviewed her to find out?"

"Toni, tune into the local TV news some day. The year has months to go and already Baltimore has seen more than two hundred killings. I don't have time to go poking into a murder that's ancient history."

"What about Alice Ritco's murder. Or isn't a homeless old woman worth your trouble? What about Professor Harold McDaniel? I think the person who killed him may be the same the one who got Alice."

"The two didn't even know each other. The only thing they had in common was their age."

"And their connection with the Margraf Experiment."

O'Dell looked exasperated. "Alice had no connection with Margraf, and neither did McDaniel, really. People get held up and murdered all the time. McDaniel was just in the wrong place at the wrong time. Toni, I haven't forgotten Alice Ritco, and I'm going to track down the names on Bodner's list. It just isn't going to happen tomorrow, that's all. Okay?"

"Sure," I said and climbed out of O'Dell's Pinto. But when his taillights disappeared into the night, I knew it wasn't okay. I couldn't wait for him to find time to work on cases low on his totem pole. Until I knew the truth about what happened to Alice, she would haunt me. So would Connie and McDaniel.

The next morning, I phoned Maloney. "You going to see your chiropractor any time soon?"

"Tomorrow afternoon, as a matter of fact."

"Would you take me with you?"

He sounded surprised. "Why? You want a treatment?"

"I'd just like to talk to her face to face."

THE OVERCAST sky and blustery wind that had chased away the Indian summer heat made me glad Mahoney was giving me a lift to Doris Ritco's.

"Got any more jobs for me," I asked as we cruised down Falls Road. He looked more like himself now that he'd given up the neck brace.

"Something came in this morning," he said, answering my question. "If you like shopping, you might get some fun out of it. Man named Mark Martin wants to know how his wife spends his money."

"What does that mean?"

"Means he can't understand how she manages to get rid of her monthly $3000 household allowance."

I gasped. "He gives her three thousand dollars a month? That's a fortune!"

"That's his opinion, too. But by the thirtieth the account is always flat. She says it goes for clothes, lunches with the girls and other necessities. He's afraid she's supporting a boyfriend or a drug habit. Anyhow, he's willing to pay to get the story.

"Sounds intriguing."

"If you're intrigued enough to take it on, it's yours."

We discussed the details until Maloney pulled his Chevette into Doris Ritco's parking lot. When he turned the motor off, I said, "Heard anything about the Brockloffs?"

He shrugged. "She's being treated for an emotional disturbance. They're both going into counseling. It wasn't going to do Karla's reputation any good to press charges."

"No, I guess it wouldn't."

He gave me a considering look. "You don't like Karla much, do you? Believe it or not, she has a lot of good points."

"You don't have to convince me, Angus."

"Oh, hell," he said and shoved open the driver's side door. "Let's go in."

Inside everything was the way I remembered—piped birdsong, greenery, restful colors. The receptionist let me accompany Maloney to a room where he stretched out on a bench with a doughnut shaped hole for his nose. When he was lying face down, she attached little pads with wires to the back of his neck. She explained that they sent electrical impulses which would help relieve the pain Maloney was experiencing in his neck.

She left me there to keep Maloney company. But it was clear he didn't want to talk. I wandered out into the empty hall. A couple of doors down, I found Doris Ritco doing paperwork in her office. When she saw me, she put her pencil down and smiled.

"Can I help you?"

"I don't know if you remember me. My name's Toni Credella. I came here with Mike Mitchum a few days ago."

"Of course, I remember you. You wanted to talk to me about my mother's death. I saw you at her memorial service. That was kind of you."

"I liked your mother. I miss her and feel very bad about the way she died." I thought of Alice the way I'd seen her last, begging me to let her in. In one of my confessional moods, I might have told Doris. But, realistically, I didn't think that information would do either of us any good now. "I'm sorry I didn't get a chance to say hello at the memorial service."

She shrugged. "I wasn't exactly up for a meet and greet. I didn't have a close relationship with my mother when I was growing up, or in her last years, either, really. I didn't know her street friends, except some of them by name only."

"I thought I saw you say hello to Jimmy."

"Jimmy?" She looked blank.

"Jimmy, the guy in the wheelchair, the one who hangs around with the kid who plays the harmonica." I didn't know Jimmy's last name.

"Oh, you mean Jim Drury. Yes, it's such an odd coincidence. It really is a small world. When I first set up my practice in Baltimore and contacted my mother, she used to talk about her pals Jimmy and Harmony. I never dreamed I actually knew Jimmy until she pointed him out down at the harbor one day. He's changed a lot, of course, but I'd recognize those shoulders anywhere. We were at Salisbury State together. He was my roommate's boyfriend."

She played with the pencil in her fingers. "Boy, was he a different guy then—captain of the Lacrosse team, honor student, a real hunk. It's terrible to see what bad luck has done to him."

I assumed she meant how Jimmy had been crippled in the war. "Yeah, Vietnam really did the poor guy in."

"That and losing Beth. I don't think he was ever the same after losing Beth."

"Beth?"

"Beth Shane, my roommate. She was killed in a freak accident during some kind of psychological experiment. It happened right here in Baltimore."

Chapter 19

ALL THE WAY back from Doris Ritco's clinic my head buzzed. Jimmy, the boyfriend of Beth Shane, the girl who'd been killed in a melee during the Margraf Experiment?

I'd never suspected Jimmy of killing Connie Swenson. Now that I knew about the connection between them, that changed. What if Jimmy had blamed Connie Swenson for what happened to Beth? What if he'd entombed Connie in the very building where she'd provoked the fight that killed Beth? Knowing Jimmy, it didn't seem so impossible. There'd always been something a little scary about him.

Thinking back, I recalled Jimmy's story of losing the use of his legs while trying to save the life of a buddy named Todd. Wasn't the guy who'd thrown the fatal brick at Beth named Todd Lawrence?

"Angus, you were in the military," I said to Maloney.

He turned his head.

"How easy would it be for one soldier to kill another while they're both in a battle with an enemy?"

"You mean when they're both on the same side?"

I nodded.

"Happens all the time by accident, and probably more often than we know by design, too. When you're fighting for your life you're so scared you don't really know what's going on around you. Most of the war stories you hear are pure myth, invented by mutual memory lapse after the event."

While I fretted over that, Maloney headed the Chevette down my block.

"Got a call from your pal, O'Dell yesterday," he said.

"Oh?"

"He's going to bring a new student to my dojo next week. Kid named Jerome Robinson."

I smiled and gave Maloney a brief account of O'Dell's connection with Jerome, to which he listened attentively. When we pulled up in front of my house, he turned toward me.

"Answer a question before you get out, will you? You've said that you and O'Dell are just friends. Are you just friends with him the way you're just friends with me?"

"No. You and I are something besides friends. You're my boss."

"How important is that to you, Toni?"

All of a sudden, I felt breathless. "Why do you ask?"

"Because I need to know. How important is it that we keep this relationship strictly platonic?"

"Are you asking because you think it could be something else?"

"We've both known that for a while, wouldn't you say?"

"But Karla..."

"Let's leave Karla out of this, Toni. This is you and me. I've been thinking a lot about us, about how it felt to kiss you the other night. Before I do something stupid, let's be honest with each other."

I took a deep breath and forced myself to think. I needed to give Angus the right answer. But did I know what the right answer was? "The job is very important."

As he gazed at me, there was no expression on his face at all. "Okay."

"Angus, try and understand."

"You don't have to explain anything, Toni."

"I want you to understand. When I came to you and begged for this job, I was at a low point. I didn't just need to earn money, though that was certainly part of it. I needed a direction for my life, something that would give me self-respect."

"You think detective work is it?"

"Yes, I do. And I also think you're the only PI in Baltimore who will teach me."

A slow grin dug brackets at the corners of his mouth. "You could be right about that."

"I know I'm right. I can't drive, I can't read, and I shot and killed a Baltimore city cop. I was incredibly lucky to meet you. No one else would take me on as an associate. I can't risk messing that up."

"Okay," he said matter-of-factly, "that's settled, and there's no need to discuss it again. I forgot to ask. Get what you wanted from Doris?"

Twinges of loss and disappointment tugged at me. Had I made

the right decision? I could only hope that I had. But if I wanted it to stick, I'd better play it just as cool as Maloney. "Maybe more than I wanted," I said. "What about you?"

He moved his neck gingerly. "I'm satisfied. The woman's got great hands."

"You need all the help you can get to spend the night sitting up in this car."

He laughed. "Yeah, well, the pay is decent and I don't have to work hard. George is the one who makes the rounds. I'm not going to get much sleep tomorrow, though. Karla's going out of town on a business trip. I'll have Andy with me."

Maloney looked happy when he mentioned his son's name, so I knew he wasn't complaining. We said goodbye and I went inside. To keep myself from brooding, I dialed O'Dell at work. I needed to tell him what I'd learned from Doris. The sooner he had the information, the sooner the weight of it would be off my shoulders.

"He's off duty," they informed me. Frustrated, I dialed O'Dell at home and got his answering machine. "Call me right away," I insisted. "I just found out something that could solve Alice Ritco's murder and Connie Swenson's, too."

Of course, it wasn't too smart for me to leave a message like this where somebody besides O'Dell might hear it. But so much was going on in my head that I wasn't thinking too clearly.

After I opened a can of hearty vegetable soup and fixed myself a grilled cheese sandwich, I settled down to do some sanding in the upstairs hall. About nine o'clock my sister phoned.

"Good news," she crowed. "They're going to reinstate Al?"

"You mean he's going back to being a BPD cop? What about the van?"

"We're selling that, at a huge loss, I'm sure. He'll have to start over with his retirement fund. At least he'll be bringing home a paycheck."

"What about his leg?"

"They'll keep him in the office until he's fit. Oh Toni, I'm so relieved!"

I was happy for her, and I told her so.

"Maybe you'd like to come out for dinner with the folks sometime next week," she said almost shyly.

"Is this an invitation Al knows about?"

"He suggested it."

I wasn't sure I believed that. On the other hand, if it was true, I felt pleased. Family members shouldn't hate each other. It was time Al and I called a truce. I accepted.

Shortly after my conversation with Sandy, exhaustion set in, and I went to bed early. Almost instantly I fell into a deep sleep.

I woke up smelling smoke. My eyes popped open. I scrabbled out of bed and ran down the hall to the stairs. Thick veils of smoke hung on the staircase. I tried to fight my way through them, but they drove me back. I collapsed on the landing, eyes watering, chest burning. I remembered hearing that people in fires usually die of smoke inhalation.

The smoke alarm I'd installed in my bedroom started to screech. Fat lot of good it did me now. I cursed myself for being too cheap to hang one downstairs.

My bedroom is in the back of the house. I ran to the front and threw up the window of the guest bedroom. Sticking my upper half out as far as it would go, I peered down. A red glow flickered in my living room window.

"Oh my God!"

Fortunately, the upstairs phone still worked. I called the local fire station. That done, I grabbed an armful of sheets from the linen closet.

By now smoke billowed up the stairs and poisoned the air in the hall. Throat and eyes burning, I shut my back bedroom door against it. Ignoring the wailing smoke alarm, I tied sheets end to end as I'd seen it done in movies.

Actually, the distance from my bedroom window to the ground can't be more than fifteen feet. I'd survive a jump to the pad of concrete directly beneath, but I'd probably break something. Situations like this bring home to you just how much you like your body intact and unbroken.

When I'd strung four sheets together, I anchored one end to the corner leg of my oak bureau and threw open the window. Why weren't firefighters drenching my living room, I wondered. The station was only two blocks away. Even if they had to walk, they should have arrived by now.

I tossed my bundled bedding out the window. The sheets weren't quite long enough, but I figured at least they'd break my fall.

I glanced at the bureau. My weight might drag it to the window, but it was too big to actually go through. What about the oak leg? Was there any chance it would snap?

Dark windows stared blankly from the surrounding houses. Couldn't the people behind them hear my smoke alarm?

Whatever the reason, nobody was offering to rescue me. I had to help myself. Pulling the sheet taut from the bureau, I stuck one leg over the window sill, then rolled over on my stomach as I maneuvered the other leg over and out.

For a couple of minutes I let my legs dangle, balancing my middle on the sill and pulling at the sheet to test its strength. It occurred to me that I wasn't trying to save any of my belongings and that I wasn't wearing many clothes. In fact, I only had on the panties and tee shirt I'd been sleeping in. Beneath my thin cotton top, I wore no bra.

I heard the clang of fire engines roaring up to the front of the house. Behind me a light in a window sprang to life.

Dangling there, I felt like a bug in a spotlight. The chill October wind iced my nearly naked rear end. My bare feet scraped at the bricks. Was I crazy, dropping into an alley in my neighborhood like this? Why hadn't I thought to throw down a pair of shoes, jeans and a jacket?

I had started to crawl back in when the sheet let loose. I only had time to yelp "Shit!"

Maloney caught me. My weight sent us both to the ground, but since I was in his arms, he broke the fall for me.

"Oof! Jesus!"

Sheets swathed my head. One of Maloney's elbows dug into my rib. He groaned in my ear and struggled beneath me. Stunned, I lay on top of him, inert as a sack of oatmeal.

"Jeez, Toni, are you all right?" Once again, Maloney made an effort to sit up. This time he succeeded and carried me with him.

"What happened?"

"You fell and I caught you. Good thing you're such a lightweight. If you were any bigger, we'd be permanently merged. Nothing's broken, is it?"

"Yes, no, I don't know. My house..."

"It's on fire, Toni, but they're putting it out now. From what I could see, it was just the living room."

"Just the living room?" I thought of all the work I'd done on that living room. The scraping, sanding, painting, varnishing. Just the living room.

A COUPLE Of hours later, I huddled on Maloney's couch. He'd been right about the fire. It hadn't taken long for the guys with the axes and hoses to put it out.

I'd tried to talk them into letting me go back to my bedroom. That wasn't legal until the Fire Marshall gave the okay. They did, however, retrieve some clothes for me, so I was now decently dressed.

Maloney came in carrying a mug of coffee and a plate of toast. "Thought maybe you could use something hot in your stomach."

"Thanks. Hey, that chair you bought from Chad looks great next to the fireplace."

"Does, doesn't it?" He contemplated his furniture arrangement, then set the toast on the coffee table. "How're you feeling?"

"Rotten. How about you? Did I do anything bad to your neck again when I fell on you?"

"Don't worry about me. Let's worry about you, Toni. Who would want to firebomb your house?"

The verdict wasn't officially in yet, but the firemen who'd been inside my living room had smelled kerosene. From that and the evidence of a broken front window, it looked as if someone had deliberately set my place on fire.

"I'm so tired," I muttered. I just wasn't up to thinking about all this.

"Bedroom's free. Why don't you go in and lie down?"

"What about you? You've been sitting up all night in that Chevette. How did you happen to be in my backyard, anyway?"

He shrugged and looked faintly embarrassed. "Sometimes when I'm driving home from work, I take a route past your place just to make sure everything looks okay. You remember, you said you'd been broken into once."

I nodded, nonplussed. True, the construction site Maloney guarded wasn't far from my street. But it was definitely out of the way from there to Maloney's apartment.

"It's a good thing I checked on you this morning," Maloney went on. "I saw flames through your window. By the time I was out of the car, fire engines were pulling out their hoses. I knew you slept in the back of the house on the second floor."

"How did you know that?"

"You mentioned it when you described your robbery."

Remembering that discussion only vaguely, I said a prayer of thanks that he had such a retentive memory. "You saved me from winding up in the hospital, Angus. Thanks."

"Don't mention it."

"Of course I should mention it." I took a sip of coffee from the mug he'd placed before me, then set it down and burst into tears.

"Hey, hey, Toni. Take it easy. What's wrong, honey?" He was next to me on the couch, now, his arm around me. One of his big hands patted my head and shoulders as if I was a hysterical kid or a frightened dog.

My face was in my hands, which were already slick with my tears. "My house," I moaned through my fingers. "It's the only thing I have. I've worked so hard to make it nice, and now it's ruined."

"It's not ruined, honey. Only the living room."

"Only the living room! That's half the house!"

"It's not so bad, Toni. You've got insurance, don't you?"

I nodded. Fire insurance had been one of the conditions for getting an abandoned house from the city so cheaply.

"You might even come out of this with your place in better condition. For sure, you'll get a new plaster job." Maloney's arm tightened around me. At that moment it felt like a warm, strong barrier protecting me from my troubles. I leaned into him, comforted by his solid chest and the soothing tone of his deep voice.

"Tell you what," he said, stroking my hair. "After you've had a rest, we'll go over and take a look."

"They won't let me in."

"We can look in the windows, see what we can see. Okay?"

"Okay." I pulled back from Maloney's shoulder so I could lift my face to his. The buzzer downstairs went off. It was Karla dropping off Andy.

While Maloney explained why I was there, I finished my toast and coffee. A few minutes later, I let him persuade me to take a nap on his bed.

I didn't really sleep. Though Maloney's walls were thick, I could still catch Andy's voice now and then as he and his father watched television together. With that in the background, I dozed while images from the last few weeks ran through my mind. Alice begging to get in, Professor McDaniel flipping through his notebook, Connie Swenson's reconstructed head, Jimmy in his wheelchair, me waking up to the smell of smoke in my house.

I came out of the bedroom in time to take a shower before lunch. After Maloney fixed Andy and me a gourmet meal of Beefaroni, he took us back to my house. It was not a pretty sight.

The acrid odor of smoke and destruction hung around it. To my surprise, my door—the lock of which had been hacked to pieces by the fire guys—hung open. I stuck my head in and saw O'Dell and a man I didn't recognize standing amidst the destruction in my living room.

"Hey, what's going on?"

The two came out to talk to me.

"I got your message last night," O'Dell said as he approached the doorway. "When I called this morning, all I got was a busy signal. When I came over to talk to you, I found this. What the hell happened?"

"You tell me. All I know is one minute I was in dreamland, the next I was smelling smoke."

O'Dell's gaze swept over me then paused as he spotted Angus Maloney and Andy.

"Angus took me in last night," I explained.

"Oh." O'Dell looked less than thrilled by this information. He greeted Maloney coolly and then introduced Harvey Mason, an arson investigator with the city. "Harvey and I have worked together on several cases. So long as I was already on the spot, I decided to stick around and hear what he had to say."

I focused on Mason who was a tall, thin man with a close-cut Afro and sad, dark eyes. "Do you think arson was involved here?"

"I'm afraid there's no doubt. Arsonists imagine that when they use gasoline or kerosene, the fire will destroy the evidence. That's not true. The smell in there is overpowering. It's also clear from burn marks and melted glass just how it was done."

"How?" Andy piped up from behind me.

Mason glanced at the boy and Maloney. "Looks as if somebody filled a bottle with kerosene, stuffed the top with a rag and lit it just before tossing it through your window."

"I was firebombed?"

"You were firebombed. Do you have any idea who might want to do that?"

My gaze went to O'Dell. "Miss Credella and I need to have a few words in private," he said. "Toni, there's something I want to show you."

A couple of minutes later, I stepped gingerly over a pile of burnt rubble that had once been a bookcase. O'Dell beckoned me further into the room and then pointed at some twisted plastic. I recognized it as the remains of my telephone.

"I found this when I was looking around with Mason," he said.

"Found what?"

O'Dell had taken a clear plastic bag out of his pocket. It contained something small and metallic. I peered at it. "What's that?"

"It's a bug," he said.

"A bug?" I stared at it. "Where did it come from?"

"You tell me. These days anybody can buy and install the equipment to bug a phone. Toni, somebody's been listening in on your phone conversations."

Chapter 20

A FEW MINUTES later O'Dell ushered me back outside. I told Maloney I'd meet him at the harbor in front of the Science Center. After he and Andy went off in the Chevette, I slid into the passenger seat of O'Dell's car.

"Okay, let's talk," he said. "Tell me everything that happened last night. Start with the reason why you called me. The message you left on my machine was that you'd found out something about Connie Swenson's and Alice Ritco's murders. What was that all about?"

Still in shock that someone had tampered with my phone, I described my interview with Doris Ritco. O'Dell asked a couple of questions, but mostly he just looked grim. When I got it out that Doris knew Jimmy from college and that Beth Shane had been her roommate and Jimmy, Shane's boyfriend, O'Dell shook his head.

"You had the right idea about Doris Ritco. I should have talked to her sooner. But I haven't been ignoring Alice and Connie. Some interesting information came in yesterday about the Margrafs."

I sat up a little straighter. "I thought they were dead."

"They are. It's how they died that's interesting."

"They were killed in a plane crash, right?"

"Right, but it wasn't a commercial airliner. They went down in a small private plane while flying across the Chesapeake Bay to the Eastern Shore. The plane was theirs. Robert Margraf was the pilot. It was a routine flight to attend a conference in Ocean City. According to the report filed with the FAA, their aircraft ran out of gas."

"Ran out of gas? But that's not exactly a long-distance journey."

"From what investigators could determine after the plane was recovered from the water, the gas tank had a hole. How the hole got there and why it wasn't noticed earlier, they couldn't say. The crash was called accidental, but there was some question even then. This happened not long after the Margraf experiment. I think there's a good chance their accident could have been engineered."

"By whom? Jimmy?"

"No one thought of him at the time. But if he held the Margrafs responsible for his girlfriend's death and was carrying on a vendetta against everyone involved, it would fit, wouldn't it?"

I tried to imagine the kind of grief that would take such a violent turn. The Jimmy I knew came across as cool and contained. Harmony seemed to be the only person he was fond of. Yet, if O'Dell's theory had any validity, he must have been crazy with grief over Beth's loss and consumed with hatred for those he considered at fault.

"Here's another interesting tidbit," O'Dell added. "Todd Lawrence, the guy who hit Beth Shane with a brick, is listed as having been killed by friendly fire in Vietnam. That is, the bullet they found in him was one of ours."

"Are you theorizing that Jimmy did that, too?" The same thought had run through my mind.

"He was in Vietnam. Whether he was in the right place at the right time, I can't say. But I'll set the ball rolling to check it out."

"What about the bug in my phone?"

"Whoever installed it heard the message you left on my answering machine last night. That might account for your fire. They were afraid you were about to finger them and wanted to fix it so you couldn't."

I shuddered. "What are you going to do?"

"I think we have enough to bring James Drury in on questioning."

"For what? The murder of Connie Swenson or Alice Ritco?"

"Maybe for both, maybe for more than those."

I thought of Professor McDaniel. Why would Jimmy have killed an aging professor with only a slight connection to the Margrafs? I thought about the bug in my telephone. What if it had been planted during my break-in? If someone had been listening to my phone conversations all that time, could they have heard me say McDaniel was giving me information about the Margraf Experiment? Was I inadvertently responsible for McDaniel's death? I felt sick.

"Jimmy's stuck in a wheelchair. How could he climb into my place through a broken window and plant a bug?" I asked aloud.

"That remains to be seen. As far as the bug is concerned though, his military training could make him very comfortable with such a device. When I make inquiries about his career in Vietnam, I'll check out his background in explosives and listening devices, too. Now, about this fire, did you see anyone, hear anyone?"

"Nothing like that. I was asleep until the smoke woke me up." I gave O'Dell a careful account of what had happened. When I finished, he eyed me cooly.

"So you went home with Maloney."

"I wasn't going to stand out on the street in my underwear."

"Jesus, you were in your underwear?"

"Not for long. The fire people got some of my clothes out."

"Did they offer to dress you, too?"

"No."

"Yeah, well I bet they enjoyed the show. You didn't need to go with Maloney. You could have gone to your parents' place. You could have called me."

"Why would I have done either of those things? It was the crack of dawn and Angus Maloney was there, willing and able."

"I bet."

O'Dell's accusatory tone rubbed me the wrong way. "Listen, Gus, what business is it of yours? I'd had a hell of a night, so I took the first offer of shelter that came along. Maloney's my boss and a heck of a nice guy."

"A nice guy with a kid and the nice guy's also hung up on his ex-wife."

"So?"

"So keep that in mind when you go meeting him at the Science Center." O'Dell checked his watch. "Which, you'd better do pretty soon if you want to catch him."

"What's your plan of action?"

"Go knock on James Drury's door and have a little talk."

"You might not find Jimmy at home. Sometimes he hangs out at the harbor, sometimes around the Cross Street Market. You might even find him in the lunch line at the church on Light Street. Listen, he has a pal he's tight with, a kid named Harmony. He's a little strange."

"Maybe Harmony's the one who planted that bug."

"Could be. Jimmy could talk him into anything." I remembered crackers and coke that had disappeared from my kitchen. Harmony was always hungry. And the missing card box and candlesticks were just the kinds of pretty things that might appeal to him. I also remembered that the book on the Harzine had disappeared that night. How would Harmony have known to take it? I'd certainly never mentioned it to him or Jimmy. Had Jimmy seen me with it and told him to take it? I thought back, trying to remember how this could have happened, but drew a blank.

Wherever this Drury is," O'Dell promised, "I'll track him down. We're going to find out what happened to Connie and Alice, Toni. And I'm going to fix it so you can sleep in your house and feel safe."

BEFORE GOING off to search for Jimmy, O'Dell dropped me at the harbor. My head was filled with what I'd just found out. I thought of Connie Swenson, dead all those years because of a psychological experiment that got out of hand. And what about Alice? Why would Jimmy have wanted to kill Alice?

When Doris recognized Jimmy, she'd been shocked that he was a panhandler not all that different from her mother. Had she told Alice about his girlfriend getting killed in the Margraf experiment? Alice had seen Connie's bones unearthed. Had she questioned Jimmy about the bones and perhaps drawn a connection between them and Margraf?

Jimmy was no talker. I couldn't imagine him telling Alice his story. But they'd been pals and drinking buddies. Perhaps he'd let something slip that allowed her to make inferences after she heard her daughter's story and saw Connie's bones. Alice had been a wily old girl. She might have tried to blackmail Jimmy. Sure, she could get money from her daughter. But she might have preferred to get money her own way. I knew I was just speculating. There were still too many missing pieces.

When I met Maloney and Andy, they had just emerged from a movie at the Imax. They invited me for lunch at the coffee shop in the Science Center. After we ordered, Andy went off to play with one of the children's displays on magnetism. When he was out of earshot but still comfortably in sight, Maloney asked what had gone on between me and O'Dell in my house. Though I knew I should probably keep it quiet, I blurted out the whole story.

As Maloney listened, his thick eyebrows kept inching up. "Why didn't you tell me any of this before? I knew your house had been broken into, but I thought that was just burglary. It was much worse. You were in danger. Last night somebody tried to kill you."

I pictured my ruined living room and felt teary again. Only the kids and moms and dads chattering away in the other booths embarrassed me into keeping my eyes dry. "Maybe it's over now."

After finishing our hamburgers and milkshakes, we wandered outside. The sun had finally struggled through the cloud cover. It shed a thin white light over the harbor that brought the color of the brick promenade and the flags snapping in the wind into sharp relief.

Tourists in a neon rainbow of jackets and headgear were a moving patchwork. Mothers urged toddlers along and pushed strollers between the Science Center and the Light Street Pavilion. Gulls pirouetted in the wind. As one of the water taxis that ply the harbor motored up to a piling, the white birds scattered.

"Where to now, sport?" Maloney asked Andy. We had started to amble north, past the excursion boats.

"Can we rent a paddle boat?" Andy pleaded.

Maloney shook his head. "Too rough out there."

I seconded that. The gray water chopping up against the docks looked forbidding. The wind had risen and was lifting my hair so that I had to keep a hand over it.

Andy looked downcast. "The Aquarium," he suggested next.

"You went there with Toni just a while ago."

"We could go again."

"The Aquarium will be a mob scene. How about the City Life Museum or the Public Works Museum? Wouldn't you like to know what happens when you flush a toilet?"

While this negotiation was going on, we made our way through the crowds milling in front of the Pavilion. I stopped short and tugged on Maloney's sleeve.

"What?" He turned toward me.

"That's Harmony and Jimmy over there."

They were stationed in their usual spot. Harmony was juggling apples. Next to his feet, his upended cap held change and a few dollar bills. Nearby, Jimmy sat with a Styrofoam cup and a cardboard sign scrawled with "Help the Homeless."

I whispered to Maloney, "I expected that O'Dell would have tracked Jimmy down by now."

"Your timing's just a little off. That's him over there."

I turned my head and spotted O'Dell coming around the corner of the Pavilion. He saw us before he spotted Jimmy. When his eye caught mine, I grimaced and gestured with my head to the spot where Jimmy and Harmony were working the crowd. He nodded and walked quickly past, making a beeline for Jimmy.

Andy jigged at Maloney's feet, tugging on his arm. "C'mon, Dad, what are you waiting for? Let's go."

"Hold your horses, son. I'm looking at something."

"What? Let's go!"

I grabbed Andy's hand, knelt and wrapped my arms around him. "Shhh. Something's happening. Just wait."

"What? What? What is it?"

O'Dell was within ten feet of Jimmy when he swung his head and stared. I wasn't aware that Jimmy knew O'Dell. Yet, a look of recognition came over his face. I saw his fingers clench on the arms of his chair.

Holding tightly to Andy's hand, I stood, unable to take my eyes off a scene that horrified while it fascinated.

O'Dell leaned over Jimmy's chair and palmed his ID. The two men stared into each other's faces, O'Dell talking rapidly while Jimmy's heavy jaw tightened. The intensity of their one-way conversation captured the notice of several passersby who shot them curious looks.

Harmony didn't seem to be aware yet that anything unusual was going on. He had four apples in the air and one hand behind his back, catching and tossing with dizzying rapid-fire coordination. His face expressed total concentration and joy in his work.

Jimmy made a sudden rough gesture that catapulted his Styrofoam cup to the pavement. Pennies, quarters, dimes and nickels exploded out of it.

"Oh Look. That man dropped his money!" Andy yanked free of my hand and ran to scoop up a quarter careening toward the brick promenade's edge.

"Andy, no!" I ran after him, but Maloney was ahead of me. As he scooped his son up, Jimmy's electric wheel chair shot forward. Simultaneously, he sprang up and shoved his cardboard sign into O'Dell's face. Unprepared, O'Dell stumbled back.

With an agility truly astonishing in a man who'd been collecting disability payments from the government for years because he couldn't walk, Jimmy sidestepped his still rolling chair. Pivoting, he broke into a headlong run, whacking tourists aside as if he were a bowling ball and they ten pins.

"Jesus!" Maloney shoved his son into my arms and took off after the escaping man. At the same time, O'Dell righted himself and sprinted through the crowd. People screamed and pointed.

Several had been knocked off their feet, some by Jimmy, others by his wheelchair. It plowed through the mob like a berserk robot. One old lady lay on her back in its wake waving her arms and legs.

As the wheelchair plunged over the edge of the promenade and sank into the harbor with its wheels still whirring, Harmony's apples dropped. His happy expression had changed to one of horror. He stared after the fleeing Jimmy and his pursuers. "No, no," he wailed. He dashed through the crowd, setting up another round of protests and exclamations. "No, no!" he kept keening.

He was too late to help his friend. Maloney and O'Dell had cornered him on the end of the wooden dock where the City Clipper ties up to board passengers for evening Reggae cruises. Jimmy jumped onto the white sailing ship's deck, pushed a protesting crew member out of his way, and bolted for the bow. There was no place for him to go after that but out onto the bowsprit. He hopped onto the long pole of varnished wood that projected over the water and walked it like a gymnast.

That's as far as you go, Drury!" O'Dell's shouted words wafted back to me as I stood clutching Andy. "Turn around and give yourself up."

Jimmy whirled, teetered slightly, then found his balance. He glared at his two pursuers. Behind them, Harmony hurled himself aboard and came pounding up. "No, no, no!" he still wailed.

Jimmy glanced over O'Dell's and Maloney's heads at Harmony and then back at O'Dell. Wordlessly, he dived into the choppy gray water.

Chapter 21

I WONDERED if O'Dell would jump in after Jimmy. He didn't. A posse of official vehicles, apparently alerted by one of the foot patrol who roam the Inner Harbor, came roaring up. Every mobile siren in Baltimore seemed to open its metal throat. Police cars, ambulances, fire engines and rescue units converged into the parking lot behind the information booth. Uniformed officers scrambled over the promenade area like ants at a honey spill.

At the same time, a police boat plowed through the inlet between the Aquarium and Domino Sugar. Its siren, too, blared as its twin diesels sprayed frigid plumes in its wake. The combination of so many forces probably only made it harder to fish Jimmy out. By the time they extricated him from the water, he'd been in it a good twenty minutes. The last I saw of him, he was tied to a stretcher and being loaded into the back of an ambulance like so much unclaimed baggage.

"Why did that man jump into the water?" Andy tugged on my hand.

"I'm not sure. I guess he did something bad and when they tried to ask him about it, he got upset."

My eyes were on Harmony. As he stared after the departing ambulance, his face was the picture of utter devastation. I wanted to go over and say something comforting, but I couldn't imagine what that might be. Andy pulled on my hand again, distracting me. When I looked up, Harmony was gone.

Still, I couldn't get him out of my mind. I was worrying about him when O'Dell called early the next morning.

"I phoned Maloney first," he informed me. "He said you'd moved in with Randall. Good choice."

"Randall has an extra room. Maloney doesn't and he's got his son staying with him right now."

"You don't have to explain to me. You're a big girl. You can impose on whomever you want. I'd invite you to impose on me, but right now I have a houseguest, too."

O'Dell sounded so bemused as he told me this that I had to ask him who it was.

"Would you believe Jerome Robinson? He showed up at my door last night saying his mama's new boyfriend kicked him out. Kind of rough for a kid."

"From what you told me, you had it just as rough when you were his age."

"Yeah, I did. Matter of fact, he and I talked about that some. You know how it is when it's late at night and you get to talking."

"Yeah, I know." A picture of O'Dell and Jerome commiserating with each other about their unhappy childhoods popped into my head. Was it possible? It seemed like a bleeding heart fantasy.

"You find yourself saying some surprising things. So, in a funny way, Jerome and I have something in common. Anyhow, either I took him in or he spent the night on the street. So what choice did I have?"

"None. How did it go?"

"Score one for righteous causes. He didn't murder me in my bed, and I still have a television set."

"What about tonight?"

"I don't know. He's at school now, the price I exacted for letting him sleep on my couch. We'll just have to play it by ear. That's not what I called you about."

"What did you call me about?"

"Just thought you'd like to know, James Drury signed a full confession."

"How full? Did he confess to murdering Connie Swenson and Alice Ritco?"

"That and more. Not only did he admit he did Swenson, he also admitted to rigging the Margrafs' plane to crash and blowing away Todd Lawrence in Vietnam. Says he told Alice the story one night when he was drunk and killed her when she threatened blackmail."

"Was it Jimmy who broke into my house or did Harmony do it for him?"

"He says it was him and that he was the one who bugged your phone. Learned how to do that sort of thing in the military. So long as he's confessing to multiple premeditated murder, there's no reason why he shouldn't throw in breaking and entering and invasion of privacy. I'm surprised he didn't top it all off with loitering and spray-can graffiti. Anyhow, he says he broke in when he saw you carrying a book on the Harzine Institute. While he was in your house, he took the book and did your phone. He was aware you were fond of Alice and worried about you coming up with something on him. Rightly so, I might add."

As O'Dell's voice filled my ear, I flashed back on being smothered the night of the break-in. The choking weight on my face, the burning in my chest as I struggled and thrashed, then the final sinking into blackness. Why didn't Jimmy finish the job? If a big guy like Jimmy had actually been trying to smother me, there was no way I could have fought him off.

"What about McDaniel?"

"Him, too. I tell you, this has done wonders for my clearance rate. Drury says he bashed McDaniel's brains in when he realized he was feeding you information about the Margraf Experiment. Look at it this way, Toni, it's a tribute to your detecting skills. You really had the nutcase worried."

"The only way Jimmy would have known about McDaniel was because I must have mentioned him on my bugged phone. Bodner's lucky his name never came up in one of my phone conversations."

"He is. But it's not your fault, Toni. You're not the one going around murdering people here."

"Why didn't Jimmy bash my brains in, since my sleuthing was the source of the trouble?"

"He almost got you, too, Toni. That was no love letter he tossed through your window. You're lucky you're not a crispy critter."

My conversation with O'Dell didn't go on much longer. I put the receiver back in its cradle and sat staring at a puddle of light on Randall's Italian tile cooking island.

"Why so pensive, doll?"

Randall stood in the entry. He wore a gray silk warm-up suit. Beads of moisture from the shower gleamed in his close-cut afro, and his skin in the warm sunlight held mahogany tints that I'd never noticed before.

He headed for the coffee maker and poured himself a full mug of the Jamaican grind he got from a specialty coffee shop at the Gallery.

Over the rim of his coffee cup he gave me an assessing look. "I can see something's got you upset. Anything I can do to help?"

I told him about the conversation I'd just had with O'Dell.

"So, you should be feeling proud of yourself."

"Proud because I got a harmless old professor killed and sent Jimmy to jail and messed up Harmony's life?"

Randall choked and set his mug down fast. "Have you ever considered that feeling guilty about everything and everyone is a form of egotism? You didn't knock McDaniel on the head, Jimmy did. The man is a cold-blooded multiple murderer, Toni. Not to mention that he was guilty of fraud against the government for claiming a disability he never had! He's responsible for ruining his own life and by helping to unmask him, you did a public service."

"I know you're right, but what about Harmony? What's going to happen to him now? The poor kid had finally found a safe berth. Jimmy may have been a murderer, but he's the only person who was ever good to Harmony and gave him a real home. I wish you could have seen them together. They were like father and son. It was really touching. Now Harmony is on his own again."

"Spare me. If you're serious about this private eye shtick, you're going to have to toughen up. By the way, are you serious? Do you want to go on working for Maloney?"

"Yes, despite everything, I still want to learn how to be a private investigator."

"Even when it means you have to associate with mental cases like Gus O'Dell?"

"Gus isn't all that bad. Hey, this ought to interest you. Last night he let Jerome Robinson sleep at his place."

When Randall lifted a rude eyebrow, I smacked him on the shoulder. "It's nothing like that! Jerome's mother's boyfriend kicked him out and he had no place to go."

"I'm glad to hear O'Dell has something besides a water pump beating in his chest. What about Angus Maloney? Now that you've had a chance to get to know him, what's your take?"

Randall studied me shrewdly. He didn't get to be a partner in a pricey law firm by being naive or unobservant. I knew what he was asking me.

I had to work at it, but I managed to smile and return his look steadily. "I think Angus is a great guy," I said. "I'm going to learn a lot from him, and he's going to make a wonderful boss."

TO THAT END, I spent the rest of the week working on the surveillance Maloney had assigned to me. Following Mrs. Martin around to malls and exclusive dress shops gave me a real workout. But by the end of the week I had good news for Mr. Martin— depending on how you look at it. His wife, Melanie, really was spending her generous monthly allowance all on clothes.

To do this without busting the seams in her closet, she had to make regular donations to the city's second hand clothing shops. Since she was close to my size, trailing her gave me a fashion bonus. I was able to pick up some pretty nifty duds from her giveaways dirt cheap.

At week's end I used Randall's computer to put together a report which I took to Maloney's dojo. It was a busy place. In addition to the regular guys who are always there tossing each other around on mats, O'Dell was working out with one of Maloney's advanced students while Maloney watched and shouted instructions. Jerome was off in a corner learning some moves from Sean, who was being very cautious with Jerome's injured arm. When I walked in, Jerome shot me a guarded wave and then focused all his attention on his instructor.

I watched the two of them. Though Sean was older and quite a bit more muscular than Jerome, they were both about the same height. Sean, however, had a kind of self-contained serenity and economy in all his movements that Jerome conspicuously lacked. Something about the way Jerome hung on the older boy's every word told me Jerome wanted for himself some of what Sean had acquired through study and hard work. I gazed at him, taking in how fully engaged he was in a non-felonious activity that involved discipline and self-knowledge, and felt pleased.

At that moment I noticed Doris Ritco. Trim in navy slacks and a yellow turtleneck sweater, she was standing on the sidelines and watching the action on the mats. She greeted me warmly and explained that, after what happened to her mother, she was considering letting Maloney teach her some self-defense. I told her I thought that was a good idea and that he was teaching me. I wasn't ready to take on any ninjas yet, but I was beginning to feel a little safer on the street.

"I know James Drury has confessed to my mother's murder," she went on. "I want to thank you for all the trouble you took over that. Angus tells me that if it weren't for you the case might never have been solved."

"Oh, I don't know."

"Well Angus thinks you're a very good investigator. I'm glad Jimmy's been stopped, of course, but I'm still in shock. To think that he killed Connie and Todd and so many other people." She shook her head. "If only I hadn't told Mom about him."

"You can't blame yourself. Jimmy was the murderer, not you." I gazed at her curiously. "You knew Jimmy when he was a young man. You must have had some idea about his character. Does what's happened seem impossible to you?"

She nodded slowly. "Yes, it does. He always seemed like such a sweet guy. Once Beth told me he was the only guy she ever dated who got teary-eyed in movies at the same places she did. But do we ever really know anybody else so well they can't shock us?"

I had had the identical thought many times. At a loss, I turned my attention to O'Dell and his sparring partner and Doris did the same. Though I'd seen lots of practice fighting in Maloney's dojo, I'd never seen this guy before. He was big, Maloney's size, and he was muscular and quick.

"They're really going at each other," Doris commented. "I hope no one gets hurt."

"It's just practice. They know better than to hurt each other." To be honest, I wasn't so sure. I watched O'Dell deliver a flying kick that Maloney's student deflected by rolling over backward and then taking O'Dell down with him by grabbing his ankles. O'Dell responded with a cutting blow to his adversary's wrist. This was the closest thing I'd seen to a no-holds-barred Aikido match. Most of Maloney's other students had stopped their own workouts to watch.

O'Dell had wriggled free, only to be taken down again. He sprang up, double whirling and then kicking high and wide. The blow he aimed at the other man's gut failed to land squarely because he sidestepped, at the same time clubbing O'Dell with his forearm. If O'Dell's kick had connected, the other guy might not have enjoyed his dinner that night.

"They're well matched, aren't they?" Doris commented. "I mean you wouldn't think it because one is such a big fellow, but this other man is quick and surprisingly strong." She stared, fascinated.

A few minutes later, the two quit savaging each other. Sweating, their chests heaving, they slapped backs as if it had all been in fun—

and maybe it had been. I'll never understand men.

They came over to the sidelines to grab towels and take long drinks of bottled water.

"Hey, man, cool!" Jerome exclaimed. He looked at O'Dell with admiration.

Maloney caught my eye and ambled over to the spot where I stood with Doris.

"Your friend was feeling lively today," he said indicating O'Dell.

"He's your friend, too. You were teaching him Aikido long before you met me."

"True. If it weren't for my neck, I'd be sparring with him myself. Got that Martin report?"

"Right here, boss." I produced the report and watched anxiously while he glanced through it. He chuckled when he got to the part about Mrs. Martin's shopping habits. "Got any plans for the evening," he asked when he finished and stuffed it into his duffle bag.

"I finally got the okay from the Fire Marshall, so I'm going over to my house to see what I can salvage."

"I hate to ask you to change your plans, Toni, but I have to take care of Andy tonight, so I can't watch the construction site. Sean was going to take over for me, but now he says he can't. Any chance you can do it? It should be perfectly safe now. There's a night watchman on duty. All you have to do is keep an eye out and use the car phone if anything comes up. Nothing will, though. It's been quieter than the morgue over there."

Sure. Will I be sitting in your car, or do you need it?"

Maloney frowned. "I need it. I'll have to make other arrangements. Tell you what. When the time comes, just show up and ask whoever's on duty. They'll have something for you, okay?"

"Sounds fine. Say hello to Andy for me."

I SPENT ANOTHER couple of hours at the dojo working on my Aikido. Then I headed for home. Unfortunately, home these days had boarded up front windows and smelled like a rained out barbecue.

When I unlocked the door, the odor hit me—charred wood, kerosene, burnt upholstery, scorched plaster—and all of it blended to a tasty black paste by water under pressure from a firehose.

I spent most of my time upstairs, stripping the beds, windows and closets so I could try to launder the smoke and smell out of sheets, curtains and clothing. Afterward, I wandered around trying to make a mental catalogue of the damage, so I'd be able to hold my own with the insurance adjusters.

It was not happy work and as afternoon shadows lengthened, I was feeling bummed. I was just examining my cupboards to see if any of the packaged food was edible when I heard it. From one of the many windows I'd opened to air the place out came the distant strains of "Home on the Range."

I'd heard Harmony play it before and had thought he made it sound sad. I'd never heard it rendered so plaintively as I did now. Somewhere out there he was wandering the streets like a lost soul and playing that song as if it were a dirge.

How was he doing, I wondered. Was he taking his medicine? He'd relapse into his schizophrenia and start hearing voices again if he didn't. It had been Jimmy who'd made sure Harmony did what he was supposed to. Now Jimmy was locked up.

I hurried out into the street and tried to follow the strains of the harmonica. I turned corners, ran through alleys, peered into backyards. Always, it was just ahead of me, both beckoning and eluding. Finally, when the cheerless music seemed to be just around the corner, I called Harmony's name.

The music stopped, and I felt certain he was standing nearby with his head cocked, waiting for me to appear.

"Harmony, are you okay?" I cried. "It's me, Toni Credella. I've been worried about you. I want to help you."

But when I rounded the corner the street was empty.

Chapter 22

AT THE appointed hour, I rode my bike to the construction site. Decked out in his customary yellow hard hat and cement-streaked jeans, Mario Caprini greeted me. "I heard you helped catch the creep who killed that old lady."

"Not really."

"That's not what your boss says. Anyhow, I spoke to Maloney just a few minutes ago. You can use my car tonight." Mario pointed to a little black Honda parked about twenty feet from the base of the crane. "It has a phone, so you'll be all set."

"What will you do for transportation?"

"I don't plan on going anywhere tonight. One of my men will drop me off at home and pick me up in the morning. Just leave the keys with George."

Glancing around, I saw the night watchman standing at the other end of the site. After I thanked Mario, he continued to gaze at me, a half smile on his face as he studied mine. He was better looking than he'd been in high school. I remembered him as a skinny, intense kid with acne and an Adam's apple that wouldn't quit. The acne had gone away. His throat looked normal and the rest of him had filled out nicely.

"You don't look much different than when we were in high school," he said.

"Why Mario, you make a girl blush."

"You never did take me seriously. Not now, and not when we were in high school, either."

"Not true. I liked you a lot, Mario."

"Maybe we could get together for dinner sometime?"

"Maybe we could."

"Hold that thought, Toni. I'll call tomorrow, after you've had a chance to catch up on your sleep. Okay?"

"Sure." Why not, I thought. My relationship with the other men in my life didn't seem to be going anywhere. Maybe it was time I branched out.

Mario left with the rest of his crew, and I settled into his car and broke out the hero sandwich and canned juice I'd picked up on the way to the site. I was stuffing the last of the sandwich into my mouth when George tapped on my window.

"How you doin' in there?"

"Fine. How about you?"

"I'm okay, but that might not be for long. Looks like quite a storm coming."

"You're right." We both studied the landscape. The wind ruffled up white caps on the water in the harbor across the road. Miniature sandstorms swirled and eddied off piles of dirt and gravel mounded around the construction site. George shielded his eyes with the back of his hand. The sun had set behind one of the downtown skyscrapers. In the light reflecting off it from the city the sky looked ominously dense, a clotted slate colored mass. A jagged crack of lightning ripped through it.

"Whoo, look at that! Think I'll go find me some shelter. You be all right here in this little car?"

"I'll be fine." Wind snatched the words away.

George disappeared into a pale green construction trailer just as the first wild curtain of rain swept over Mario's car. I peered out the window. At first rain poured down so thick and heavy that all I could see was an opaque glaze of liquid coating the glass. Above me, the boom on the crane whined. Though I couldn't see it, I could easily imagine it jerking and dipping in the wind.

I wished I were parked outside the fence. I didn't like being so close to the crane. I told myself there was no chance of the thing toppling on me. Giant slabs of cement pinned it to the earth. Even so, the creaks and groans it made as the wind swung it to and fro gave me the shivers. Its metal shrieking made it sound like a trapped animal.

I pictured the huge steel clamshell that dangled from the cable at the end of the crane's boom. As new floors appeared on the condominium, the crane operator used the clamshell to hoist building materials to work crews. I'd seen it lift enormous weights in its steel jaws, including a generator the size of a small pickup truck. What if the clamshell came loose from its cable and fell on Mario's Honda? I'd be mayonnaise.

"Won't happen," I told myself. "Not a chance." Still, if it hadn't been raining so hard I would have found shelter in the trailer with George. For sure, I wasn't doing much of a job watching the construction site. But who would bother the place in weather like this?

After a while the downpour let up some. Though the windshield was still opaque as mother of pearl, the rain on the roof turned into a steady patter. My thoughts drifted. I have no idea when I closed my eyes or how long I'd been dozing when I felt it.

My first indication came in another dream of Alice. I was in a canoe on a quiet green river. The sun beat down damply through wide, leathery leaves. Unfamiliar birds chirped in branches overhead. Lazy dragonflies whirred and dipped in erratic patterns, their busy wings throwing off iridescent blue sparks. Below the surface, pale fish lurked and blew small mysterious bubbles.

Alice sat opposite me, twirling a torn parasol between her grimy hands. I stared at her curiously. She wore a dirty white lace prom gown of vintage 50's design. It was strapless and the tops of her breasts poured out of its bodice in luxuriant mounds of mottled flesh. Matching white lace gloves covered her forearms but left her pudgy fingers bare. "Alice," I said, "why did Jimmy kill you? Did you know about Connie Swenson? When you saw them dig up her body here, did you threaten to tell the police what you knew?"

She never answered me. For at that moment our canoe started to shake like a beach umbrella overturned in a typhoon. I dug my fingers into the sides and screamed. Alice jumped to her feet. She winked at me and did a graceful swan dive. The last I saw of her was her white satin slippers twinkling as they disappeared overboard. When I peered after her, I looked into the pitiless eyes of a sea monster. He had the bottom of the canoe locked between his jaws. As I stared in horror, the fragile wood bottom of the craft splintered and the long knives of his teeth burst through smeared with blood.

My eyes popped open. I was fully awake and aware in every cell of my body that something was terribly wrong. Though I was in Mario's car and not the canoe of my nightmare, I was still rocking violently. For a split second I thought it might be the wind.

It wasn't the wind. A crunching, ripping sound whined above me. I twisted my neck back. There were holes in the roof and something shiny punching through them. "What the ..."

The car rocked violently. It was no longer on the ground. It was in mid-air. The shiny things poking through the roof were teeth on a pair of steel jaws. Somewhere above me pulleys and cables squealed. The clamshell had broken into the top of the Honda like a lobster punching through the soft carapace of a water beetle.

Still muddleheaded from sleep, I wondered for a split second if the clamshell had fallen on the Honda, as I'd feared. Then how could it be lifting the car? I rolled down my window and stuck my head out. The car was five feet off the ground. I should have jumped out then. But I was still too dazed to think clearly.

I scrambled for the other side so I could look for the crane's cab. I saw it parked at the top of the crane high above me. Inside it, someone was operating the clamshell to haul the Honda off the ground with me trapped inside.

"Hey! Stop!" The car was now fifteen feet off the ground. Dumb, Credella, I realized. This wasn't happening by accident. Whatever the person in the crane's cab intended, I wasn't going to like it.

I grabbed the car phone and dialed 911. "Help me!" I croaked and tried to explain what was happening.

The car jerked and I dropped the phone. When I picked it up, the connection was gone. A quick look out the window told me the Honda was twenty feet off the ground and swinging back and forth like a pendulum. The motor operating the pulley on the clamshell roared hungrily, stopped abruptly, then jolted to life again. The person in charge was definitely not a professional.

I dialed Maloney. Miraculously, he answered on the second ring. "Help me!"

"Toni? What's wrong?"

Hysterically, I tried to explain. As I squeezed the words out, I realized how futile they were. There wasn't time for either the police or Maloney to help. I knew who was in that cab and what he intended.

Panicking, I dropped the phone and grabbed for the door handle. When I looked down, my guts did flip flops. I was at least twenty-five feet above the ground.

The car was a coffin now, getting out of it my only hope. Keeping my feet wedged under the side of the car seat, I circled my hands over the bar of the car's roof rack. Then I half straightened my jackknifed body.

The rain had settled down to a fine drizzle. The night air wrapped itself around me like an icy rag. Moisture slicked the top of the Honda.

My fingers found the edge of the clamshell. Hot to the touch and rough textured, it vibrated with the motion of the pulley threaded through its top. I could feel the tension on its steel jaws.

It was the only thing besides the car I could hold onto, and the car was doomed. The person inside the cab intended to drop it, and soon. We were now perhaps thirty feet above the construction site. The pulleys stopped grinding and the clamshell floated, eerily pregnant with its burden. My scrabbling fingers explored the clamshell.

One of the jaw's teeth had not sunk into the Honda all the way. I was able to wrap one hand around it and then the other. My feet remained jammed under the base of the car seat. Gingerly, I walked them to the flat ledge of the seat and hoisted myself up to the next half buried tooth. Then I put both feet on the seat's backrest and pushed. My right hand grabbed another tooth. The other grasped the second tooth more firmly.

I was horribly aware that the cab operator could see me in the light bouncing off the fog on the ground. The crane's spotlights weren't on. Either the operator didn't want them on, or he didn't know how to put them on. Out on the harbor I heard the bellow of a foghorn. It sounded like a death knell.

Riding my bike around Baltimore has made my legs strong, not my arms. Could I hoist myself out of the car and find a spot on the clamshell where I could stand? Already my arms trembled from terror and fatigue.

The clamshell roared again. My heart fought like a lab rat facing the guillotine. I kicked my right foot and tried to roll up onto the car's roof. My head hit the clamshell, but at least I could now get both feet on the car's hood. Light appeared between the clamshell's jaws. I scrambled onto the roof, grabbed the sides of the jaws and crawled between.

It started to creak open. The giant hinge that operated it whined and moaned. The Honda's metal skin screamed as the roof ripped away from the jagged teeth. One instant I stood on the car roof, the next I dangled over open space listening to a clap of metal thunder reverberate over the construction site.

Desperate not to follow the Honda, I stretched as tall as I could. Hooking my fingers over the top of the clamshell jaw, I managed to put my tiptoes on the teeth. It wasn't comfortable, but at least I was still in one piece.

The cab operator didn't like this. The other side of the jaw started to close. As I watched it come at me, I pressed myself back into the steel hollow of the clamshell's mouth and drew my legs up. The teeth slammed together, missing my sneakered feet by about half an inch.

The clamshell seemed to quiver with rage at missing its prey. The jaws opened and closed again, and then again, like a monster gnashing its fangs. I clung to the inside, rattling up and down like a pea in a blender.

The clamshell shook and waggled. It rocked and swayed, but I hung on. Where was George during all this, I wondered idiotically. Could that be him in the cab? But I knew better. I knew who it was.

Finally the crane's motor stopped grinding. The clamshell hung motionless. I could see the crane. Fog wreathed and coiled around its base. Fronds of mist blanketed the wreck of the Honda which lay on the gravel like a squashed puppy. Out on the harbor I heard a tugboat hoot.

The cab's window was shiny black in the darkness. It slid open. A form crawled out. It swung lithely up onto the cab's roof and then out to one of the boom's girders. Harmony.

"Toni." His voice was muffled, as if the fog and damp were sucking at it. "I know you're in there. You can't stay. I'm going to come and get you."

I watched him walk along the inside of the boom, graceful as Nureyev.

"Harmony, why are you doing this?"

"You know why."

"No, honest, I don't. Where's George?"

"Who?"

"Where's the night watchman?"

"Oh, him. The storm was so loud he didn't even hear me come up behind him. I tied him up. He can't rescue you, Toni."

"Harmony!"

He shook his head at me. "It's your fault, just like it's your fault they took Jimmy away. Jimmy was my only friend. Now they've locked him up."

"What happened to Jimmy isn't my fault. He did bad things. He killed some people. He killed Alice."

Harmony laughed. He had always struck me as fey, but now his laughter had a wildness I hadn't heard before. "Jimmy didn't kill Alice."

"He didn't?"

"I killed Alice."

"You? Why?"

He had walked out of my limited range of vision. I knew from his voice that he was at the end of the boom, directly overhead where the clamshell's cable was attached. As the clamshell shuddered with his shifting weight, I guessed he was sitting, legs dangling over the edge.

"I had to kill Alice," he said. "The voices told me I had to."

"Voices?"

"You wouldn't understand. It's because I'm special. The voices always tell me what to do. Now they're telling me I have to kill you. I'm sorry, Toni. Until you started making so much trouble for Jimmy, I liked you. I didn't kill you the night I broke into your house. I could have. It would have been easy."

"So it was you!" I remembered the pillow over my face, the smothering sensation.

"Jimmy told me he saw you carrying that book. I had to get it away from you. It might have been better if I'd just killed you. All I had to do was hold the pillow over your face a little longer. But you fought and I got tired. You looked pretty in your underwear."

I had wondered if Harmony were taking his medicine. He wasn't. Somehow I had to keep him talking and hope that Maloney or the police got here—though what could they do?

"Harmony, Alice was a harmless old lady. She never hurt a fly."

"She wasn't so harmless. She told me about that girl's bones they dug up, and I told her what Jimmy did."

"You told her that Jimmy killed Connie Swenson?"

"I didn't mean to," Harmony wailed. "It wasn't my fault I told her Jimmy's secret. It was Alice's."

"How was it Alice's fault? I bet Jimmy warned you never to tell anyone."

"She tricked me. It just came out and I couldn't take it back.

That's when I knew I had to kill her. If Jimmy found out I told Alice what he did, he'd never trust me again."

So Alice hadn't been trying to blackmail anybody. She'd had the misfortune to persuade Harmony to blab Jimmy's secret and then suffered the consequences. "Oh Harmony, how could you kill Alice?"

"I did it for Jimmy. I did all of them for him."

"Professor McDaniel, too?" My voice quavered on the moist night air.

"He was a mean old man, and I could tell from what you said on the phone that he was going to tell you too much."

"From what I said to him on the phone?"

Harmony sneered. "Jimmy learned electronics in the army. He taught me how to bug a phone. It's easy. I could sit in my room at Jimmy's place and hear everything you said."

So, Harmony had planted the bug the night he'd broken into my place, and my phone conversation about McDaniel had led Harmony to him. I felt sick.

"I didn't mean to hurt that old professor," Harmony was going on plaintively. "I just wanted him to promise not to say any more to you about the Margraf Experiment. But when I asked, he told me to get away from him. He walked faster. He ignored me."

"Harmony, that's no reason to kill a person. Everyone's life is precious to them."

"Jimmy's life is precious to me. If it weren't for you, we'd be together now. I would have pushed you off the crane before, Toni, only Jimmy was watching, and I knew he didn't want me to. When I told him about killing Alice and McDaniel, he was mad at me. He said after he got rid of that girl and the Margrafs and Todd, he wanted to put all the killing behind him. Still, I wish I'd given you a shove. Maybe if I had, Jimmy wouldn't be in jail now."

"Hurting me now won't help Jimmy. It'll just make things worse for him."

Harmony didn't seem to hear. "I have to kill you now," he said dreamily. "Why don't you make it easy and just jump."

I cowered back into the clamshell. "No."

"Jump, Toni. Then it'll be over and I can go home."

Headlights pierced the fog. Brakes screeched and someone rattled the lock on the gate. Muffled by the fog, a deep male voice reached my ears. "Toni? What's going on in there?"

"Maloney!" I pressed my face against the teeth of my prison. "Maloney, help! I'm inside the clamshell. Harmony wants to murder me!"

I heard metal rattle, then a thud and running feet. A curtain of mist parted, and I saw Maloney's face staring up. He stood next to the broken hulk of the Honda. "What the hell happened here?"

"You can't help her," Harmony screamed from high above me. "I'm going to get her. She's mine!"

"Jesus!" Maloney exclaimed as he took in the situation. He ran to the crane and hauled himself up over the cement weights. He began climbing the metal framework. "Hold tight, Toni."

"You can't help her!" Harmony screamed defiantly. "I've got her."

As Maloney climbed, the clamshell shuddered. I knew Harmony had jumped upright. I pictured him stepping over the pulley, positioned close to the end of the boom. I imagined him grasping the cable attached to it and, monkey-like, swinging himself down. Fresh shudders warned me that he was sliding down the cable like a fireman down a pole. "I'm coming to get you," he chanted.

Cowering back, I heard the clang of his shoes on top of the clamshell. As Harmony shifted his weight to survey his new position, my metal prison echoed with more clangs and thuds. I realized then that I had an advantage. It wasn't going to be so easy for him to get at me. The closed jaws of the clamshell were smooth. They wouldn't offer a foot or handhold for sliding safely to the teeth.

He beat at the top of the shell with either his fist or the bottom of his shoe. "Can you hear me in there, Toni? That man can't help you."

I could no longer see Maloney. But I knew that if he could reach the cab, he could lower the clamshell back to the ground. Somehow, I had to keep Harmony at bay long enough for him to do that.

"Listen to me, Harmony. You can't do Jimmy any good by hurting me. He's confessed to everything, including the murders that you did. You'll only make things worse for him."

"That's not what the voices say."

"The voices aren't real, Harmony. You only hear them because you're not taking your medicine. Jimmy wants you to take your medicine. You know he does."

"Jimmy is my best friend. Because of you, he's in trouble."

In the distance I heard the whine of a siren. At the same time, something that sounded like sandpaper scraped along one side of the clamshell. I had been mistaken. Harmony had found a handhold, for he was inching his body down over the rough skin of the clamshell's locked jaws.

"Harmony, don't. You'll fall!" I screamed.

The crane's motor roared to life. So Maloney must have climbed to the cab. As the clamshell shuddered, Harmony screamed with rage. Smoothly, my cage started down. I gazed through its teeth and saw the broken hulk of the Honda come closer. For a split second, I was elated. That didn't last long. What would happen when Harmony and I were both close to the ground? Harmony would be able to get at me without fear of falling, and Maloney would still be up in the cab.

The siren neared. I heard brakes squeal. But I was too obsessed with the squeak and grind of the cables and Harmony's threats to pay close attention.

"I'm going to get you, Toni! I'm going to get you!"

The crane's motor switched off, leaving the clamshell perhaps ten feet above the Honda's corpse. "Come on down from that thing, son!" a familiar voice called. Two uniformed officers emerged from the mist and stood next to the Honda, gazing up.

"Al!"

"Toni, where are you?"

What had been terrifying, suddenly became ludicrous and sad. Harmony, who'd been hurling curses and threats, started to weep. The clamshell shook as he dropped off it. He landed a yard from the Honda and curled into a ball of misery at Al's feet. "It's not my fault, it's not my fault," he chanted through his sniffles.

While the other officer snapped cuffs on him, I did my best to explain the situation to Al. "Can you get out of that thing?" he asked.

"I can probably slide through the teeth, but I'm afraid I'll hurt myself if I fall." My teeth chattered from shock, and my muscles felt frozen in place.

Maloney appeared next to Al. "Toni, everything's okay now. Jump."

"I can't."

"Yes, you can." He climbed up on top of the Honda's roof. Steadying himself, he stood and held his arms out. "I'll catch you."

He was now no more than three or four feet from where I cowered inside the clamshell. I maneuvered my body over the teeth and slipped through them. In the next instant Maloney had caught me and I rested safe in his arms.

Epilogue

HARMONY confessed to killing Alice Ritco and Professor McDaniel. At first Jimmy insisted that he did all the murders, but when he realized lying wasn't going to help Harmony, he amended his confession. He admitted he only murdered Connie Swenson, the Margrafs and Todd Lawrence.

Still, he was an accessory in the other deaths. He showed Harmony how to bug a phone and where to get the equipment. When Jimmy saw me carrying the book on the Harzine Institute at the harbor, he encouraged Harmony to break into my place, take the book, and listen in on my phone conversations. Jimmy insisted that he never realized that would lead to Harmony killing Professor McDaniels. Nevertheless, McDaniels was a nice old man who died for no reason.

It's a sad story that depressed me for weeks. Since then, however, some good things have happened. Harmony is getting treatment and, hopefully, Jimmy will get justice. The insurance came through for my house. Tomorrow my living room gets replastered by professionals.

The good things don't end there, either. Al is back with the Baltimore Police Department and happily harassing gypsies and whoever else has the misfortune to run into him in the wrong place at the wrong time. I'm getting along a little better with my family.

O'Dell and I don't see much of each other. On the occasions when our paths have crossed, I've learned that Jerome's physical injuries are healed, he's pulling decent grades at school and he's become a regular at Maloney's dojo.

Another plus—Maloney doesn't moan and groan about Karla so often. In fact, he's even started to date. Right now he's going out with a couple of ladies. One of them is Doris Ritco.

Yes, I know. Possibly, he could have been mine if I'd said the word. But neither of us is ready for a serious commitment. We both have a lot of healing to do. For now, Maloney and I are better off as friends and colleagues. For the future—who knows?

Frankly, right now the present looks just fine to me. Maloney is teaching me the PI business, and I'm doing everything I can to be good at it. I'm even taking driving lessons—from a professional this time. My social life doesn't look so bad, either. Lately, I've been seeing a lot of Mario Caprini and one or two other guys I've met recently.

Oh yeah, and I just started work on a really interesting case.

~ The End ~

Louise Titchener

Louise Titchener is the author of over forty published novels in a variety of genres. She loves to set her books in Baltimore where she lives with her philosophy professor husband.

When she isn't writing fiction, she paints, sails, bicycles and figure skates. She particularly enjoys long walks around the harbor where many events in her most recent story, Buried in Baltimore, take place.

Visit Louise's Baltimore web site, with links to her personal web page at: http://www.mysteriousbaltimore.com